FRASER VALLEY REGIONAL LIBRARY

3900350967629

D0516512

THE HEALER'S TOUCH

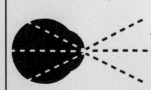

This Large Print Book carries the
Seal of Approval of N.A.V.H.

The Healer's Touch

Lori Copeland

THORNDIKE PRESS

A part of Gale, Cengage Learning

GALE
CENGAGE Learning·

Farmington Hills, Mich • San Francisco • New York • Waterville, Maine
Meriden, Conn • Mason, Ohio • Chicago

GALE
CENGAGE Learning·

Copyright © 2014 by Lori Copeland, Inc.
All Scripture quotations are taken from the King James Version of the Bible.
Thorndike Press, a part of Gale, Cengage Learning.

ALL RIGHTS RESERVED
This is a work of fiction. Names, characters, places, and incidents are products of the author's imagination or are used fictitiously. Any resemblance to actual persons, living or dead, is entirely coincidental.
Thorndike Press® Large Print Christian Fiction.
The text of this Large Print edition is unabridged.
Other aspects of the book may vary from the original edition.
Set in 16 pt. Plantin.

LIBRARY OF CONGRESS CATALOGING-IN-PUBLICATION DATA

Copeland, Lori, author.
    The Healer's Touch / by Lori Copeland.
        pages cm. — (Thorndike Press Large Print Christian Fiction)
    ISBN 978-1-4104-7024-9 (hardcover) — ISBN 1-4104-7024-5 (hardcover)
    1. Single women—Fiction. 2. Family secrets—Fiction. 3. Christian fiction. 4. Love stories. 5. Large type books. I. Title.
    PS3553.O6336H43 2014b
    813'.54—dc23   2014020886

Published in 2014 by arrangement with Harvest House Publishers

Printed in the United States of America
1 2 3 4 5 6 7 18 17 16 15 14

But he was wounded for our
transgressions,
he was bruised for our iniquities:
the chastisement of our peace
was upon him;
and with his stripes we are healed.

Isaiah 53:5

INTRODUCTION

Missouri. Fertile rolling hills, craggy caves, and early morning mist slowly lifting in deep hollows. That's the beautiful setting where I grew up.

The Ozark Mountain scenery is hauntingly exquisite in the spring. One of the reasons I'm thankful God made me a Missourian is because of the state's four distinctive seasons — all with their own drawbacks, but lovely indeed. Today, as I'm writing this, winter is showing off its finery in melting snow-packed trails and in sparkling icicles hanging from ice-covered bluffs.

When spring finally comes, those same riverbanks and steep cliffs come alive with redbuds, dogwoods, reddish pink tall thistle, the proud and purple Beggar's Lice, showy white blackberry bush, and wild Sweet William.

Long summer nights are lit by fireflies, sweet scented yellow honeysuckle, and window-rattling thunderstorms.

Fall shimmers with the yellow and orange of Tickseed Sunflower and Sheep Sorrel. The vast array of trees produces radiant reds supplied by sugar maples and showy oaks.

Among the Ozark's beauty lie deep secrets, old wives' tales, and superstitions. Some tales are sworn to be factual, but others are rather dubious. Some are out-and-out unbelievable. But the story you're about to read — the story of the "Spooklight" — is true.

Or so it is said.

I have seen this mysterious light. I have witnessed it roaming the small stretch of gravel road near Joplin, Missouri, where it still lurks today. It's a country road tucked away from sight. Cars have been noted to sit bumper to bumper there, waiting to see the "Spooklight."

This isn't a small light. It's sometimes as large as a house. To this day, when it appears cars scatter and gravel flies. The faint of heart don't dare to linger. But those who live in the area say the light is getting dimmer now and appears with less regularity. Others say it's getting old and cranky.

In the 1980s a graying, stooped man by the name of Garland Middleton established a Spooklight museum. Folks stopped by the tiny building located alongside the gravel road within easy viewing distance of where the spectacle was likely to appear. The short intersecting road wasn't much to look at, but all eyes were trained on the spot where the light was likely to emerge when darkness gathered. Garland (later dubbed "Spooky") was always delighted to talk to you about the light. He'd tell eye-widening stories and legends about its source. Old Garland would sell you a cold bottle of soda pop — and maybe some potato munchies and a candy bar. A bare ceiling bulb held by a frayed cord illuminated the frayed magazine and newspaper clippings tacked to the wall.

What most fascinates me — a born romantic — about this spectacle: The light appears to respond best to love. And children. It is thought to feel love and if possible tries to return it.

Over the past hundred years, area residents have hired their share of "supernatural" folks to tell them what this strange phenomenon is and why it's there. The first recorded sighting is said to have taken place in 1886, but some say it was noted long before that.

The elusive light keeps a respectful distance these days. And if the circus-like atmosphere gets too loud, it chooses not to show itself at all.

Numerous legends exist about its origin. A few are written about in *Ozark Spooklight,* by Foster Young. I've loosely utilized these tales in the following storyline. Certified investigations have resulted in numerous explanations for the light, but none that satisfy. One man said it was coming from car lights on busy Route 66. This could be true, but the first sighting was in the late nineteenth century when there were no cars, or highway, or Route 66.

The light's brightness varies. Sometimes it's dim, like a small, blinking flashlight. Other times the light is bright enough to reflect off cars. Sometimes the light is a solitary radiance that frequently divides itself into as many as a dozen floating colored lights, moving and dancing. On rare occasions it has been captured by time-lapse cameras.

The phenomenon drew NBC's attention in the 1980s. They sent a crew to see if the light would appear, and it did. Later the segment aired and the moderator, John Barbour, confessed he thought the light was real.

To suggest that the light exists only in the

imagination of some is to say that it exists in the camera's eye.

When I witnessed the light, it wasn't bouncing or coming up to the car window. It was in the distance, moving, almost shy. Hesitant.

During the writing of this book, I invited a few old friends from our teenage years over to talk about the Spooklight. Everyone had their recollections of the first time they saw it. One lady said she was on the floorboard covering her head with her arms, begging her boyfriend to drive away from it. Others said they got out of their cars and walked the lane, getting as close as they could. When I saw it I can't recall much more than thinking, *Huh. There really is a light.*

My husband and I drove back to the area last week. He remembered the Spooklight route; I didn't. The museum is gone, fallen to ruins in thick winter undergrowth. The gravel road is still there. I counted two mobile homes and a house along the isolated four-mile gravel strip that is mostly farm and cattle land, tall oaks, and red clay. I so wanted to knock on doors and ask questions, but my husband restrained me.

By now you're either interested in the light or you're dubiously shaking your head. I

11

have done both during my lifetime. If you're ever near Joplin, Missouri, take time to drive to the gravel "Spooklight Road." There aren't any public signs — none that I could find, anyway — but ask most anyone in the area and they'll point the way.

What is the light's source? Is it burning out after all these years? Has it lost heart? I have no idea. I am certain the source is explainable, but to date nobody knows why it's there or what it wants. I have used many of the numerous legends and "for real" stories told about the light in this book, so you decide.

Lori

1

Four miles south of Joplin, Missouri, 1887

"Give it up, Cummins! Don't make me shoot you!"

U.S. Marshal Ian Cawley let his horse have his head. Towering sycamores flashed by in the deepening Missouri twilight. Darkness threatened to overtake him, but that was no excuse for giving up the chase. He had this scruffy little thief this time. The back of the outlaw's dirty bowler drew closer. Ian could smell the stench of unwashed body and filthy shirt. Hunching lower in the saddle, he urged the horse. "Come on, Norman. Let's get this over with and head home."

Home being Kansas City, one hundred fifty miles to the west.

The whimpering outlaw wasn't getting away from him this time. Twice Jim Cummins had slipped Ian's net, and the fact rubbed the marshal raw. There wouldn't be much of a bounty — when the outlaw robbed banks the take was always small — but the man was a huge thorn in his side. He was tired of this game. Jim was *his* this time. He gripped the reins, urging his horse to a painful stretch. A few feet more and he would make the leap from his horse to Cummins'.

The scummy little criminal had the reputation of being meek, but Cummins was acting anything but docile right now. He wasn't highly thought of as criminals went. His own gang viewed him as a sniveler and crybaby, but he was adept when avoiding the law.

Ian's buckskin pulled closer.

Hunching lower in the saddle, the outlaw whipped his animal to a frenzy.

Sighing, Ian prepared for the pain. The little runt wasn't going down without a fight. No one ever did. Half a mile out of town he'd tackled Jim off the horse. The two men had scuffled on the roadway, and Cummins had thrown a hard right that left Ian reeling. The lapse allowed the outlaw time to mount up and take off, but in the process he'd dropped a Liberty Bank bag which was now in Ian's possession. Somewhere during the brawl Ian had lost his wallet with his badge and papers, but he'd have to go back for them later. He couldn't let Cummins gain any more distance.

This time Ian had him.

Preparing for the jump, he braced for the jolt. Last time he'd done this he'd broken two ribs and shattered his pelvis, but he'd brought in Hobbs Kerry alive. Ten thousand wasn't bad for a day's work, overlooking the soreness. The money had bought Grandpa a new plow and Grandma one of those fancy Home Comfort cookstoves. She'd baked cinnamon rolls and fruit pies for everyone in the county there for a while.

But Ian was getting too old for this line of work. He ought to hang it up and settle down. Live a normal life.

A brilliant light suddenly appeared in front of the racing horses. Momentarily distracted, the marshal focused on the strange object. What in the blazes? It hadn't been there a second ago. Involuntarily slowing, he threw up a forearm to shield his eyes.

Cummins reacted to the strange sight, swiftly hauling back on the reins. Both horses spooked, going crazy. Ian spoke in a low, even tone to Norman. "Don't bolt on me." Ian wouldn't put it past the animal to pitch his rider over his head. If the ill-tempered, contrary beast hadn't been such a fine piece of horse flesh Ian would have sold him five years earlier. Cummins' mare danced over the rutted road as the outlaw shrieked, shielding his eyes with a lifted shoulder from the light's dazzling brilliance.

Bouncing closer, the light hovered between the two men.

Norman blew and stepped backward, but Ian's eyes were glued to the strange light. What was it? He'd never seen anything like it. He'd read newspaper accounts of folks making claims that they had seen strange glowing objects in the sky, but he'd not heard of a bouncing light.

The object shifted, jauntily moving to perch on Cummins' saddle horn.

Screaming, the outlaw spurred his mare and the animal took off in a gallop, Cummins batting at the bizarre object that hovered around his head.

Ian sat frozen in place, eyes trained on the spectacle. He'd help, but he'd never fought a . . . a light. The outlaw's screams filled the impinging darkness as the bobbing light ballooned and then deflated but never moved from Cummins' saddle horn. The astounding sight suddenly zipped off and disappeared over a rise and Ian sat, transfixed.

Back over the rise the light came, heading in his direction.

Stuffing the bank bag in his saddle roll, he

urged Norman forward and took off like a hen with singed feathers, as Grannie would say. Galloping back the way he'd come, he risked a couple of glances over his shoulder and saw that the light was gone. Automatically slowing, he turned and then started when he saw the light was perched on his horse's rump, round as a water barrel now.

Stumbling out of the saddle, he stepped a distance away to see what the thing would do. It split into five bouncing balls, frolicking about like a spring colt.

"What do you want?" Ian shouted. Not only had he let Cummins get away, he was trying to initiate a conversation with a light.

The light skipped about, rolling to a nearby plowed pasture and tumbling like a child at play. When Ian stepped to his horse the light returned, forming a halo above his head.

He fixed in place. He had a hunch that if he ran the thing would stay right beside — or ahead — of him.

Calmer now, he said, "What do you want?"

The light hovered. Ian could have sworn it tilted slightly as if to say, "What?"

"Who are you? What do you want?" More to the point, where was Cummins now? Three miles down the road and still screaming, probably. He had escaped him again. Norman snorted, staring at the sight.

The light steadied, grew dimmer, then radiant. Minutes stretched as he watched the strange ball cycle. It appeared it wasn't going to move until Ian did. By now he had worked up a heavy sweat in the mild spring night. Perspiration trickled down his neck and he wiped moisture from his eyes. Wasn't this a fine mess? Nobody would believe this story. His gaze wandered down the desolate road. A man could go a long time in these hills and hollers and never see a soul. Tree frogs croaked in nearby ponds.

Suddenly the light shot away at breathtaking speed. It reached the top of the rise before Ian realized it was gone. Springing into action, he swung aboard Norman and spurred him into a full gallop. The horse obliged, racing down the uneven road at a perilous clip.

Peering over his shoulder, Ian suddenly drew up. The light was clinging to his shoulder now. He shoved it away but his hand only moved through air. Squealing, Norman swerved back and forth on the road as Ian struggled to battle the light and hang on. The object tired of the battle, divided again, and became five pinging balls, skipping, dancing in front of the horse's path.

Wild now, Norman plunged through heavy thicket and galloped headlong into open pasture.

"Whoa! Steady, boy!" Ian grabbed for the reins that had escaped him when the horse veered off the road. For the first time in his life the marshal felt completely helpless. A thin moon slid out, illuminating his predicament.

Galloping at full speed now, the stallion headed straight for a barn in the distance. The light bounced in front of the animal, teasing, goading. "Thank You, God," Ian muttered. Norman would stop when he reached the barn.

The light hopped on top of Norman's head and a watery moon shone on the rutted pasture as Ian hung on. By now he heard hysterical screams and realized they were coming from him.

The barn door had been shut for the night. Norman's stride lengthened, his heavy muscles slick with sweat. The ball bounced up and down, back and forth, and from side to side. If the thing had hands, Ian sensed it would be clapping with glee over the merry flight.

And then he looked up, and understanding coursed through him like a bolt of lightning. Norman wasn't going to stop. Ian instantly recognized the horse was going through whatever stood in its path. "Whoa, boy! Whoaahhhhh!"

The sound of shattering lumber echoed throughout the holler as Norman, Ian, and the bouncing light entered the barn without benefit of an open passage.

As his body flew toward the barn floor and the sharp, broken shreds of lumber, Ian caught one last glimpse of Norman's rump as the horse pivoted and galloped away. Ian had one last coherent thought.

I'm going to sell that miserable horse if it's the last thing I do.

A boom shattered the kitchen's peaceful silence, and Lyric started and jerked her hands out of the pan of sudsy dishwater. She glanced over her shoulder at her sister. Lark was sitting at the table, reading. "Was that thunder?"

Lark had her head buried in a Charles Dickens novel, apparently oblivious to the clap that had shaken the timeworn two-story house. "I didn't hear anything."

Lyric's sweet but slightly inattentive sister wouldn't hear a tree felled beside the house if she was reading. Lifting the window over the sink to allow a hint of fresh night air into the kitchen, Lyric conceded that March was extremely warm in the holler this year, which usually meant a stifling summer ahead. The garden vegetables, newly planted, would be burned to a crisp by fall, no doubt. Tomatoes would blister on the vines and second-planting string beans would wither. Pausing, she listened for another clap, but all was silent. She shrugged and returned to the dishes.

The back door burst open and Lyric's hand flew to her heart until she saw Samantha — known to friends and family as "Boots" — standing in the doorway. "It is customary to knock," she gently reminded the fourteen-year-old.

"Sorry. Did you hear that blast?"

"I heard something. Is a storm brewing?"

"Not a cloud in the sky." Boots took a deep breath and continued. "Can't imagine what it was. Scared the waddin' out of me. Lark, you have got to hear this! You know how Caroline is sweet on Henry and they've been sort of, you know, courting? Well, tonight Henry came over early because he's not allowed to stay out much past dark and Caroline's mother said that she could go for a short ride in his father's new buggy . . . and of course you know where Henry took her. Right straight down that creepy road, and lo and behold the light is acting up again. Why, they saw two poor men, each riding in opposite directions like the old devil himself was on their tail, trying to outrun the thing. But it was pestering them something awful." She paused to draw another deep breath. "Henry said the light hadn't shown itself in a while and he wanted to impress Caroline with his bravery, so he brought the buggy up here . . ."

Lyric glanced out the window. Darkness encroached and a light fog hung in the air.

"Anyway, he got Caroline all settled with a nice thick lap robe — which she didn't need because it's so mild outside, but you know Henry. He's a real gentleman. Anyway, they settled down to watch for the light. Caroline said he put his arm around her. Don't you think that's a little forward, putting your arm around someone on your first — well, maybe second — outing? But he did, and they settled back to watch for the Spooklight."

"Boots, I wish you wouldn't refer to that . . . that thing as the *Spooklight.*" They had enough to worry about without concerning themselves with frightening legends. Life was difficult enough living in this holler, isolated from everyone by the strange spells her mother's illness caused. She now lay in her bedroom, frail and weak, awaiting death.

Lyric had spent her life protecting Lark from folks' cruel barbs and innuendos about how they were different than others, not worthy to be a part of the community. The entire town isolated themselves from Edwina Bolton, the strange woman with two young girls.

Boots's excited voice droned on. ". . . and then just before dark, Henry suggested that they spread the lap robe on the ground and watch for the light from there. Moony-eyed Caroline agreed that was a grand idea, so they climbed out of the buggy and made themselves real comfortable."

A simply grand idea, Lyric silently mocked, aware of how easily a young woman like Caroline could be led astray. She just bet Henry was all for getting all comfortable. Caroline and Boots needed better adult supervision than their grandfather provided. Given no choice, Neville had assumed the care of Caroline and Boots when their mother passed a few years back. The father was never found . . . or known, if the scarce bit of information Lyric heard during her brief trips to town for supplies held true.

Those hurried excursions gave her goose bumps. Folks turned away as though she was scarlet fever on legs. That silly light that appeared in the holler often did so closest to the Bolton property line. Folks put two and two together and made four: surely the light had something to do with Edwina Bolton and her strange fits.

That was nonsense and Lyric knew it. That "spooklight" was just a trick of nature. But try convincing the townspeople of that! But it wouldn't be much longer before her mother passed on, and then Lyric would take her sister and leave this place. Together they would build a new life hundreds of miles from this isolated holler hidden deep in the Missouri hills — somewhere far away, where no one knew about them. She remembered being a young girl and peering at the globe that sat in the parlor. The tiny spots on the paper had turned into exciting new adventures Lyric would experience someday.

"And then," Boots continued, breathless, "Henry started sweet-talking her. Seems the horse spotted the light first. He reared and took off like someone lit a fire under his rear."

"Boots," Lyric cautioned. The girl's language often tended to be highly improper, a trait she'd acquired from her salty-talking grandfather.

"Backside," she emphasized. "The horse *dragged* Henry's father's new buggy that he'd just bought today. Caroline said the light came right up to them, bold as brass, and just hovered there like it was looking them over. She said she got goose bumps the size of cotton wads. Then it was gone . . . but so was the horse and buggy, and they had no way to get home. Caroline said Henry knew his pa would be mad as hops when he discovered he'd let the horse and buggy get loose. After a bit they started walking. I bumped into them when I finished up milking. They were none too happy, either. Caroline was wearing her best patent leather slippers and they were all dusty and scuffed from the briars and dust."

Boots pulled a chair closer to the table. "And you know what else?"

"What?" Lark's eyes fixed on the book page, her voice bordering on monotone. Different as they were, the two girls were as tight as a cheap pair of shoes, even though Lyric was certain that Boots's grandfather didn't overly approve of the friendship.

"That wretched Jim Cummins was spotted earlier today. Walked right into the general store and was about to purchase chewing tobacco when this feller walked in — a stranger, Earl said. Nobody knew the

25

outsider but he must have changed Cummins' mind about the tobacco. Earl said he took off out of there like a scalded cat and last he saw of him he was hightailing it out of town and the stranger was right behind him."

"Outlaws." Lyric shook her head. The hollers were full of them. Lowlifes who kept their families hidden from the law. Lyric listened to the girl's chatter as she dried a skillet and put it away. Boots's occasional bits and pieces of area information were all the news they had, and Lyric welcomed the diversion. No one in Bolton Holler ever ventured up to the house unless forced to. Stories abounded about the "evils" that lay within the walls of the old house, and even the strong of heart avoided the place.

A slow smile formed on her lips. She used to feel sorry for the townsfolk, even pitied them for their misbeliefs that a black cloud hung over the Bolton home — a sinister one, it was said. Most of the folks in town had decided the strange light that shown regularly in this holler was a direct product of Edwina Bolton. Lyric knew that to be nonsense, but the people in town were far more willing to trust in superstition than logic.

She lifted the curtain over the kitchen

26

counter window and peered out. Funny, there wasn't a cloud in the sky. She could see every single star. If not thunder, what had she heard earlier?

She wiped off her hands on her apron. "Boots, don't stay long," she said. "It's well past dark and your grandfather will be alarmed if you're not home soon."

"I won't. Anyway, back to Henry. He is in so much trouble! I doubt that his father will let him take the buggy and horse again for some time and Caroline so looks forward to their rides home on Sunday night."

Slipping into a light sweater, Lyric stepped onto the back service porch. Milk cans and churning pots littered the small enclosure. Outside, she glanced up to see a beautifully rounded moon rising. The sight was so pretty she paused to enjoy the night.

Talk of beaus and courting often caused a stirring in her soul. She would never marry. There wasn't a man around who would dare to come courting for fear Edwina would have one of her mad fits. *Maybe I'll have to settle for one of the Younger brothers,* she thought with a grin. Although the Youngers were nothing to smile about. She'd seen the hoodlums around, shooting up the town and causing trouble. She had prayed the rowdy gang would disband but they hadn't;

they'd grown even more worrisome. The whole lot was at their best when they banded together. The Younger brothers — Cole, Bob, Jim, and John — were a thorn in every decent side. Talk drifted to her when she visited the general store. Occasionally a Younger shot up the town and bullied folks something awful and the men in town didn't lift a hand. They were terrified of the hoodlums and gave them plenty of space.

Drawing the sweater closer around her shoulders, she set off toward the barn. That noise had to have come from somewhere. She had closed the door earlier and everything had been peaceful. Maybe ol' Rosie had spooked and kicked her stall down . . . but even that wouldn't have made such a thunderous sound. As she approached the dwelling, moonlight emphasized a gaping hole where the barn door had once been. Gasping, she picked up speed, her eyes searching for the source of such destruction. Her barn door! What in the world . . . ?

Now, where was she going to scrape up enough extra money to replace that door?

Drawing closer, she stared at the pile of ankle-deep rubble. The Youngers. How *dare* those thugs destroy her property! The town might have difficulty confronting those men, but she didn't. She'd march down there where they lived and give someone a good piece of her mind!

Leaning around the corner, she fumbled for one of the matches she kept in a box on the wall. A flame ignited and she lit the lantern wick. Light illuminated lumber strewn this way and that. The milk cow, Rosie, stood in her stall, eyes wide open. Lyric stepped deeper into the shadows and squinted, giving a quick intake of breath when she spotted a man's body spread haphazardly across the dirt floor.

A *Younger.* Her pulse quickened.

Creeping closer, she centered the light on his still form and realized that this Younger was dead.

A dead Younger. In her barn.

She whirled, searching for his horse. Only Rosie stood in the dimly lit structure, however. Maybe he'd walked in here . . . but it looked for the world like something enormous had been ridden though the door.

Her eyes darted to his chest, where she detected a slight rise and fall. He was still breathing? She set the lantern aside and knelt beside the still form. In a daring moment, she laid her head briefly on the wide span of chest and listened. A slow, faint beat met her ears.

Straightening, she took a deep breath. *Almost dead,* she mentally corrected. If she'd step back and show respect for the dying the good Lord would finish His job. The town would be rid of one of the Younger brothers and maybe, for once, they would show a Bolton a little respect for delivering them of such a nuisance.

Worrying her lower lip between her teeth, she mulled the dilemma over in her mind. If she could do anything to sustain his life, she must. It was nothing less than her Christian duty. She hadn't learned the healing arts for nothing. And besides . . . if he died who would pay for the new barn door?

But he was such a worthless man, causing Bolton Holler and every nearby community nothing but trouble.

Yet she was not to judge others.

Though this outlaw needed a good judging.

Judge not, that ye be not judged. For with what judgment ye judge, ye shall be judged: and with what measure ye mete, it shall be measured to you again.

Bending close, she checked his breathing. The rise and fall of his chest was hardly detectable now. If she was going to act she'd have to do it quickly. Stripping off her apron, she hurriedly bound the deep slit

30

oozing across his forehead. It took several moments to locate and staunch the flow of blood from multiple cuts and gashes. He must have been riding a horse when he burst into the barn. She clucked her tongue. He'd ridden a horse straight through a barn door and been thrown from his saddle. Wasn't that just like a Younger?

She sniffed for the stench of alcohol. Nothing met her attempt but a rather pleasant manly scent — not too strong like that of some men she passed in town.

The spring night had begun to cool and she shivered as the breeze blew straight into the barn. How was she going to get him to the house? Moving to the back of the barn, she rummaged around until she found the old Indian travois that had been there for as long as she could remember. The conveyance was in sad shape, its hide stretched thin with prior use.

In minutes she had hitched Rosie to the transporter and then stood staring at the unconscious man. How would she get him on the sled? He was twice — no, three times her size. "Well, Rosie? Any suggestions?"

The old milk cow chewed her cud.

Moving to the stranger's head, she grasped his shoulders and pulled. His lifeless bulk barely budged. After three attempts, she eased his upper torso onto the sled. Moving to his boots, she swung his legs onto the travois and then stood back, puffing.

She led Rosie out of the barn pulling the travois. Was Younger still breathing? She couldn't spare the time to check. She had to get him to the house and to her box of remedies . . . although it might already be too late. He was lying so still, as though waiting for death to snatch him away.

She paused long enough to prop a few boards against the barn opening, praying that the flimsy protection would guard her meager stock tonight. She relied on their few sitting hens for eggs, and couldn't afford to lose them to fox and coyote.

She glanced at the wounded man, resenting the intrusion. If she didn't need that barn door so badly she would gladly let him return to dust as quick as he could.

2

Boots set her empty glass in the dishpan and glanced out the window. "Hey, Lark?"

"Mm hmm?"

"Why is Lyric hauling a man to the house on a travois?"

Lark absently lifted both shoulders in a shrug and then glanced up. "She's *what*?"

"She's got a man on a stretcher and Rosie is hauling it up the hill."

Table legs scraped the floor as Lark sprang from her seat and moved to join Boots at the window. "For goodness' sake. Where did she get a man?" Whirling, she stepped to the back door and flung it open. "What's going on? Who's that?" she called.

"Just hush up and help me get him into the house." Lyric removed her blood-splattered sweater and pitched it onto an empty milk can.

"Get him in the house *where*?"

"We'll put him in the parlor for the time

being. He's in bad shape. He may even be dead by now."

Boots scooted around the stretcher and the three women eased the patient upright. "He's big," Boots said. "Big and strong. Who is he?"

"I'm not sure." Lyric paused to catch her breath. "I think he might be one of those Youngers."

Boots gasped and took a cautionary step backwards. "How do you know?"

"I don't know for certain, but someone was snooping around and somehow tore up the barn door. It's busted into a hundred pieces. This man was unconscious on the barn floor. Who else but a liquored-up Younger would do such a thing?"

Boots glanced up. "To a Bolton?" she said. "I mean . . ."

"I know." Lyric sighed. "We're not the most revered family in the holler, but no one's ever destroyed our property. Not like this. They wouldn't dare. They're scared to death of us."

"No one's afraid of you. It's your ma and her fits," Boots corrected.

Nodding, Lyric murmured, "He must be a Younger, for sure. No one else in town would cross our property line." She bent to take a closer look at the man's coal black

hair and high cheekbones. He was darkly tanned, even this early in the year. Though the man's face was bloody and swollen, he was still a right fine-looking male. "I didn't know those Youngers were so handsome."

She shook her head. Lyric couldn't imagine why he'd picked the Bolton place to wreak havoc, but one thing was certain. This man was vile and dangerous.

"Lark, you and Boots support his right side. I'll take his left. Move him slowly. He's lost a lot of blood." Underneath the tan, his features were almost ashen.

Perspiration soaked Lyric's dress as they approached the parlor. The room was almost never used these days, and dust balls skittered across the wood floor as they entered. "We'll put him on the sofa. Chances are he won't make it another hour. Lark, run and get something to cover the furniture while we support him. Boots, remove his boots once we lay him down. The least we can do is make his last moments comfortable — even if he is a Younger."

Lark raced to get clean blankets and Boots removed the man's bloodstained riding boots. She looked at him skeptically. "Don't you think we should clean him up a bit?"

"I suppose we should, though he doesn't deserve it." Somewhere this man undoubtedly had family who prayed for him — or a wife. For their sakes, she would do what little she could in his last moments.

"Get a cloth and a pan of warm water." Lyric stepped over to light the oil lamp, dusty with neglect. Light flickered to life, revealing overstuffed chairs and heavy tables. It was a dark, depressing room — not the most comforting place to lay a man whose life was draining away. She wouldn't miss this room. She wouldn't miss any part of the house that held so many unhappy memories. Once Mother passed, Lyric would take Lark far away and they'd begin a new life, a normal one, someplace where folks didn't stare with accusing eyes and whisper hurtful lies.

Boots returned with an armful of blankets and pillows and the women set to work making the wounded man as comfortable as possible. Twice Lyric pressed her ear to his broad chest to assure that he hadn't passed on. His breaths were shallow and came with a struggle. She shook her head. She knew enough of medicine to know that he didn't have long.

She ushered the two young women out of the room. "It's late, Boots. Your grandfather will worry if you're not home shortly."

"But I want to stay! I've never seen anyone

croak before."

Lyric shooed the curious girls to the doorway, her temples throbbing. "He should have an uneventful passing." Even now his breathing was so shallow she could hardly detect it.

Boots persisted, whining now. "This might be my only chance to watch a Younger die."

"I certainly hope it will be." Lyric took the girl by the elbow and ushered her out of the parlor. "Lark, look in on Mother and make sure the ruckus didn't disturb her. I'll stay here until . . . until it's over."

When the door closed behind the girls, she lowered the lantern wick and then took a seat across from the sofa to wait.

A rooster's crow roused her. Slowly opening her eyes, she noted the thin shaft of daylight streaming in through the heavy drapes. Sitting upright, she pushed herself up out of the chair and knelt by the sofa to meet a pair of clear green eyes. Her heart shot to her throat. There was too much life in those eyes. Way too much. He was still alive. Alive and wide awake on Mother's sofa.

"Good morning."

His deep tenor startled her speechless. For a moment her throat worked, but words refused to come. Finally she whispered, "You're alive."

A half-hearted chuckle escaped him. "Am I? I've been trying to decide."

Backing slowly away, she murmured, "Don't try anything funny. I'm armed." Or she could be soon enough. A Colt revolver sat as close as the desk drawer, and though he was awake he couldn't move swiftly enough to prevent her from shooting him. She took a second precautionary step backward. "You're a Younger, aren't you?"

"Am I?"

"And you, in a drunken stupor, tore my barn door apart. I hope you have the proper funds to replace it."

He lightly touched a finger to the deep gash across his forehead and winced. Silence dominated the room. When he didn't readily answer, she asked. "Which one?"

He glanced up. "Which one . . . ?"

"Which Younger are you? Bob? Cole? Jim?"

He closed his eyes and shook his head. "I'm sorry, ma'am. My head's throbbing — what are you asking?"

The outlaw was playing games with her. Was he lying there gathering enough strength to attack her and rob her? Goosebumps swelled on her arms. "I think you'd better leave now."

He obediently rose but then wilted back to the sofa. Fresh blood oozed from his various cuts. "I'm afraid I'm a bit weak to oblige. Could I beg a glass of cool water?"

For the briefest of moments compassion overrode her fear. He looked so pale — and pathetic and fragile. She was supposed to be a healer, wasn't she? She should be helping him. But maybe he was stronger than he was letting on. Maybe he was testing her. A Younger would do that.

"I'm afraid I'll have to tie your hands and feet first."

He glanced up.

She kept her tone firm and in control. Giving a wounded man — even an outlaw — a glass of water wasn't unreasonable. "Is that agreeable?"

"It that's what it takes to get a glass of water."

She eased around the sofa, keeping a close eye on his movements as she rummaged in the desk drawer and drew out a ball of twine. If he had normal strength the binding would be useless, but he appeared weak as a newborn kitten. And it wouldn't take long to draw a simple glass of water from the pump in the kitchen sink.

"Please cross your hands at the wrists,"

she instructed.

He slowly lifted both hands to comply. "A simple glass of water and I'll be on my way."

"Nothing's simple with a man like you." She wound the twine tightly at the base of his arms, taking care to make the bond secure but not so constricted that it would cut off his blood supply. The good Lord knew he needed what little still trickled through his veins.

Her words appeared to penetrate his fog. "A man like me? Do you know me?"

"Oh, I know *of* you." She turned slightly so he wouldn't notice the scissors she carried. She snipped the twine and tied a double knot. "Everyone in ten counties knows of you."

"Really?"

"You're not a celebrity, if that's what you're thinking."

"No, ma'am. Truth be told I'm not thinking anything other than I'm thirsty. At the moment, I don't know who I am or how I got here."

"I'm sure both will come to you shortly." He had taken quite a lick to the head. No doubt he'd have a splitting headache if the loss of blood didn't get him first. "I'll get that water. Don't try to go anywhere." She tucked the scissors into her pocket and

40

strode to the kitchen. Taking a clean glass from the cupboard, she filled it from the pump. Her eyes fell on a pot of thick oatmeal bubbling on the stove. Lark had started breakfast, then. Dipping a small bowl into the pot, she added cream from the pitcher, butter, and two heaping spoonfuls of dark brown sugar. She knew of no rule that said a wicked man had to die on an empty stomach.

When she returned to the parlor he was lying on his back, eyes closed. Pausing in the doorway, she studied his chest for signs of life. A slow rise and fall assured her that he was still breathing.

"I thought you might be able to get a bite of oatmeal down."

His eyes slowly opened and he stared at her. "Do you have the water?"

She crossed the room and set the tray on a nearby table. "Better drink slowly." She steadied his head while he drank thirstily, draining the glass before he slumped back to the pillow.

"Would you like to try a bite of oatmeal?"

He shook his head. "Later," he said hoarsely.

Understandable. Most likely there wouldn't be a later, but the eating was his choice. She set the empty glass on the tray and then turned to inspect him. Dried blood caked his swollen face. His injuries were so grave that his features were barely discernible this morning. Angry dark purple bruises dotted his arms and forehead. "I would send for the doctor but he wouldn't come — leastways not for a Bolton, and I have to think a Younger wouldn't fare any better in his esteem. He wouldn't come unless somebody made him . . . and nobody would."

Actually it took an arm and leg to get the man up here when Mother was at her worst. He'd be here and gone before she knew it, hightailing it back down the hill, scared out of his mind by Mother's fits.

Not many people had seen Mother when she was having one of her episodes, but the few who had made sure everyone else heard the stories. Lyric and Lark still lived with the stares and outright fear that shown in the townfolks' eyes when they ventured to town. Anything odd — anything that couldn't be easily explained — was blamed on Edwina.

Lyric didn't appreciate the notoriety. She couldn't attend church because of the stares and whispers, but she had a Bible and she studied it. Seemed to her that the only One who got to judge a person was the Lord

Jesus Christ — and He wouldn't judge her on rumors.

The man's scraped fingers fumbled weakly in his pocket.

"Money won't help; the doctor won't come." Sighing, she sat down to wait another hour to see if she would be forced to apply her talents. She knew about herbs and salves and poultices. If he made it another hour, she would do the right thing and make a sincere effort to help.

His hand dropped away. "There's nothing in my pocket."

"You don't carry identification?" With his lifestyle the choice was probably a wise one.

"There's nothing on me — not that I can find."

She stood up, intending to brew herself a cup of strong hot tea. It had been a long, tiring night. She had dozed off and on and then dropped into a fitful sleep near dawn.

The plain truth was the last thing Bolton Holler needed was another live Younger, though for the life of her she couldn't imagine why she would spare this town a drop of empathy.

Yet she knew she wouldn't let the man die without lifting a hand.

Lyric paused in front of the freshly planed

door and breathed deeply of the spicy scent of new wood. The new neighbors had arrived last week but she hadn't gone to welcome them. She'd sat on her back porch and listened to the music and festivities coming from the rowdy housewarming celebration in honor of the young couple's recent marriage, wondering what it would be like to be included in such fun and merriment. She'd never been to a party or a housewarming, but someday she would go and she would dance and laugh the night away without fear of reproach.

Last time she'd shown up on a new arrival's doorstep the Bolton name had preceded her, and she had been ushered off the property with a shotgun. From then on she had stayed home instead of paying social calls, but today she was forced into extraordinary measures. Younger had more grit than a sandbar.

She lifted her hand to knock and then paused. She hesitated to alarm the newlyweds. Surely they'd heard rumors regarding the Bolton place, but they must be the brave sort if they'd chosen to build their new home half a mile away.

The sun was only now peeking above the horizon, and the few roosters milling about the yard sounded a bit sleepy as they crowed in the new day. Finding a Bolton on your doorstep at the crack of dawn would not be a good start to the day for Levi and Katherine Jennings, but the stranger was still breathing and she was fresh out of witch hazel. She rapped softly and then drew back when the door flew open to reveal Levi, hair mussed, wide-eyed, shotgun in hand. "What?"

"I . . . good morning. I. . . ." He reached out, drew her inside the house, and slammed the door behind her, throwing the bolt shut. Her gaze traced the room and rested on Katherine, who was sitting on the bed sobbing.

"I . . ." By the look of fright on Levi's face her reputation preceded her, but why would he be eager to draw her into the house? "Please — don't be frightened. I'm here to ask if you could spare a bit of witch hazel. I have a wounded man —"

"Did you see it?" Levi cut her off, stepping to the window to peer out.

"I . . . could you spare any witch hazel? A few sprigs will do . . ." Her eyes focused on the shattered windowpane above the sink. The newlyweds must be feuding something awful.

Katherine rose from the bed and threw herself in Lyric's arms. "It was *awful*! My heart is still beating so hard I can barely breathe."

Turning slightly, Lyric eyed the new groom. Had she walked in on a marital spat? Her eyes skimmed the length of the tall man, sturdy to be sure. She'd need a sizable club to quell him. She turned back to meet the bride's flushed face. Such a lovely woman — long shiny hair that fell to her waist and a soft, pale complexion. Her gaze ran the length of the new house. Two large rooms, one an actual bedroom — everything a new bride could hope for. Lyric's eyes returned to the husband, who was still watching out the window. Surely he wouldn't mistreat this lovely creature. "I'm sorry. Did I see what?"

"That *thing*!" A shudder escaped the new bride. "Didn't you see it?"

"I saw roosters," Lyric offered. Maybe Katherine was one of those citified Joplin women — one who wasn't accustomed to living in the woods and hollers. If so, she was in for a real surprise. In these parts there were bobcats, mountain lions, and snakes galore.

Stepping away from the window, Levi shook his head in apology. "I'm sorry, ma'am. My wife and I have had quite a night. Won't you sit down?" He pulled a chair away from the table and motioned for her to sit down. Lyric noticed he kept the rifle close at hand. "Is there something we can do for you?"

"Yes, I'm your closet neighbor, Lyric, and —"

The new husband's face drained of color. "Lyric? Lyric Bolton?"

She nodded.

"Eekkkk!" Katherine flew into her husband's arms as he fumbled for the rifle and brought it to one shoulder. "You just stay where you are, missy. You move a muscle and I'll shoot!"

"Wait!" Lyric squeezed her eyes shut, waiting for the explosion. "The rumors you hear are wrong. There's nothing wrong with me. My mother isn't well, but I'm . . . I'm not crazy."

"You jest stay right where you are, woman." Levi leveled the barrel squarely at her chest.

"I'm here to beg a few sprigs of witch hazel. They may help a wounded man. Please." Lyric slowly opened her eyes and saw a flicker of hesitancy in his glare. "Please. Lower the barrel. I'm not here to do harm. I have a gravely injured man at my house and I need witch hazel to help with the swelling. He's going to die if I don't

47

tend him."

"Who's injured?"

"I'm not certain — a man. I found him half alive in my barn last night."

The man's suspicion fixed coldly on her. "How do I know you're telling the truth?"

"You don't. You'll have to trust me." She indicated the gun. "You may keep it pointed at me, but please remove your finger from the trigger."

The groom eyed his bride and she slowly nodded. "She doesn't look like she means any harm," Katherine said.

Levi slowly lowered the barrel. "Now, what's this about a wounded man?"

"I found him last night in my barn. Apparently he's one of the Youngers. He ran his horse straight through my barn door."

"Younger, you say."

"Yes sir — although I don't know that for a fact. He could be any other of the hoodlums that hang around here."

"If he's no good, why save him?"

"I wasn't going to, but when he was alive this morning — well, are you a God-fearing couple?"

Both nodded.

"So am I — though everyone thinks I'm not. I have a Bible and I read it and I choose to believe what it says and it says I'm to help my neighbor."

"Amen," Levi nodded. "But you're mighty good-hearted to go this far. Can't say I'd do the same." He took a seat and his wife came to sit on his lap, resting her head on his shoulder.

"If you had a few sprigs of witch hazel I could repay it in a few months once my herb garden gets going again."

Levi shook his head. "You can have your witch hazel. We got far worse problems." He glanced at Katherine. "Do you want to tell her, honey?"

"This strange light —"

Lyric nodded. "The spooklight."

"It has a name!"

"Yes ma'am. It's been around a while."

"What *is* it?"

"Can't rightly say," said Lyric. "Some folks . . . well, some folks say my mother's behind it, but I can assure you the Boltons have nothing to do with that pesky thing. One thing I can tell you is that it appears to do no harm. Never once heard of it hurting anyone, or doing anything upsetting other than appearing . . . and bouncing around."

Folks didn't like that in the least — the oddity even upset her at times.

Katherine slid off Levi's lap. "Do you know that — that thing kept us up all night?

Peering in the window, bouncing around the room . . ."

Levi broke in. "We'd just gone to bed when I heard the horses. They were mighty upset about something. My pa gave us the pair for wedding presents and I thought, well, the longer I lay here the more upset Katherine will get and when I heard them start to run I knew I had to go check. I thought horse thieves were trying to steal them."

"I wanted to go with him but I just couldn't," Katherine said. "I was afraid it would be the Quapaws . . ."

"Honey," her husband soothed, "I've told you those Indians are peaceful and not likely to bother a soul. Anyway, I thought it was either horse thieves or a bobcat. I got out of bed and fumbled for my trousers. Suddenly Katherine screamed and grabbed my arm something fierce. All of a sudden I noticed this peculiar yellowish light — a ball of light — peering through the bedroom window."

Katherine moaned and hid her face in her hands. "It was horrifying."

"Well, I gotta admit that for a moment I was speechless," Levi confessed. "Course I'd heard stories of some strange light over here, but I never took them seriously. I don't believe in spooks and sure never figured to find one in my bedroom. Now Katherine yelled, 'Lord, have mercy! Who are you? Get away!' I was standing there in shock when that darn thing just up and entered the room, big as you please! Suddenly it divided into a bunch of colors, three, four . . . I plain lost count. I couldn't do a thing but stand there and gawk. The thing shot up to the rafters and disappeared and then swooped back over there in the corner of the front room." He pointed to the spot. "Beat all I've ever seen. My bride was wailing and tearing at my clothes — she was near hysteria. I finally came to my senses enough to lunge for my rifle, but my hands were shaking so badly I couldn't load the thing."

"And where was the light then?" Lyric asked.

"By then it was resting on the windowsill. Just sitting there like it belonged. Beats all I *ever* seen," he repeated. "I told Katherine that not a soul would believe us when we told them what we experienced."

"No, it was there," Lyric conceded. "It acts that way to some folks. With others it doesn't act so strange. Seems to have a personality."

"Why, I've never heard of such a thing." Katherine dabbed a hanky to her nose. "If

51

anyone had told me about that light I would have never came here."

"Someone said you folks came from Joplin?"

"We did — but I never heard a thing about a strange light."

"That seems odd," Lyric mused. "I assumed most everyone in these parts have heard about it." She glanced at Levi. If he came from Joplin surely he would have heard about the mysterious light. "A couple of years ago the light caused such a panic in Hornet, folks abandoned their homesteads — perfectly nice farms."

He shrugged. "I'd heard about it, but I didn't put any store in the folklore." He turned to look at the shattered pane. "It shore owes me a new window. I was so upset I threw my gun at it and shattered the glass." He gave Katherine a sheepish look. "I had to go outside and get the gun."

Lyric released a pent-up breath. Well, that explained the broken window.

"When he returned I'd stoked the fire and gotten dressed." Katherine wiped her eyes. "Neither one of us has had a moment of sleep."

"I'm sorry." Lyric rose, patting the young woman's arm. "Nobody knows what the light is or where it comes from, but I can assure you it means you no harm — least-ways it's been showing itself for a while now and other than being a little playful and scary, it appears to be harmless."

Levi pulled his bride closer. "It'll be fine, honey. Probably one of those things that'll never be explained, and except for our nerves being a bit on edge we're none the worse for wear."

"You're right." Katherine managed a timid smile. "But if it continues to happen . . ."

"If it continues to happen we'll move away, but I'm guessing we'll never see that thing again."

Lyric wasn't as optimistic as Levi but she remained silent. The Jennings weren't the only folks in the area skittish of the light, but she had her hands full with the wounded stranger.

Katherine offered her husband a timid smile. "But we only just built the house, Levi. Our dream home. It's so lovely and you and your father worked so hard to construct it." She glanced at Lyric. "Levi and his father work in the mines."

Lyric nodded. Joplin was rich in ore, lead, and zinc, and most men in the area made their living there. The work was hard, dirty, and dark, but it paid well.

Levi playfully ruffled Katherine's hair.

"Then we'll hope it never happens again, or we'll learn to deal with it."

She shuddered. "I think we should keep the option to move open."

He chuckled and set the gun aside. "Miss Bolton, if you'll come with me I'll get you that witch hazel from our stores."

"Thank you — and I'm sorry if I frightened you." They seemed like such a nice couple. Wouldn't it be good if Lyric could make a friend of young Katherine, if the young bride's mind and opinions had not been tainted by others? She couldn't imagine having anyone other than Lark to share her fears and dreams with, to help plan a future when Mother was gone. She'd read that having a close friend was like medicine — friendship cured many an ill.

Levi shook his head. "No — a little thing like you don't frighten me but . . ." He turned to glance over his shoulder at Katherine, who had disappeared into the bedroom. "But that light plain scared the molasses out of me."

A somber-faced Lark and Boots sat on the front porch when Lyric returned carrying the witch hazel. Judging by the girls' expressions a new crisis awaited. Picking up her steps, Lyric hurried up the road as Lark rose and came down the steps to meet her.

"What's wrong? Is it Mother?"

"No. It's the man. He's not breathing."

Lyric suddenly couldn't think. He was dead? He'd looked weak but awfully alive when she left. "Are you sure?" In some ways she welcomed the news but a small part of her felt defeated. Disappointed. She should have offered help sooner. Used her medicines earlier. Only God had the authority to say if a man lived or died, but she might have helped save him. Perhaps even the slightest attempt would have failed, but she would now live with the knowledge that she'd done almost nothing to save a life — a life God had given. Regret trickled from her heart.

"Positive," Lark verified. "We watched him like you told us to. His breathing got real ragged and his lips turned blue and then he didn't move anymore."

"Did you check his pulse?"

"Of course not. I wouldn't touch a dead man."

Boots's eyes widened. "We watched him like a hawk, Lyric. Honest. He snores a little — not much but some. When we last checked him he wasn't snoring; he looked like he was plain dead."

"If you didn't check his breathing then

you can't possibly know if he's dead or alive." She shook her head and began climbing the porch steps.

"Are you going to touch him?" Boots shuddered, but her eyes were bright with curiosity. The front screen closed and the girl's remark went unanswered.

The parlor door was open. Lyric moved to the sofa, almost dreading the task. She wasn't overly fond of working with the deceased, though she had helped prepare bodies before. Her gaze fell on the deceased outlaw. He was bloody and bruised and she detected no sign of life. The girls were right: He was gone, passed from this earth and from a life of shame. She murmured a prayer for his soul, focusing on the firm chin and black-and-blue swollen features. His time had been short and violent and the Good Book told her there was a certain place for men like him. She shuddered at the thought and reached to pull the light blanket over his face.

Rains had been plentiful this year so the burying wouldn't be hard; the dirt was soft and pliable. Then it occurred to her that the Youngers and their gang reportedly lived a scant few miles from Bolton Holler. Decency said she should send word to the family to come bury their own. Because a man robbed and even killed didn't mean he had no folks who loved him.

And perhaps — no, surely — there was some kind of bounty on this man's head. A bounty that would provide her with funds to build a new barn door . . . and the means to leave Bolton Holler and start a new life.

The thin, freshly shaved man sitting behind the sheriff's desk glanced up when Lyric entered late that morning. His chair scraped the floor and overturned when he recognized her.

"Please." She held up a calming hand. "I'm here to collect a reward."

Visibly uneasy, the younger man hitched up his gun belt, straightened his bony shoulders, and assumed a calm expression. "Who you got?"

"I believe that I have a dead Younger in the parlor. I think it only decent that someone ride and inform his kin that they should come get him."

The man's face turned blank. "A Younger? Which one? Not Cole, 'cause I jest heard he was over in Hot Springs checking on one of his racehorses."

"Cole Younger races horses?"

"Sure enough — he's a big sportsman. I hear tell that Cole is quite the horse lover."

He took another hitch in his pants. He didn't have enough flesh on his lanky frame to keep his britches up. "Those Youngers take care of their animals."

She didn't have the slightest interest in the Youngers' pursuits, but being friendly appeared to set the jailer at ease. "I don't know which Younger I have — you're not the sheriff, are you?" She had seen the sheriff around town on occasional visits and this man wasn't him.

"No — sheriff's away on personal business. Gonna be gone for a spell. He left the town's security to me." He straightened, proud-like. "I'm in control whilst he's absent."

"Then you should be the one to ride out to the Younger place and inform them they have kin to bury."

"Ma'am." Color crept up his neck. How old was he? Maybe in his very early twenties — certainly not experienced enough for this job. "If I was to ride into the Younger place for any reason, I'd have my head blowed off."

"Even if it's on official business?"

"Them Youngers shoot first and ask questions later."

"Well, it hardly seems fair that I have to bury the man. He's responsible for destroying my barn door and I have no funds to rebuild it." She paused, her eyes scanning the rows of posters tacked to the wall. "I'm assuming there is a reward?"

"If he's any part of the Younger gang there's likely a bounty on his head. Do you recognize his face on any of those posters?"

Stepping closer to the long row on display, Lyric scanned the assortment of horrors. Every last man looked like he'd shoot his grandma for a stewing hen. Her eyes moved down the row. It was so hard to tell. Most of the men wore beards and had missing teeth. The man in her parlor was a clean-looking sort, except for his injuries, and the swelling made it hard to make out his true features. After a bit, she turned away. "None of them look like the man in my parlor, but I heard Jim Cummins was seen in the area yesterday. Perhaps the man isn't a Younger but a Cummins."

"Could be, but I don't know much about Cummins," the man admitted. He stepped to the board and ran his gaze the length of the posters. "This here is Bud Pence. Does the man you got resemble him?"

She stared at the faded image. "Not really — but I can't say for certain. When he went through the barn door he got banged up pretty bad. I didn't think he'd make it through the night, but he did. He passed earlier today." Sighing, she turned away. "I don't know who he is but maybe he has kin in the area. Is it possible for someone to come and identify the body? Surely someone knows the hoodlums that plague the area."

Gunshots often shattered the stillness, and she could hear the ruckus clear up on the hill. Those gangs sure liked to cause trouble. The men rode through town, whooping, hollering, tearing down clotheslines of clean wash, shooting out windows, and terrorizing anyone in their path. A stray bullet had caught Wilson Brown three years past, and the town clothier was still in a wheelchair.

"There's several who'd know if it's Cummins, though you got one problem."

"Only one?" She laughed lightly. If only this were her one problem.

"You're not going to get a soul to come up to your house and identify him. You up to bringing him to the jail?"

Put a dead body in her cart and drive it all the way into town? She shook her head. "Can't you do this?" The very idea that a young, strong man like him couldn't get past his superstitions was plain silly. If he couldn't muster the courage to cross the Bolton threshold, how was he ever going to control the Holler's outlaws?

He removed his hat and laid it across his chest. "Ma'am. That spooklight — that there does something to me I can't explain."

"Don't folks see it down here?"

"Not as often. I haven't and I don't intend to if I can keep from it."

"My family has nothing to do with that light," she snapped. "You are surely a man of common sense."

He nodded. "Common sense tells me to stay far away, ma'am."

Shaking her head, she lifted the light scarf around her hair. "I don't see how I can get a dead man to the jail, but I'll try. Will you be here tomorrow morning?"

The delay would mean that she and the girls would have to carry the body from the parlor to the wagon. Were the three up to moving his bulky weight again? Lark and Boots wouldn't relish the task, but she couldn't allow the deceased to turn back to dust on Mother's sofa. And she wanted him out of the house — and out of her life.

"Yes, ma'am, I'll be here in the morning, and I'll have someone here who can tell you for certain who your man is."

"He isn't my man — and once he's identified I pray there's a bounty." The dead man on her mother's sofa was not only *not* her man, he wasn't her problem — but that seemed beside the point. The barn door was the real problem. Rosie wasn't likely to wander off, but wild animals could easily get to the cow and the chickens without the door to stop them. And if anything got the cow or chickens there would be no fresh butter, milk, cream, or eggs in the Bolton household.

The acting sheriff nodded. "If he's any part of the Younger gang, there'll be a reward. And a nice one."

"Then I will return early tomorrow morning to collect that prize." With a nod she turned and left, closing the door firmly behind her.

A balmy sun shifted to the west as Lyric reached the top of Bolton hill. Winded, she paused to catch her breath.

The Bolton house did resemble a house of fear.

Two stories, sagging shutters, warped paint. The all-weather spring-fed creek filled with limestone slabs gurgled alongside the path that led over the hill to the barn. Water poured from the spring, cascading over the bluff. When the wind blew, the old house creaked with noises even Lyric couldn't identify. The woodstove was enough to heat the downstairs but the upstairs bedrooms were cold and drafty in the winter and hot and stuffy in the summer.

The repugnant thought of moving the deceased rested heavily on her mind. It was hardly fair to involve Lark and Boots again, but she had no choice. He must be moved one final time in the morning, and then she could hand him off to the sheriff and be done with him.

A more repugnant thought crossed her mind, one that made blood rush to her head. What if there was no bounty? What if the man the sheriff brought in to identify the body couldn't make a positive match?

Visions of the few coins she kept in a jar in the pantry danced before her eyes. There were barely enough there to see them through the winter and a new spring planting.

Lifting her head, she let the slight breeze cool her thoughts and calm her fears. The Lord always provided.

Her eyes caught sight of a young woman coming down the back path carrying a dish covered with a red and white checked cloth.

Katherine Jennings.

Waving, Lyric hailed the visitor. Surely she was on her way somewhere and a mere wave wouldn't offend her.

The woman smiled and turned in her direction. Dumbfounded, Lyric watched her slowly make her way toward the Bolton back door. Breaking into a run, she raced to meet her.

"Afternoon," she called when her neighbor was within hearing distance.

"Good afternoon!" A breathless Katherine arrived with the most warming smile. For a moment Lyric couldn't find her voice. Visitors were a rarity — especially female visitors — and she mentally prepared to wish her new acquaintance well and watch her walk on. But Katherine continued toward her with a purposeful stride.

Extending the pie, the young woman said, "I came to apologize for my earlier behavior. I'm not usually the weepy, frightened sort."

Offering a welcoming smile, Lyric took the dish and sniffed the pleasant aroma. "Lemon?"

"The only kind that turns out right for me."

"Thank you — but there's no need to apologize. Your fright is completely understandable under the circumstances."

"Oh, Lyric — may I call you Lyric?"

Lyric nodded, her smile widening.

"When Levi and I married, I was so disturbed to think there wouldn't be any women my age around, but when you showed up this morning I felt much better."

"Katherine, I am delighted to see you. Come — let's sit a moment on the porch."

"I'd like that."

The two women crossed the porch and Lyric stopped dead in her tracks. The pie in her hand wavered. Sitting on the left side of the porch, big as life, was the Younger.

Peering closer she noticed he wasn't sitting; he was slumped — with a rope coiled around him. Eyes closed in death.

Turning on her heel, Lyric bumped into Katherine. "Let's sit on the other side. It will be warmer there."

"What . . . ? Okay. Well, as I was saying. . . ."

Words faded and Lyric's mind raced with possibilities. Lark and Boots must have wanted the body out of the house pretty badly if they'd been willing to carry him themselves. That was fine — he could stay there until properly identified. Then the sheriff would have to deal with the remains until kin arrived to claim him.

Taking a seat in the sunlight, Katherine said, "I can't stay long. Levi is expecting a roast for supper and I haven't put the meat in the oven yet." She glanced down the road. "And I certainly don't want to go anywhere alone after dark."

"I'm so glad you stopped by." Lyric took the chair opposite her, not sure where to put her hands. She'd never had a real conversation with a peer and she wasn't sure what to say. The spooklight certainly wasn't fodder for friendly chatter. "So you're newly married? How long?"

"Almost a month now." Katherine extended her right hand, where a tiny gem sparkled on the third finger.

"It's very lovely."

"It was Levi's grandmother's." Katherine drank in the jewel, pride shining in her eyes.

"You say you hail from Joplin?"

"Yes. We've been there since the boom started. Papa's mined for just about everything there is in these parts. Raised his family digging for ore and zinc."

Smiling, Lyric tried to keep up with the conversation, but her mind was on the body sitting not twenty feet away on the opposite side of the porch. She prayed Katherine wouldn't notice. Little did her friend know that the spooklight wasn't her only problem.

She managed to respond to the woman's friendly chatter calmly. "I've never been to Joplin. I hear it's very nice." She'd never been farther than the small settlement that sat at the foot of Bolton Hill: a general store, blacksmith, livery, jail, and a man who worked on teeth when he was sober. Someday she planned to leave this all behind. Someday she would visit Joplin and places far beyond — maybe even Oklahoma. She shifted, her eyes traveling to the corner post. Katherine couldn't see the Younger from where she was sitting, and there was no need to unduly alarm her. They'd chat for a while longer and the young woman would be on her way, none the wiser.

"Joplin nice?" Katherine sat back and her expression turned thoughtful. "Not really. The folks are friendly enough, but it's a typical boom town. Saturday nights are the worst. Drunken cowboys and miners crowd the saloons with dust from the mines still on their clothing. There's a lot of brawling — mud —" She turned to trace Lyric's gaze. "Is something amiss?"

"Nothing." Lyric smiled. "The town sounds interesting. Perhaps if I ever go there you'll go with me and show me around."

"I'd love that! It's pretty normal, I suspect, but I have family and good friends there. Levi assures me we'll visit often." She bent closer. "Are you and your mother close?"

Lyric wasn't sure how to answer. Close like mothers and daughters who shared secrets and smiles and hugs? No. Edwina had always been the strict authoritarian, not a nurturing mother. Lyric couldn't remember a single time she had ever felt close to her. "Mother's been ill for a long time . . ."

"Oh, of course. How insensitive of me. She hasn't been able to do much, has she?"

"Not much." Her manic fits had mostly passed, and now Edwina spent most of her days in bed. At the moment Lyric couldn't think of a single thing that made her more of a daughter than a caregiver.

Katherine leaned forward, lowering her voice. "About that strange light."

"The light won't hurt you," Lyric repeated. "But it is a bit unnerving."

"Have you seen it?"

"Many times — but not as closely as you have." Lyric had dreaded the question. The two women seemed to be off to a good start, but she might as well come clean about the rumors. "There are various speculations about its source. Katherine, you should know that — well, that people think my mother has something to do with it. They don't understand her sickness, you see — and they've heard her say some crazy things. But I can assure you she has nothing to do with the light. If you want my opinion the light can be explained. I just don't have that knowledge."

"Yes . . . you mentioned your . . . family earlier this morning. And truthfully Levi and I have heard the stories, and we thought long and hard about building so close, but the land was exactly what Levi wanted. I won't say I wasn't a bit hesitant to meet you but now you seem . . . well, normal."

Lyric cast an eye toward the porch and wondered if she'd feel the same if she knew who was sitting with them. Could she share her deep need for friendship with this kind lady? The two had only met this morning and yet she had taken an instant liking to Katherine Jennings.

Katherine leaned in closer. "Do you think we're nearing the end of the world? The New Testament mentions 'signs and wonders' that will precede Jesus when He comes again. Do you think that's what this light represents?"

"I've heard such speculation. Some say the light is something that comes from way beyond the sky. A traveling minister told the people the light was an evil spirit, not a ghost. The stories say this particular evil is trapped in this location for reasons unknown to mortals." Endless legends of missing miners, headless soldiers, and swamp gas tried to explain away the light.

"Oh, my." The girl's face now turned ashen.

"There are many theories, but none proven. Most are simply silly." Lyric shifted, glancing at the corner post. "I would offer you a glass of lemonade, but I used the last of my lemons and sugar. Would you like some spring water?"

"No, I really should be going." Katherine stood, shaking the wrinkles from her skirt. The dress was a pretty store-bought one, unlike the one Lyric was wearing. "I wanted to bring the pie and make my apologies for being so inhospitable this morning. We should have tea soon."

"I would love that."

Katherine picked up her wicker basket. "You mentioned your mother. Does she feel up to me peeking in on her? I'd love to meet her."

Lyric couldn't think of a worse idea. "I'm afraid mother is very weak," she said. "She has been bedridden the past few months and sleeps most of the time. She awakens only for light meals and then only for a few minutes."

"Oh. I'm so sorry."

"Thank you so much for asking. Her time is short. We're . . . waiting."

"I understand. Please call on me if you

need anything. And Levi has a strong back. If you need wood . . ."

The unexpected and unusual offer brought swift tears to Lyric's eyes. She quickly turned away so Katherine wouldn't notice. "Thank you, but that's not necessary. My little sister and I are quite familiar with an ax."

"Well, if you should need anything, don't hesitate to send for us. We want to be good neighbors."

"I won't hesitate, and thank you for the pie. Lark and I will enjoy it immensely." The treat would be most welcome.

Moving to her visitor's right side, Lyric walked down the steps with her. Katherine was headed north, so with any luck she'd never spot Younger on the side porch.

"Oh, dear. I fear I should have put that roast in the oven before I walked over. It may not be done by supper, but Levi will eat most anything — perhaps we'll have leftover stew. We had it for dinner, but with a pan of fresh biscuits Levi shouldn't complain." The women briefly embraced and then Katherine set off for her homestead, swinging the empty wicker basket. Lyric watched until she disappeared far enough down the road that her voice wouldn't carry and then bellowed, "Lark!"

She couldn't wait to hear those two young ladies explain why they had set a dead man on the front porch.

3

The sound of feet clamoring down the stairway alerted Lyric to the two girls' presence. When the screen door opened, Lark peered out. "Did you scream at me?" she asked.

Keeping an even tone, Lyric asked, "Why is that man wrapped in a blanket sitting on the front porch?"

Lark's eyes traveled to the corner post. "Mr. Younger?"

"Who else would be dead, sitting on our porch, wrapped in a blanket?"

"Mr. Younger. We didn't want him stinking up the house so Boots and I moved him out here." She glanced at the sun. "It's getting pretty late now to start digging a hole. Can we get it done before the light fades?"

"Of course not, but it doesn't matter. We aren't going to bury him; we have to take him into town first thing in the morning. The sheriff will have someone there to identify the remains and they will assume responsibility for his disposal."

Boots's eyes lit up. "You mean we might not have to bury him? Good. Carrying him out of the parlor was bad enough."

"Why should we? His family will need to deal with his remains. He isn't our problem. I'm only interested in the bounty."

Lark glanced toward the corner post. "He's not damaged or anything. He's only been out here a little while and I'm getting tired of dragging him around. Can't we leave him on the porch tonight? You don't look much like you want to tackle getting him back into the house."

The young idealist was correct on that assumption. Tracing Boots's gaze, Lyric studied the sky. "There's no sign of rain. I suppose it won't hurt anything to leave him where he is, but we'll need to shelter him from animals. Get more blankets and make sure all blood is wiped cleaned. We don't want to attract wild critters. I need to feed Mother supper now. Did you check on her often today?"

"Three times. She was sleeping. She's getting real tired now, Lyric."

Nodding, Lyric brushed past her sister and stepped into the house. She'd wasted a full night and day on the blanket-wrapped stranger sitting on her porch.

She didn't intend to waste another moment.

Tree frogs sang as Lyric sank down on the back porch step a few hours later. A full moon lay on the horizon; the faint but distinct scent of earth trying to push its way to new life reassured her that life went on.

Mother had eaten nothing tonight. The liquid had poured from the corners of her mouth instead of being swallowed. Edwina's shallow breathing was barely a wisp of rise and fall. Lyric had taken the broth and fed it to the barn cats.

Resting her head on a corner post, she closed her eyes and tried to ignore the fact that a dead man was resting just around the other side of the house. She shook her head as she thought of all that poor man had endured. Dragging him from the barn to the parlor to the porch . . . but surely he'd only gotten what he deserved. Those Youngers were nothing but trouble, and if another one was gone, well, good riddance.

She sniffed, thinking she could already smell the decomposing body. The whole situation was starting to alarm her. She wanted it over and done with.

Something stepped from the shadows and

she straightened, straining to make out the object. It was much larger than a fox but leaner and taller than Rosie. The shotgun sat inside the doorway; she should have thought to bring it with her.

Bumping up the step on her backside, she made ready to leap when the object appeared in the clearing.

It was a horse.

A saddled animal dragging reins. The enormous buckskin nosed the dirt, snagging pieces of tender green shoots starting to poke through the ground. When he spotted her, he made a blowing sound.

Easing slowly to her feet, she stepped down, her eyes fixed on the riderless animal. He lifted his head high and whinnied softly as she approached. "Easy there, big fellow. What are you doing out here this time of night?" She latched onto the bridle, her gaze skimming the heavy thicket that lay behind the cleared path. The animal caught the scent of water and quickly moved to the rain barrel. He drank thirstily.

Lyric took advantage of the distraction to search for saddle bags or anything that might identify the horse's owner. There were no bags, just a rolled-up bedroll. A saddle and bedroll and a Liberty Missouri Bank bag. It contained a few deposit slips with recent dates and seven dollars and twenty-three cents in change and currency. Puzzled, she stepped back and removed the bit from the horse's mouth. Apparently he'd been roaming for a spell; small bloody cuts lined the inside of his mouth. "There, now. That should feel better."

Her eyes returned to the underbrush, her brow furrowed. The animal could belong to Levi and Katherine Jennings, though Levi didn't seem like the careless sort. No one would leave a bridle and bit on a horse overnight. Suddenly her breath caught. Younger's horse? The bank bag pointed to a recent robbery.

Possible, a silent voice agreed. Something large had busted through that solid doorway. And the horse could have been roaming since the accident.

The frogs turned noisy, saturating the spring night air with constant singing croaks. The horse was a splendid animal. He bore no signs of neglect other than temporary carelessness. On closer inspection she discovered a few tiny cuts and scratches but nothing serious.

The frogs fell silent.

For a moment the change was deafening. Stars shone overhead and the moon rose. The horse drank deep drafts from the barrel. Her eyes searched the heavy thicket for signs of the spooklight. *Please don't show yourself now.*

She didn't fear it but neither did she welcome its presence. Not now. Not tonight, when the whole day had been a series of nerve-rattling mysteries. Goosebumps rose on her arms and a tight knot formed in her stomach. Something felt strange. Unusual.

Something was close by.

She shook her head. This wasn't like her; she'd never feared the light or darkness. She preferred to believe the old Indian legend that the spooklight traveled the area where a band of Cherokee Indians, at the end of their rope from hunger, disease, and exhaustion, sold their women into slavery near the end of the long and torturous Trail of Tears. Legend said the spooklight glowed as an eternal reminder of the cruelty and inhumanity of the forced evacuation of the Indians from their homeland.

Still, at this moment, she sensed a foreign presence — one more formidable than she'd ever felt when the light appeared.

It's nothing. Now take the horse to the barn, feed it, remove the saddle, curry it, and bed it down for the night. All this talk and nonsense about the spooklight had her on edge — that was all.

Reaching for the horse's mane, she turned and encountered a solid wall of flesh.

Panicked, she caught her breath and looked straight into the dead man's eyes.

4

Lyric set a bowl of hot oatmeal in front of the outlaw, willing herself to breathe normally. Her heart thumped in her chest and her cheeks burned when she thought of the way she'd fainted earlier. The injured man had been left to help her back to the house.

"You could have at least warned me you were there. I thought you were dead."

Those were the first words she'd spoken since his unexpected appearance had thrown her into a tizzy. Now she sat him down at the kitchen table where he sat staring feebly at the meal, head faintly bobbing. "The last thing I recall is talking to you when I was on the sofa," the man said. "I must have drifted off. When I woke up I was on the front porch, bound like a piece of meat. Who did that to me?"

"Lark and Boots. They thought you had . . . passed."

Stepping to the service porch, Lyric got

the pitcher of cream and returned to the kitchen. She found it impossible to keep the peevishness out of her tone. "Who are you?"

He glanced up. "Ma'am?"

"Which Younger are you?"

He shook his head. "I can't rightly say. I've been trying to figure that out."

"You don't know your own name?"

"Ma'am, it's not only my name. I can't recall anything. My name, where I am, and most of all who I am." He brought both hands to his head. "I was hoping you could help."

"You're in Bolton Holler, in the Missouri Ozarks, and I know nothing about you other than that you rode your horse through my barn door and I strongly suspect you are a Younger or one of their gang. The impact must have left you temporarily addled."

"What makes you suspect I'm an outlaw?"

"I . . . because the Youngers are thick in this area, and who else would be drinking and tearing up folks' property? This is a small holler and we don't get strangers riding through often."

Slowly lifting his head, he frowned. "I rode a horse through your barn door?"

"You did — and I don't mean to add to your troubles but you'll need to pay to replace that door. If you don't, I don't know where I'll find the money. The house needs paint, and I could use another milk cow. I don't have the extra funds to go replacing perfectly good barn doors, you know."

"Of course . . ." His hand dropped to his pocket and started fumbling. She interrupted his search.

"No need to look for money or a wallet. You don't have either one. There was no identification on you." Heat flooded her cheeks. "I wasn't being nosy. We needed to know who you were — to notify kin."

"We?"

"My sister, Lark, and her friend, Boots."

"Oh . . . those two."

If anything could jog a memory, it would be Lark and Boots.

His gaze slowly roamed the kitchen and confusion lit his eyes. They were a clear green — very striking. She hadn't noticed the exceptional hue before. The warmth in her cheeks heightened when she realized what he must be thinking as he looked around her home. Barely decent shelter, an old woodstove, inadequate counter, scarred kitchen table, and three wooden chairs. She took pity on his puzzlement.

"I'm sorry about the way you found yourself when you woke." Her cheeks burned now when she thought of how he'd been tied up and set on the front porch like trash. "Well, we thought — assumed — that you'd passed."

His gaze switched back to her. "Well, I'm still here. Now what?"

"First thing tomorrow morning, I'm to have you at the jail for identification. There's a bounty on your head and I intend to collect it." She took the chair opposite him, watching various emotions play across his features. Shock. Disbelief. Fear. Her compassionate side felt sorry for his state. It was a pitiful one indeed. Both eye sockets were yellowish black, swollen to slits, and he was covered with bruises and cuts. And now she'd had to tell him that he was a wanted man with a bounty on his head.

She hoped the reward was worth the misery and effort.

"What am I wanted for?"

She lifted a shoulder. "Can't say for certain, but if you are a Younger, as I suspect, the authorities have plenty of charges to choose from."

"And if I'm not a Younger?"

She hadn't considered the prospect. It was possible, of course, but highly unlikely. The main road was miles away and strangers didn't come through the holler often. It was conceivable that he wasn't a wanted man, but the chances of anyone new riding through Bolton Holler were slim to none. Unless he was a new bandit who'd come to join one of the gangs that made their home in these hills. The caves, running creeks, white and black oak with scattered shortleaf pines, and a ground cover rich in legumes and goldenrods were the ideal cover for the wanted.

She met his gaze directly. "If you're not, you better be able to prove it by tomorrow morning."

"How can I prove something I'm not clear about?"

"You recall nothing?"

"No. Where am I?" he asked a second time.

"You're in Missouri — some miles from Joplin. You don't recall ramming through the barn door?" Seemed to her a man ought to recall something like that.

He shook his head. "Last thing I remember is talking to you, here, in some room with books."

"The parlor." She noted that he hadn't taken a single bite of the oatmeal so she nudged the bowl closer. "Maybe eating something will clear your head. A body can't think on an empty stomach."

Shaking his head, he pushed the bowl

aside. "I've lost my appetite." He glanced out the window. "What time of day is it?"

"It's late. I was about to come into the house and go to bed when you — appeared." She wasn't sure if she could ever wander out after dark again. Her heart was still beating like a war drum in her ears.

"And you're handing me over to the sheriff at first light?"

She nodded. "He'll have someone there to identify you. And should you awaken early, be careful to stay hidden. My younger sister is asleep, but she thinks you're dead. I'd like to spare her the shock you gave me."

His eyes roamed his surroundings again. "You and your sister live here alone?"

"My sister and my mother . . ." She paused, checking her thoughts. He was crafty even in his impaired state. "And the big armed hired hand who sleeps in the barn. He checks on the house every hour or so," she lied. "Nothing goes on here that he doesn't see. He has a gun and he isn't afraid to use it."

"Does he know I'm here?"

"He knows — and he's watching."

"Well —" The stranger pushed back from the table. "Much obliged for patching me up for the gallows."

"Gallows?"

85

"I don't remember who I am or where I'm from, but I seem to recall they hang outlaws in most parts."

Hang. She hadn't thought about that probability. She'd heard the hammers and saws a few times when the town built the gallows for a hanging. The event always left butterflies in her stomach, but she'd never *known* one of the men scheduled to hang. She tried not to think about the man who would face that platform soon. A smidgeon of doubt crept into her mind. What if this man wasn't an outlaw or the bounty on his head didn't amount to a hill of beans? When she'd gone to town she'd not seen one poster that even resembled the man sitting before her, though puffiness marred his features.

If he wasn't an outlaw there wouldn't be a bounty. And without a bounty Rosie would go without a door on the barn — and Lyric wouldn't have the funds to begin her new life when Mother passed.

The man shook his head in an apparent attempt to clear it. "If you don't mind, I'll sleep on the sofa."

His voice brought her back to the present. "You won't try anything, will you? If you sleep there, I'll have to sit with you with my gun close by."

"Do I look like I'm capable of trying anything?"

No. He looked like death warmed over, but she couldn't throw caution to the wind just because she felt sorry for him. He could be telling a bald-faced lie. He might know exactly who he was and be looking for the moment to escape.

"I'll get a fresh blanket." They both rose and she steadied him as they slowly eased to the parlor. He was wounded but strong; she felt the tight muscles and sheer power in his arm when he leaned into her slight weight. "I wish you would eat something," she fretted. "You'll need your strength."

"If I can't make the climb to the noose I'm sure the sheriff will assist me."

The coming hours weren't a pleasant thought — even less agreeable if she was wrong about his identity. It would be awful to hang an innocent person. She knew all too well what it was like to be wrongfully judged.

She shook the unwanted thoughts away. Who else could he be but an outlaw? Didn't Boots mention that Jim Cummins had been run out of the mercantile the same day this man destroyed her property? He could even be Cummins, though his poster wasn't on the sheriff's wall. Just because this stranger

87

was weak as a newborn calf was no reason for her to go all soft and compassionate now. She settled him on the couch and then went for the blanket. By the time she returned his eyes were closed and soft snores met her ears.

Tucking the warm blanket around him, she noted the pump knot on his forehead and winced. She supposed that after tomorrow morning he'd have more than a knot to worry him.

An hour before sunup, Lyric crept down the stairway in her bare feet. The old house was quiet; no one was awake this early. She'd lain in her bed for hours, her conscience nagging her. Was it possible she had jumped to the wrong conclusion? Odds were if the wounded man wasn't Cummins or one of the Youngers he was part of a gang, but her enforced solitude made her more aware of hypocritical and unjust beliefs. If the man on the sofa couldn't recall who he was, was it fair to tag him as a criminal without absolute certainty?

A life was at stake. In this case a mistake meant certain death instead of turned backs and outright shunning. The town had had its fill of outlaws, and they wouldn't think twice about hanging this man without

88

adequate proof of wrongdoing.

Her strong penchant for fact surfaced. Fact was, nobody in the household could be certain who this man was or where he belonged. And even if someone in town recognized him, nobody in these parts told the whole truth.

Lord, allow me more than my share of wisdom today. I can't let a man hang if he's innocent and only You know the truth at the moment. Help me to verify his true identity before I stand by and watch him be put to death.

Not that the town would believe a word *she* said. But the stranger would be safe here until she got this matter resolved. It was the least one human could do for another. Not a soul would venture near this place, even if a bounty was in plain sight. It wasn't likely the injured man was going anywhere soon, and she could afford half a morning to avoid a mistake she'd have to live with if she followed through with her original intent. She could slip into town, do a little investigating, and be back before she was due to meet the sheriff. Lark would milk Rosie, gather eggs, feed Mother, and —

An ear-piercing scream from the parlor shattered the peaceful silence.

And oh, yes. She needed to inform Lark

the outlaw wasn't dead.

Murphy Hake rode his fence line searching for breaks. Cattle theft was rampant in the holler and most of his time was spent running down strays or rounding up stolen cattle. His herd wasn't the largest in the holler, but it put meat and bread on his table. He stayed to himself, went to bed early, got up before dawn, and worked hard. He had inherited the plot of ground when his folks died during a measles outbreak three years earlier. He was an only child, left to fend for himself, which he didn't mind. Folks left him alone — other than that pesky Lark Bolton. Now that he was older he had his fair share of women admirers, and he took full advantage of their attention at the occasional Saturday night social.

He spotted a fresh cut and reined up. Warm sunshine covered his back and he slipped out of the denim jacket he'd donned before daylight. With wire cutters in hand, he approached the break, not the least bit surprised when he saw the youngest Bolton girl heading in his direction. Lark.

Shaking his head, he mentally prepared for the visit. For some reason, the girl was smitten with him. His closest neighbor had turned into a pest. She helped pass the time, but he didn't welcome her intrusions. It was uncanny how she seemed to know where and when he'd be working. Of course, town gossips claimed the Boltons were all crazy. They were unusual, but he supposed they'd say the same about him. He kept to himself and unless someone happened his way he didn't look for company.

Lark walked up, her face split wide into a contagious grin. How old was she now? Twelve? He didn't look up when she approached; he didn't want to encourage the interruption.

"Hi!"

Nodding, he lifted a piece of wire fencing and tacked it into place.

"Nice day, huh?"

"Real nice."

Lark's eyes scanned the length of broken wire. "Cattle rustlers, huh?"

"Yep. Can't seem to keep ahead of them." He tacked another piece in place.

"There's going to be a hanging after a while. Are you going?"

Kneeling, he fitted the line to a post. "Nope."

"Why not?" She put both hands on her knees and bent close, crowding him. He gently eased her aside and continued with his work.

"Ah . . . that's a shame," she prattled on. "You don't go out often, do you?"

"Nope."

Undeterred, she followed him down the fence line, hands on her knees. Someone needed to tell this girl that she was headed for trouble if she dogged all males like she did him.

"I don't get to go to any hangings." She sighed. "I'd like to, but Lyric won't let me."

"Twelve-year-olds shouldn't be witnessing such things."

"I'm fourteen now. Did you forget?"

Forget? He wasn't aware he'd ever known. Or cared. When he didn't answer she leaned closer. "Do you think that's fair, or do you think she's just mothering me?"

"Mothering you. Your mother's sick, isn't she?"

"Yeah, she's real bad." She handed him a nail when he turned to reach for one.

"Thanks," he mumbled, frowning.

"You're welcome. I'm hoping Mother will live a long time because when she dies Lyric wants to leave this holler but I don't. I want to spend my life right here." She cast a glance his way. "I want to get married and live here forever."

When he didn't answer again she prompted, "Do you think that's silly?"

"Silly?" He eased to the next post.

"You should go out more often," she decided.

"That right?"

"You're too young to stay cooped up by yourself. It isn't good for a body."

He turned slightly to stare at her. "How do you know what I do?"

"Oh, I know," Lark said. "I watch out for you."

"Watch out for me?" Straightening, he looked her straight in the eye. "Why do you watch out for me?"

"I just like to make sure you have everything you need. You know, you being alone and all."

Pitching a wire cutter into a bag, he said tightly, "Don't let me catch you anywhere near my place."

"Why not? I'm not trespassing or anything. I'm just keeping an eye on you."

"You don't need to check on me. I'm doing fine."

Now he'd have to watch for her peering in his windows. When was she going to get over this childish crush?

Shaking her head, Lark grinned. "Are not."

"Look, don't you need to be somewhere?"

"Nope. Not until they come for the out-law."

"What outlaw?"

"The one we got in our parlor. We think he might be one of the Youngers. He tore through our barn door a few nights ago and we've been expecting him to die any minute, but he keeps hanging on. We're supposed to take him to the sheriff's office this morning, where someone can hopefully tell us who he is. Then they're going to hang him."

"The sheriff." The remark came out harsh and unsympathetic.

"You don't like our sheriff?"

"He's a runt. Doesn't have enough gumption to come in out of the rain." He hammered, using more force than necessary. Sheriff Dixon should have never appointed his nephew to the job. The boy had no experience with outlaws and barely knew how to pin his badge to his shirt.

"Sounds more like you don't respect him . . . or maybe you'd like the job?"

"I wouldn't turn it down." He stood, adjusting his hat brim, and leaned down to pick up a tool. "And you can bet I would do some boot kicking in this holler." He met her eyes. "Shouldn't you be running along?"

Glancing up, she appeared to study the sun. "Yes, I guess I should. Boots will be

94

over directly. We'll have to help Lyric move our outlaw to town."

He grunted. Lord have mercy. He hoped those two wouldn't be hanging around all day. He'd not get a lick of work done.

"You want me to let you know if they postpone the hanging until tomorrow?"

"No. Not interested."

"It would be better than sitting around by yourself all day."

"Watching a man die isn't my notion of fun."

"I didn't say it was fun, but it might be interesting. Do they die quickly?"

"Quick enough."

"Do you know any outlaws in this area?"

"I thought you said you had to leave."

"Oh . . . yes, I do. Want me to take your jacket and drop it off at your house on my way home?"

"Nope."

"Well, you'll let me know if I can be any help. Nothing wrong with someone helping a neighbor."

"Don't need a thing, but thanks for asking." He reached for the horse's reins and prepared to mount. Her longing gaze didn't escape him. The girl was in love.

"You take care," she said.

Touching his forefinger to his hat brim, he reined aside. "You do the same, Little Miss."

5

The jailer sprang to his feet when Lyric entered the jail. A frown crossed his pimply features and his Adam's apple bobbed with anticipation. "You got the corpse?"

"The oddest thing happened. He roused late last night; seems he wasn't dead after all."

The apple on his neck jumped. "Roused? You mean from the dead?"

"From the *chair*. Rallied ever so slightly. He'll need more time to pass away." That wasn't exactly the truth but the good Lord knew the man needed someone on his side.

"Well, I was about to order a gallows built. Can't see no use in nursing the fellow back to health if we're just gonna hang him anyways." He chuckled. "Just put 'em out of their misery. That's my theory."

"Yes." She stepped to the poster wall and one by one slowly examined the likenesses. "It seems peculiar . . ." She paused and fixed him with a stare. "It's not necessary to stand across the room from me. I'm not crazy, you know. I mean you no harm."

"Yes'm. Habit, I suppose." He straightened and sauntered to his desk, but she noticed he never took his eyes off her.

She turned back to the poster board. "It seems that if the man's face was on this board, I would recognize him."

"Could be one of them Quantrill Raiders — they're a bad lot. Could even be Hoodoo Brown — now that thar's worth a pretty penny if you was to get him. He's the baddest cowpoke there is."

"It's my understanding that these outlaws — that the Youngers make their residence nearby. Three, four miles away?"

"Yes, suppose they do. They shelter a lot of them crooks and bad guys."

"If they're so close to town why don't you simply go and arrest them? Some have handsome bounties."

Shaking his head, he fixed on her. "Do I look stupid? They might live there but I don't go looking for trouble. I got a wife and a little girl to feed. In these parts, nobody goes looking for trouble; it finds them easy enough."

"But all that reward money — isn't that an enticement?"

"You can put a price on your life?" He shook his head again. "No one around here thinks so, ma'am. Now if one was to come and turn hisself in I'd be happy to oblige, but I'm not going to their place askin' to get my head blowed off."

She turned. "But you'd have no problem hanging an outlaw?"

"No ma'am, but yours will be dead when you bring him to me. Thar's a difference. I've heard that Hoodoo Brown's been seen in the area as late as last month — and even Jim Cummins — but then I heard Hoodoo moved his family somewhere up around Warrensburg not long ago and took a decent job as a printer's devil. But men like him don't stay straight fer long."

If the man on her sofa was Hoodoo he was married with a large family.

"Is this Hoodoo's poster?" The poster was faded and the face was hard to make out.

"That's him."

She peered closer and noted this man wore a long white beard. Of course men shaved, but the man in the image before her was older than her outlaw. Tacking the poster back into place, she continued down the row. Not a single likeness fit her man.

"If I go to all the trouble of fixin' for a hanging you are going to bring your man here, aren't you? You're not going to turn him loose if he lives. You'd be a fool."

And she'd make a bigger fool of him. "If you'd like, you can come get him. Mother might even invite you inside."

The jailer paled. "That ain't necessary. I'll take your word on it."

She hadn't given her word. "You said this Cummins person was seen in the area recently?"

"He was — but something spooked him real good and he high-tailed it outta town like a cat on moonshine — forgot all about buying his tobacco. What makes you ask?"

"Well, I'm thinking it could be him in my parlor."

"No." The jailer lifted a thoughtful hand to his jaw. "Don't reckon so. One of Cummins's cousins was in yesterday and he didn't mention anything about Jim. If Cummins had gone missin' in your parlor, the boy would have asked about him."

The whole situation took on a troubling aspect. If the man on Mother's sofa was really an outlaw in need of hanging there should be an image of him among these . . . sterling-looking specimens. Shouldn't there?

"If you don't mind me saying so, I don't know why any of this should trouble you. Just hand him over and I'll take care of your problem. Don't matter if he feels good or not — in a split second he'll be out of his misery."

"I thought you didn't go looking for trouble."

"I ain't looking for it, but when it's handed to me I dispose of the matter. You bring him in and I'll hang him."

She turned. "And if he isn't wanted by the law?"

"Well then, I'd say he'd be having a bad day and I'd also say if he's in these hollers he's wanted for something."

Bad day, indeed. She'd consider being strung up like a smoked ham more than a bad day; it would be criminal if the man were innocent. Yet there wasn't a single reason for her to think him blameless. Just because he was dazed didn't mean he was harmless. Shaking her head she moved away from the board. "There's one other thing."

"Yes'm?"

"If there is a bounty on this man's head what would it be?"

"Don't rightly know the amount, but a man like Cummins won't bring much. But if you had part of a Younger gang, now, you'd be looking at a lot more money."

"A hundred dollars?"

"Ma'am, a bounty can to go five thousand

and up if 'n it's the right person. Depends on the charges and if he's killed anyone important."

Five thousand dollars. A fortune. The amount spun in her head. She and Lark would be set for life. They could go anywhere — on a ship, travel by coach, and stay in the nicest hotels.

The sheriff cleared his throat. "Not likely you got Frank, but anyone ridin' with that Younger gang is bad news. If you should happen to have one of them in your possession then we're talkin' real money."

Nodding, she stepped around him and walked to the door.

"So you'll deliver him tomorrow early one way or the other?"

She paused. "He's worth more alive than dead, isn't he?" She had to be smart about this transfer. If a man was dead he wasn't much good to anyone, and it seemed to her folks in this town surely took delight in their executions.

The man shrugged. "Depends who he is."

"I'll expect due pay when I bring him."

"Yes, ma'am. Once we sort out who he is."

When she shut the door his words still rang in her head. "Depends who he is."

All she had to do was figure that out.

Lark turned red in the face. "I don't want to *leave* here. Boots couldn't go with us."

"No, Boots can't go with us, but we're not staying." Lyric set a wicker basket on the table. While she'd been in town she picked up a few supplies. Sugar, flour, and cornmeal.

"That's not fair, Lyric. You're the one who doesn't like the holler. Just because we're snubbed and feared doesn't mean we can't have a nice life here. Boots is the only friend I need. She's the only friend I've ever had."

"You'll make new friends wherever we go." Granted, Lark was more reclusive than she; her sister could bury her face in a book and stay there for hours, while Lyric sometimes felt the loneliness would choke her. But if Lark set her heart to something, nothing would change it. She made up her mind quickly and rarely if ever changed a decision. She didn't need adventures — not like Lyric.

Many was the time Lyric had sat on the front step and listened to the music floating from the church house on Saturday evenings and longed to be a tiny part of the socials. Sometimes she would bake a cake and enjoy a piece on the porch while the festivities went on below, pretending that she was there. Lark preferred to stay in her room, window shut, engrossed in a story.

"May I have this dance, Miss Bolton?"

"Why, thank you, Mr. Somebody. I would be honored."

And then a handsome man would swing her into his arms and her feet would fairly fly over the wood floor, her laughter blending with that of other young women her age. Oh, she knew her dreams were foolish, and a man would never hold her in his arms. When she began her new life she would be compelled to tell any suitor that her mother was a madwoman, and she had no doubts the news would dash cold water on any potential beau's fancies. After all, what if Edwina's craziness had been passed down to her daughters? A man had a right to know that sort of thing.

Lark scooted back from the table. "I won't go. I'm not leaving the holler. I've lived here all of my life and I plan to die here."

"You plan to eventually marry Murphy Hake, but that is only a senseless, youthful dream, Lark. He's five years older than you and will most likely be married by the time you're of age."

"He won't marry. He'll wait for me."

Lark turned. "Does he know you think that?"

"If you're askin' if I've informed him, no. That would be silly. It would scare him away. I'll be grown in three years. Everything will be different then. He may want me to be eighteen or nineteen but I'm in no hurry." She smiled. "God made that man just for me."

"Lark, I have never thought of you as a foolish girl but you're talking like a child. We don't know God's plans and it's foolish to speculate that way."

"It isn't foolish. And he won't marry just any woman. He'll wait for me." She crossed her arms. "And I intend to be here when he starts looking."

"You're hopeless. You will go with me when the time comes." Lyric set a sack of flour and a tin of baking soda on the counter. There was plenty of yeast still in the pantry. Tonight the house would smell of fresh bread.

"You can't make me leave."

"I'll hogtie and drag you if I have to."

"That's so unfair! Wait . . ." Lark vacated her chair and went to Lyric's side as she pulled a sack of sugar out of her bag. "We actually have sugar?"

"I thought we'd celebrate. Once I take the

stranger to town and collect the reward we'll celebrate with a nice peach pie. I still have three jars of canned peaches from last summer." She turned to peer over her shoulder. "Where's the man?"

"He was on the porch last I saw of him."

"He made it out there on his own?" Panic filled her. Had he seen his chance to escape? It wasn't possible. If he tried to escape he wouldn't get far.

Lark nodded, slipping a pinch of sugar in her mouth. "He seems stronger today."

"That's not possible. He's lost too much blood."

"Still, I saw him try to go up and down the front steps. Twice. It took him a long time, but he made it. I don't think he's going to die. I think he's too stubborn or too strong."

The man had to be weak as a kitten. He'd barely eaten a morsel since his injury and now he was attempting to climb steps?

"He must have an iron constitution." Lyric closed the pantry door, her eyes scanning the kitchen. "What time is it?"

Lark glanced out the window. "I'd say shortly before noon." Years ago they had learned to tell time by the sun's position. The clocks in the house were rarely wound.

"I'll go look for him. You need to make

106

Mother some fresh broth."

"She won't eat it, Lyric. She barely rouses these days. I think she wants to let go and pass on, but she can't."

"Perhaps the Lord is allowing her more time." Lyric sighed heavily. The years had been long, but she would miss Edwina when she passed. Her mother was cold and indifferent at the best of times, but Lyric did care. She'd seen moments when Edwina softened. She had cried when her favorite cat died. They'd sat on the back step that night and Lyric had cradled her like a small child.

"Do you think we'll end up crazy like her?"

"I don't know. I pray not."

"If we do, there's no escaping it . . . so why not stay here and be content?"

"Because I can't be happy here; I want more than accusing stares and cold backs turned on me." She lifted the window for a bit of fresh air. "I want to go to a dance someday."

"You can go anytime you want. They have one twice a month at the church."

"Wouldn't that be a sight? Me, Lyric Bolton, walking into the church. The room would empty."

Lark stepped closer. "Only if you stepped

into Mrs. Grannier's face and hissed."

The sisters broke out laughing. Mrs. Grannier was a fussy old fiddlehead who ran the town and spread gossip thick as molasses. The picture Lark painted made Lyric hold her sides in merriment. She could see birdlike Mrs. Grannier screaming like a banshee, latching onto her husband's arm. Mr. Grannier couldn't fight his way out of butcher paper, but he was a pleasant enough soul. At least he didn't step to the opposite side of the street when one of the Boltons came to town.

Lyric's smile gradually faded. She could never go to a dance in this town; no use even considering it. "I'm going to search for the wounded man. Can you start the broth?"

"Sure. Boots is coming by later and we're going to pick greens this afternoon."

"Good, bring some dandelion — and the polk might be up by now. Pull a few wild onions while you're at it." Fresh vegetables were always a welcome sight on the table. The tender plants grew wild along the creek bank.

Sighing, she longed to just take a peaceful wade in the creek instead of searching for that bothersome stranger. He couldn't have gone far, not in his pitiful condition.

When she stepped onto the porch she spotted him, way down by the fence row. Frowning, she realized that her outlaw had more fortitude than good sense.

But at least he was still here.

The mild weather was so pleasant that Lyric had decided to air the house. March in Missouri could be warm, windy, and pleasant, or else bring some of the deepest snow of the year. Tender tree buds and blooming daffodils were often buried in soft white mounds. The old saying was true: If you didn't like the weather, stick around for an hour and it would change. And change it would, because winter wasn't finished with them yet. The low bank of clouds in the north promised rough weather, but today held the firm potential of spring, with lilacs and wild asparagus sneaking around the corner.

She stood on tiptoe and peered out the window, hoping to see the wounded stranger. She had spotted him all the way down at the barn shortly after dinner and marveled at his slow but determined steps. He was still a very sick man, but he appeared to be overcoming his injuries far sooner than most.

A second knock sounded at the open back

door and when she glanced up she saw Katherine Jennings in the doorway holding a small basket. "Katherine! Come in."

The young lady stepped into the room and took a deep breath. "What smells so heavenly?"

"Peach pie. I'm baking one for dinner." Now that the stranger would be sharing a few meals she wanted the fare to be satisfying.

"If only I could smell cream and hot coffee to go with it." The girls laughed and Katherine removed her light wrap. "I hope you don't mind an uninvited guest, but Levi is working such long hours and I get lonely. Do you have time for a visit?"

Did she have time? Time was her only commodity. "Please, sit down. I do have coffee." It was the one thing Mother never refused, though she only sipped the hot brew.

"Any sign of the light?" Lyric asked.

"None, thank goodness. But then Levi and I haven't ventured out at night. I don't want to tempt it."

Sobering, Lyric pulled up the second chair and invited her to sit. "Katherine . . . you do know that you may see the light again. Over and over."

"Seriously?"

"Seriously. I believe it feels like it lives here. I've heard it's been seen as far as Oklahoma and Indian Territory, but that's not that far away. If you and Levi plan to spend your life here then you should be aware it most likely will be around."

"Oh, dear." Katherine apparently had to give that matter serious thought. "But it doesn't bother you?"

"It doesn't bother me. I can't say that I enjoy the showings and I'd be lying if I said they didn't unnerve me a bit, but I'm not afraid of it, whatever it might be."

"It must be something explainable."

"Surely it is, but so far nobody's found an explanation."

"Do you believe in . . . in ghosts?"

Lyric laughed. "Just the Holy Ghost."

Making light of the subject now, the women chatted, spending a few minutes catching up.

A tap at the door interrupted them. The stranger came in with an armful of kindling.

"Thought you might need some, since you've been baking," he said quietly. Before Lyric could answer, he slipped back outside and headed toward the barn again.

Katherine's eyebrows lifted. "I thought you lived with only your mother and sister."

Lyric sighed. How could she explain the

bruised and battered outlaw to her new friend? "He showed up here injured; I'm letting him stay for a bit."

That explanation seemed to suffice, although Lyric caught Katherine shooting an occasional curious glance out the window.

When Lyric got up to take the pie out of the oven, Katherine looked awestruck. "It's so beautifully brown."

Lyric recalled how Katherine had said pie making wasn't her gift, but she suspected the young woman hadn't made many. "Would you like me to show you how to bake a pie other than lemon?"

Katherine's eyes widened. "I've never had any luck with anything other than lemon, and truthfully, Levi gets tired of the same flavor."

"Then I'll teach you." She stepped to the pantry and got the flour and salt. A large tub of lard sat next to the cooking stove. Within a few minutes, Katherine had washed her hands and was preparing to do battle with the dough. The ingredients mixed easily and after a few more minutes Lyric stood beside the young woman and guided her hands on a rolling pin. The dough rolled out smoothly and evenly. One would have thought it was a holiday by the sounds of the young bride's squeals as she carefully laid the dough in the pie pan and then turned to assemble the peach mixture.

Katherine would never know what a gift she received; they almost never had sugar in the house and sharing a cup with a neighbor would mean one less pie for Lark, but having a friend was worth the price of a cup of sugar and one more precious jar of fruit.

Cans of peaches were opened, sugar, flour, and butter added, and the ingredients poured into the shell. Katherine rolled out the top crust without Lyric's help. After a moment the dough was set into place and Lyric showed her how to flute the crust and make tiny slits to vent the soon-to-be bubbling mixture. When the pie pan slid into the hot oven it was pretty as a picture.

While the treat baked, time flew by. The girls' laughter floated from the kitchen as they exchanged stories until soon Katherine removed a delectable looking pie from the oven and proudly stood back to survey the work. "Levi will not believe this."

"But he will most certainly enjoy it," Lyric promised.

As the afternoon lengthened, Lyric leaned on the back stoop and watched Katherine walk happily down the road, holding the wicker basket with the steaming hot peach pie tucked safely inside.

Her gaze was drawn to the barn, where she saw the stranger currying the horse. She focused on his slow but methodical movements. His hand paused, and he took deep breaths. Even from here she could tell he was struggling to remain upright and her heart went out to him. Did he recognize the horse? He didn't appear to have any particular feeling for the animal as he worked.

Her gaze focused on the animal. And what was she supposed to feed him? Rosie needed the available grass and there was no extra hay in her loft. If that animal didn't belong to the stranger she needed to sell it and its gear. The saddle alone would bring a nice price. The rich mahogany leather, the pommel, fender, and cantle all rubbed with saddle soap to a high sheen . . . it would bring a handsome price. Outlawing must pay very well.

An awful feeling swelled inside of her when she watched the wounded man painfully bend to run the brush over the animal's right fetlock. From this distance she saw that it took every ounce of strength he possessed to do the small chore. It would seem that the stranger was a man of great fortitude and determination.

She mentally shook her head. All of this effort and grit to recover, only to be hanged

by the neck until dead.
Lord, it hardly seems fair.

6

Lyric stirred when a crack of thunder shook the house sometime during the night. Rolling to her side she sank deeper into her pillow. The cloud bank must have moved in.

Drowsy, she realized it wasn't light yet. She should check on Mother. Storms ordinarily didn't bother Edwina, but if she awoke and couldn't get out of bed . . . Fat raindrops lashed the window and she stirred again, aware that the drops were extremely large. The intermittent peppering on the windowpane grew more persistent and in her drowsy state the word came to her: *thunder snow.* It was a peculiar event most likely to happen in midwinter. Lightning illuminated the bedroom and a second thunderous clap rattled the house. She particularly dreaded this kind of snow because it usually meant severe icy conditions for a few days or weeks to come.

Slipping from the bed, she lifted the

116

curtain and looked at the landscape already white with icy pellets. A bobbing light appeared, and she pressed her nose closer to the pane. The stranger was carrying a lantern and slowly making his way to the barn, occasionally losing his footing on the icy surface.

Pulling on her stockings and then her dress, she wound a wool scarf around her head and reached for a heavy coat.

Downstairs she lit a lantern and quietly let herself out the back door, braced against the blowing sleet. The white ground lit the darkness as she started off, slipping twice before she gained solid footing.

The stranger's light bobbed in the distance, drawing closer to the barn. He planned to take the horse and ride off while he thought everyone was sleeping. She hated to thwart his plans, but he would have to be a little more discreet with the next escape he planned. The pelting storm would awaken the whole house.

The light disappeared into the barn and she quickened her steps, slipping again. Brushing ice off her dress, she steadied her gait and trudged on. Cold, wet snow stung her face and she drew harsh air into her lungs. The temperature must have dropped forty degrees from the afternoon's unseasonable warmth.

The light inside the barn suddenly went out.

He must have chosen the lantern she had forgotten to fill before going to bed last night. The man's timing seemed as poor as his judgment.

As she approached the busted door, she paused when she heard him speaking to the animals. "It's okay. Nothing going on but a thunderstorm."

Rosie and the horse shuffled restlessly in their stalls.

He was speaking to the animals in the darkness. Calming them. Taking a deep breath, she stepped into the doorway. "May I help you with something?"

His voice returned through the black void. "A light would come in handy, if you have one. Mine went out."

"I know." She stepped inside, trying to close the broken timbers. Ferocious wind battered the shelter. "I meant to fill the lamp earlier but I forgot." Shaking sleet off her coat, she shivered. "What are you doing out here this time of night — or early morning?"

"The storm woke me, and I had a feeling the animals would be nervous."

She glanced at Rosie. The cow usually

didn't mind storms too much, but the buckskin did seem a bit nervous. He stomped in the stall, shying away when the man approached. The stranger reached out and rubbed his ears and the animal settled.

"That's the reason you're here? You've braved the storm to check on the animals?" When *he* could barely walk?

Shrugging, he threw a blanket over the horse's back and then added one to Rosie's broad width. "You seem to think I'm wanted for something. Maybe I shoot people but love animals."

At the moment only the latter seemed probable. He didn't appear to be dangerous or even mildly threatening, but then he wasn't himself. Heavy sleet pelted the tin roof as Lyric moved to the hay bin and grabbed a couple of handfuls. "I think you should have a name. I can't keep calling you . . . *You.* Or *Hey there.*"

"Pardon?"

"A name. I can't keep calling you 'the stranger.' " By now he didn't feel so "strange" to her. More like a distant relative she hadn't seen in years and had never really known.

"Don't see how a name will make a difference at this point." He knew she'd be taking him to town tomorrow morning; he wasn't deaf. Lark spoke of the trip in whispers but he'd no doubt heard the plan.

"Well," she said, offering Rosie the unexpected treat, "I believe the storm will make it unlikely that I can either get you to the sheriff's office or that the authorities can get to you." She glanced over at him, smiling. Funny, the unexpected delay was as welcome as rain in July. "Sometimes these storms last for days and the effects long after."

He remained silent, gently brushing the horse's ears back with his hands. She eased closer and offered the animal another fistful of hay. "Can I call you Joseph?"

"Joseph? Why would you call me Joseph?"

Shrugging, she smiled. "It's . . . It's manly and . . . if I were to ever have a baby boy that would be the name I'd give my son." Not that she'd have children, but she'd thought about names. And faces.

He glanced up, a slow grin forming. "You appear to have thought this through. Are you about to be married?"

"Me? Goodness, no. I'll most likely never be married, but I have thought about children's names." She dusted her hands off on her skirts when the horse finished the hay. "Joseph is a name from the Bible, you know. He was the favorite son of Jacob, sold into

120

slavery in Egypt by his brothers." She realized she was prattling. "I guess I've told you more than you need to know." She noticed he hadn't stopped her.

"You can call me Joseph, if that suits you."

"You mean — like it wouldn't suit you?"

He shrugged. "I do recall the Bible. You seem to know it well."

"I memorize passages. Are you a believer?"

His brows lifted with irony.

"Oh," Lyric said, glad the darkness hid the warmth in her cheeks. "I guess you wouldn't know."

"At this point I don't know anything other than I'm scheduled to hang in the morning."

"I've warned Boots and Lark to be more sensitive. I'm sorry they haven't been."

"They haven't bothered me; they're just talkative, like any girls their age."

"They never pipe down."

"It's true, isn't it? I'm going to hang in the morning without solid proof of my identity."

She sank to a hay bale. "The storm won't allow us to get to town or the authorities to get to us — even if they tried."

"Why would they hesitate?"

"Well — you see, my mother is . . . she has these fits . . ." She sighed heavily. "My mother is mad."

By his abrupt change of expression she gathered she should have broken the news more gently.

"She's mad."

Lyric nodded.

"She's been ill for a very long time. She'll have these . . . episodes. Sometimes she's full of energy, going days without sleep. She says things I don't understand. It scares people. And sometimes she takes to her bed and won't speak to us for days. She cries a lot." Lyric shrugged. "But her sickness now is different. It's a sickness of the body, not the mind. Lark and I . . . well, we don't think it will be much longer."

She breathed heavily. She'd been studying the healer's arts all her life. Sometimes she thought that if life had turned out differently, she would have liked to have been a nurse. She could set broken bones and stitch up wounds better than anyone. But nothing she did for her mother seemed to do any good.

"Your father?" said the man.

She lifted both shoulders. "I couldn't say where or who he is."

A clap of thunder shook the barn and the horse started. The stranger reached out to soothe the animal.

"The horse doesn't like storms," she noted.

"Looks that way."

She settled back on the bale, studying him. "So you weren't trying to escape? You really came to check on the animals?"

"Don't think I haven't considered running, but since I don't know where or who I am, I don't know where I'd go. Without money or identity I figure I wouldn't get very far before I was shot in the back."

A better fate than hanging. She shook the thought aside.

"For the time being, you can relax. As long as you don't give me any trouble you can stay here until the storm lets up." He'd been considerate, polite, and respectful to Lark and Boots and presented no threat to her. She could hardly turn him out in the cold when he was barely beginning to regain his strength. She considered his state. "Some of those cuts are deep. Will you allow me to sew them up?"

Now seemed an illogical time for compassion to finally surface. He'd been here for days but she'd thought — maybe even hoped — that he'd die, and she saw no use making an outlaw presentable. But right now she couldn't stand to see those still-oozing gashes ignored.

His forefinger absently traced the slash on his forehead. "Are you qualified?"

"I do all the mending around here, and when Rosie gets hurt I care for her. And I've raised Lark. She's had her fair share of cuts and bruises over the years."

"Have you got any strong whiskey?"

"Are you a drinking man?"

"At the thought of a needle going into my forehead, I suspect I could be."

"I don't have alcohol in the house, but I can give you something for the pain." She didn't keep strong drink, but she had ways to make medical procedures less hurtful.

"All right. I'd be much obliged." He managed a faint grin. "I'm sure my ma would want me to look presentable for the hanging, and I haven't slept on my pillow at nights for fear I'd soil the ticking."

"That is most thoughtful of you, Joseph. Thank you." Bloodstains were impossible to wash out.

He offered a cordial nod. "Just call me Joe."

Stepping to the back of the barn, she stretched on tiptoes and took a small box off the shelf. When she returned to the bale, she sat him down and faced him. "First we need to get the dried blood off. This won't be pleasant." To her credit, she had cleansed the worst cuts a couple of times, but the bleeding persisted. Now blood pooled in the wounds.

"What about the medicine?"

"We're getting to that." Removing a small vial from the case, she set it aside. "I believe this will work better if you lie down."

"Lie down? Here?"

"There, on the hay. Can you bring the lantern?"

He picked up the light and followed her to the back of the barn. She set the small box on the floor, next to the light. "Lie down, please."

"You know, maybe this isn't such a good idea."

"Joseph. Lie down."

Easing slowly to the floor, he stretched out, stiff as a poker.

"You can relax now."

"How can I relax when I know what you're about to do?"

Removing the lid from the vial, she instructed him to open his mouth and doused a bit of liquid on the end of his tongue. Joseph's eyes widened — that taste was anything but pleasant — and then drooped lethargically. His anguished gaze held a measure of trust. Trust she would not betray.

With the sound of sleet pelting the tin

roof, she threaded the needle, taking care to purify the thin cylindrical tool in the burning wick before setting to work. "Lord, permit me a steady hand," she whispered before she cleaned the facial wounds from a half-empty water bucket near Rosie's stall, and then carefully and meticulously began to sew.

Dawn's rays slowly spread across the frozen landscape. Sleet fell in sheets from a leaden sky. Nothing stirred outside the barn. The whole world was encased in ice. Lyric dozed, propped up on her elbow beside Joseph. Shortly before dawn she had started a fire in a metal barrel kept for dried corn. The effort knocked out the chill but offered little heat. Lifting her head slightly, she rested her ear on Joseph's chest, assuring herself that he was breathing properly. She'd had to give him a hefty dose of medication but his wounds were clean and neatly mended.

Mother would be awake and wondering where she was. Lark wouldn't know, and there was no way to send a message to the house.

Joseph's sleepy voice answered her silent question. "We're in a fine mess, aren't we?"

"There are at least two or three inches of

ice out there." She sat up, elated that he was awake and seemingly none the worse for wear. "We aren't going to be able to make it back to the house."

Joseph brought his arm to his forehead. "My head's spinning. Give me a minute to think about it," he managed to say.

"There are plenty of fresh eggs here. We can have breakfast if I can find something to cook them in." Her gaze centered on him and she breathed a silent prayer of thanksgiving when she noted his color was good. Rosy pink. "How are you?"

"What did you give me?" He slowly sat up, holding his head with both hands.

"It's my own concoction. Just some herbs that grow in these parts. I didn't hurt you, did I?"

"I thought you were going to give me a shot of whiskey."

"We don't keep strong liquor on hand."

"Can't see why there'd be a need, not with that stuff in your arsenal."

"No." She shook her head. "But what are we going to do about our problem? The ice is so thick I don't see how we'll make it back to the house, and neither Mother nor Lark knows where we are." They would surely think the worst: that the outlaw had taken Lyric captive and fled. But Lark would be unable to alert the sheriff until the worst of the weather had passed.

Struggling to his feet, Joseph paused, holding his head. The newly stitched cuts and few days' dark beard growth made him look a might hard. She questioned her gradual thawing — the slow but nagging sense that he wasn't a wanted man. Could such a gentle person really be a criminal? Yet logic warned the softening might be exactly what he intended.

"Why don't you fix those eggs first, and I'll think about the solution."

Shortly afterwards, a half dozen eggs cooked in a boiling pot of water. She'd found the rusty iron utensil discarded near one of the stalls. Giving it a good ice scrubbing, she'd cleaned it thoroughly and then laid a piece of fencing over the top of the barrel where a fire blazed. Rosie provided warm milk that they took turns sipping from a gourd. The simple fare tasted like a feast in the cold, crisp dawn.

"You're a fine cook even without salt or bacon grease," he remarked.

"Thank you. I'm much less worried about you now."

He cocked a brow. "You worry about outlaws?"

"Other than you, I've never worried much

about anyone but Lark and Mother. But your appetite is returning, and I'm glad to see that."

He flashed an amicable grin. "Looks that way." He touched a finger to his forehead. "This hardly hurts. You sew as well as you cook."

"Thank you. I could have used a better light, but I think I did a decent job. There should be little scarring." She allowed her smile to fade. "What are we going to do about returning to the house? We don't have sufficient wood to stay here for very long." There was nothing much here to burn except hay, and that couldn't be spared.

"It is a problem. The barn can't be seen from the house."

"No — the grove of sycamores blocks the view even in the winter."

"Can anyone hear us if we yell? Sound carries a long way in these hollers."

"Perhaps — if Lark was outside — or our neighbor, Murphy, but my sister detests cold and Murphy has probably decided to stay in for the day, so it's unlikely anyone would hear us."

"The horse couldn't make it up the hill without breaking a leg."

"Nor could Rosie."

They stood in thoughtful silence. Finally,

she noted, "I suppose I could crawl there."

He chuckled.

"I'm serious. I don't see that we have any choice. We'll have to string some sort of a guide line from the barn to the house so Rosie can be milked and the horse fed and watered."

He slowly buttoned his fleece-lined coat. "I'll get started. This will take a while."

She restrained his efforts. "You can't go. I will."

"I'm not going to let a woman climb an icy hill."

"I've climbed that hill since I was able to walk — and in storms worse than this one. One year we got seven feet of snow and it near buried the barn. I was still able to move back and forth with the line, but the effort took time." Her eyes roamed the barn interior. "Now where did I put that length of rope?" The sudden remembrance brought a heartfelt groan. "It's on the back service porch."

"There's nothing here we can use?"

She shook her head. "Lark and I cleaned out the barn last summer and we moved a lot of stuff to the house."

Running a hand through his hair, he frowned. "I won't allow you to crawl up that hill on your hands and knees."

"You would rather spend the next week in here, with no fire and only eggs and milk?"

His gaze strayed to the horse. "We could eat that contrary thing."

She turned to look. "The *horse*? What's he done?"

"He doesn't like me. He spits on me and steps on my foot every chance he gets, and he's bitten me twice since he's been here."

"Horses don't spit."

"This horse takes water in his mouth, washes the hay out, and then lets it roll onto my boots. It's as close to a full-blown spit as a horse is going to get."

"Really?" She studied the buckskin that stood quietly in his stall, big brown eyes peering out. The animal's markings were beautiful. Full tawny belly and fetlocks of jet-black coat. "He looks like a perfectly gentle animal."

"Well, looks can fool you."

"Perhaps his nature is why his owner turned him loose — but one would think they would keep the stable gear." She turned to smile. "I can't afford to feed him, so when the weather breaks I'll have to sell him."

"If I don't end up bringing much in the way of bounty, that should pay for a new barn door."

Lyric smiled. "You know, Joseph, for an outlaw, you're not that bad."

He reached out to tweak her nose. "And for a recluse, you're not a bad cook. Those eggs were the best I've ever eaten."

Relief flooded her, a heady, breathless sensation that left her puzzled. Was she coming down with something? A cold, perhaps?

"Joseph?"

He turned. "Yes?"

"You can call me Lyric."

He nodded. "That's a right pretty name."

"Mother never did anything normal, including naming her daughters."

"Then she couldn't be all bad," he noted. "Shall we take a closer look at that hill?"

"Sweet *Moses,* that looks like fifty miles of bad road." Joseph's troubled gaze traveled the huge hill, frozen slicker than a Minnesota pond in January.

"I've seen it worse — but not much," she admitted. She took a cautionary step ahead of him, slipped, and almost went down. He grabbed an arm and steadied her. "And you're going to try to walk up that hill?"

"Crawl," she corrected. "Very slowly and methodically."

"I'll be right behind you."

"You most certainly will not. I didn't stich all those cuts closed only to have them torn loose. You stay put." She pulled her coat tighter and set her jaw. "This may take a while."

"I don't plan on going anywhere."

She set off, slipping her way across the frozen ground. If she were lucky Lark might look out the window, but her hopes weren't high. Once that girl buried her head in a book nothing distracted her. She would surely be wondering where Lyric was, and common sense would say that she was stranded at the barn, but then she never went to the barn before daylight.

Her feet spread and she went down. Regaining her footing, her legs bowed and she froze in place. If she moved even the slightest inch she would be flat on her back. Slowly, she eased both legs together. Tossing a sheepish grin over her shoulder she started off again, and her feet flew out from under her.

Heat burned her cheeks. Joseph was standing in the barn doorway, and though she couldn't see him she could *feel* his amusement. She didn't know what he found so funny. Just wait until he tried the climb — he'd suffer the same humiliation.

Struggling back to her feet, she grabbed

133

for her scarf when the wind snatched it and the sudden movement threw her off balance. Lying face-up, she stared at the stormy sky. So far she'd moved maybe fifty feet. Joseph's calm voice came to her on a windy gust. "Are you sure you don't want me to try?"

"No." She sat up, brushing icy pellets off her skirts. "I'm doing fine. I said it would be slow."

"Let me know if you change your mind."

Thirty minutes later she had made it halfway up the hill — just to the point that she could see the house. Smoke curled from the chimney but there wasn't a thing stirring. No Lark peeking out the window. "Lark!" she yelled, praying the wind would carry her voice.

After a long silence, she tried again. "Lark!" By now her clothing was wet and she was chilled to the bone. She had to make it to the house shortly or she would catch her death.

"Sit down and ease up the hill," Joseph called, his voice echoing over the frozen countryside.

Nodding, she sat down and began slowly easing up the hill on her backside. The movement met with success and she steadily inched her way toward the house.

When she was twenty feet from the back door, frozen to the core, her hands red and stinging like fire, the door opened and Lark popped her head out. "There you are. Better bring in more wood; the fire's getting low."

"Exactly where did you think I had gone?" Lyric's chattering teeth made it nearly impossible to talk as she sank to the kitchen table. Lark had quickly stripped her out of her wet clothing and was now briskly rubbing warmth back into her frozen limbs.

"How did I know? I thought you might be at the barn but I didn't see how you got down there. I told Mother you were outside doing something in the yard."

"Doing something in the yard." Lyric clamped her rattling teeth together. "On a day like this, I'm outside, doing something in the yard." She grasped a mug of steaming tea and took a trembling sip.

"Well, I had to tell her something or she'd have worried. By the way, the stranger's gone too."

"Joseph's at the barn."

Lark paused and met her eyes. "Joseph?"

"I was tired of calling him a stranger, so I named him Joseph."

"And he's okay with that?"

"Why should he care? He doesn't know his name."

"Well, that's pretty cold."

Lyric set the cup aside and turned to pull on clean bloomers. "I thought it only proper to give him a name."

"He has one. Younger or Cummins."

"We don't know that for certain."

"Goodness. What's happened? You've changed since yesterday."

"Go find the rope we strung during the last big ice storm. We have to string it down to the barn so Joseph can come in out of the cold."

"Mmm . . . I'm not sure where we put it."

"On the service porch, behind the extra milk can." She pulled on a woolen dress over the bloomers and tidied her hair. Feeling had returned to her hands and fingers. "Hurry, Lark. He's cold and in pain."

Lark left, and a moment later Lyric heard the back door open. Checking her appearance a final time, she reached for a dry coat and a pair of gloves, dreading the elements.

Outside the wind blew something fierce and heavy snow fell from a lead-colored sky. Lark had dressed warmly and Lyric held the ladder as her sister climbed to the roof where a strong bolt with a looped head was in place. Lark tied the rope securely and then slid down the gutter, ignoring the ladder. She collapsed in a deep drift of snow.

"You know you're not supposed to do that," Lyric scolded. "If you tear the gutter down I can't replace it."

"But it's the only thing that makes this kind of storm any fun."

Dragging the rope, the two sisters sat down and slid down the hill. Lark squealed, apparently thinking the adventure great fun; Lyric thought it was pure misery, but Joseph's wait was nearly over. He was huddled near the dwindling fire when the women entered the barn. Lark went straight to Rosie, hugging the old cow around her neck. "Hello, love."

Joseph straightened, his face chapped by the biting cold. "I see you made it."

"It was a breeze. The rope's up. All you have to do is hang on and pull yourself up the hill — or scoot on your backside."

Lark glanced at his stitched face and grimaced. "I see Lyric's been busy." She flashed a grin. "She must be starting to like you."

The process of climbing the hill was laborious at best, even with the rope to guide them. Lyric went first. Joseph followed and Lark trailed. The process would need to be repeated twice a day during the storm's duration to milk Rosie, gather eggs, and feed the buckskin, but for now the immediate crisis was over. Joseph wasn't swinging from the end of a rope, and Lyric wasn't frozen stiffer than wash on a mid-February line.

All in all, the day hadn't been all that bad.

7

"I think you're turning sweet on him."

"For goodness' sake, Lark." Lyric snapped a clean sheet free of wrinkles and tossed one end to her sister. "Why would you say that? I'm moving the man from the sofa to a bed until the weather lets up." She smoothed the sunshine-smelling fabric and tucked one end neatly in a corner. "He can't sleep in the parlor forever. For one thing, I haven't mentioned a word about his being here to Mother. Have you?"

"Not me. I don't want her to know."

"She'll have to know; she can't just walk out of her room one night and find him."

"Then you tell her. You're the one who brought him here . . . and besides, it's starting to feel like he's moving in with us."

"I can assure you he is not moving in with us." Lyric tossed a couple of pillows on the bed and turned. "There. It's cooler up here but he will be more comfortable. And you and I will be warmer sharing your bed until he goes."

"You mean more crowded." Lark tucked the other side of the sheet in the mattress and sighed. "You know what?"

"What?"

"I'm relieved the storm came. I don't want him to be hanged, even if he has done bad things."

"Lark, you don't know the man. Right now his memory is gone, but when it returns he might very well be a wicked man." But she couldn't fault her sister. Secretly, Lyric was starting to have the same impossible wish.

"He doesn't look wicked. It's not fair to judge a person by what others think."

Lyric changed the subject. "Have you put the pot of beans on to boil?"

"I'm going to. I had to help you make the bed first."

"Go put the pot of beans on." It was like pulling hen's teeth to motivate that girl.

Late that morning, Lyric took a firm hold of Joseph's elbow and helped him up the first step. "Are you sure you can make it? There are twelve stairs."

"I can make it. Just take it slow and easy." The couple climbed with measured steps.

Every hour Joseph appeared to improve, both a good and bad sign. She'd rather him feel poorly when he was hung. That way he might welcome death at least a little bit.

"You shouldn't have gone to the bother of making up your room for me," he said. "In a few days the ice will melt, and I'll be out of your hair."

"Mother's rather fussy about her furniture." If Edwina knew who had been sleeping on her sofa she would have revived long enough to bodily remove the occupant. That would not have been a pleasant sight.

"Well, I'm grateful," he said, breathing heavily.

They reached the second landing and Lyric steered him through the first open door. The high-ceilinged room faced the back of the house with northern exposure, cold in the winter but not stifling in the summer, with a lovely view of the wooded hillside below. The ice-covered trees made quite a pretty picture had her guest been in the mood for scenery. His pinched features allowed that he wasn't.

Settling him on the bed, Lyric drew a heavy blanket up close to his neck. "Move quietly. Mother sleeps deeply but she might be able to hear you."

"I'll be quiet."

"Just don't walk around in your boots."

"Can you remove my hat?"

She lifted the Stetson and set it on a nearby dresser and then took off his boots. "Either Lark or I will be up to check on you several times before nightfall."

"Much obliged." His tone was tinged with pain; it had been a long, cold day, and the climb up the hill had sapped what strength he had regained.

Lyric quietly closed the door, leaving a crack open so some heat would filter through.

She had a hunch he would sleep for hours.

When Joseph next opened his eyes it was to the sound of a bare branch scraping the window. He blew a small puff of air and realized the room was so cold he could see his breath. Sleet mixed with rain ran in rivulets down the windowpane. Someone had been in the room and lit a glim — a relic used to light early mining camps. Lyric. A name he could recall — her and Lark — and the girl with the red boots.

Lying still, he watched streams form and then branch into symmetrical tributaries on the window. Something smelled good, like cornbread baking in an oven.

Who was he?

He didn't feel like a criminal. But if he'd done the things Lark and Boots said he'd done he deserved to be hanged. And the idea that he'd ridden a horse through the Boltons' barn door seemed laughable, but why else would he be in this shape? Every bone in his body testified to some horrific impact . . . but why would he ride a horse through a barn door? He must have been drunk — drunk and lost his identification somewhere.

He must have been mule-skinner drunk.

A light appeared in the window and he glanced up. The yellowish ball appeared to be holding invisible hands to its temples and peering inside his room. He froze in place. The medicine Lyric had given him earlier must still be affecting his mind.

Something about that light was oddly familiar. Digging his heels into the mattress, he sat up straighter, trying to ease back in the bed. The thing was actually staring in the window.

Then it was gone.

Sliding back flat, he took a deep breath. He was sicker than anyone thought.

The window lit and he slowly turned eyes on the bouncing object. Now it played, skimming across the pane, leaping up and down.

Oh, you have my attention. His gaze traveled to the table where his hat was perched. He recalled Lyric removing his boots earlier. Where was his gun? A man would carry a gun. He spotted the revolver on the dresser.

The light slowly withdrew into a tiny bright speck hovering in a treetop fifty yards from the house, and then zoomed in like a hawk in pursuit of prey, skidding up the glass and then pausing, breaking into four pieces, two zipping one way, two the opposite.

Joseph's stocking foot touched the icy floor. A man would have to be dead to sit still for this — this *thing.* Someone was trying to scare the Boltons off their place.

He crept out of bed, aware of the brightly lit landscape outside the window. Nothing — man or beast — could maneuver over that ice. That left the supernatural, something he didn't cotton to.

Picking up the revolver, he turned slowly and took careful aim, but the thing took off.

Lowering the pistol, he waited until it returned. He took aim again and fired off a round. Glass shattered and a rush of cold air hit him.

Carrying the pistol back to bed, he crawled between the sheets and then sat straight up when the bedroom door flew open and a

144

woman stood glaring at him. Her wild hair fell all the way down her back, and her eyes seemed to shoot daggers at him. She held a flickering candle and a long white nightgown encased her skeletal frame.

"Ma'am," he acknowledged when he found his voice. Lyric's words about his room being near her mother's belatedly rattled around in his head.

"Did you shoot my window out?"

"Yes, ma'am. There was this light —" He felt like a tongue-tied schoolboy facing a ruthless teacher. This had to be Lyric's ailing mother. She would think he was insane.

"You'll replace it first light."

"Yes, ma'am."

Lark appeared, carrying an oil lamp. "I heard a shot — Mother! What are you doing here?"

The words snapped out. "What is this man doing in my house? Who is he?"

Lyric glanced at Joseph. "I've been meaning to tell you — he came here injured and I've allowed him to stay until he's strong enough to move on."

"And who gave you that right?"

"Common courtesy, Mother. I couldn't turn him away to die."

"See that he leaves immediately." The sick woman turned and slowly made her way back down the long stairway, holding the candle aloft in front of her.

Lyric entered the room and set the light on the table. Rubbing warmth into her shoulders, she shivered. "Now see what you've done. Mother knows you're here and she'll fret — and just look at this mess."

"A crazy light was staring at me through the window, so I shot it."

Moving to the broken glass, Lyric *tsked*. "The light likes to visit from time to time. In the future please refrain from shooting through windows."

"Likes to visit? Are you serious?"

"I am perfectly serious. The light comes around from time to time. Nobody knows why or where it comes from, but it won't harm you." She studied the gaping hole. "I'll have to tack a blanket over this until morning. We have extra glass on the service porch. If you want, you can sleep on the sofa again tonight."

He sure didn't intend to sleep in this spook hole. Straightening his shoulders, he edged toward his boots. "I shot it. It won't bother you again."

"No, you didn't." She perused the shattered glass littering the floor, fingers resting on her chin. "I think after I tack the blanket up I'll leave this until morning."

"I did shoot it — that's what roused your mother."

"I heard the shot but if you'll notice . . ." Her eyes motioned to the side yard where the light sat on the woodpile, puffed up and proud like a toad.

Stepping to the window, he whistled under his breath. "I hit the thing squarely on target."

"Yes, well, come along. If you feel up to eating after your rest, supper's almost ready. Beans and cornbread. Lark made the trip to the barn to milk and check on the animals. The rain barrel was frozen over again so she broke the ice. Everything should be fine until morning."

"I shot that thing, Lyric."

"I'm not arguing with you. Come along. It's freezing in here."

He trailed behind her, carrying his boots. Her mother scared away any appetite he'd gathered, appearing out of nowhere like that. "I thought your mother was too ill to move around."

"It's the first time I've seen her out of bed in weeks. You've caused quite a stir."

Lyric took the steps in front of him, muttering something under her breath about idiots who didn't know any better than to shoot through glass, but he refrained from answering. He'd shot that light.

It looked as though — no, not possible.

That thing was *grinning* at him.

Black clouds lifted and the sun popped out, leaving white, high-top clouds that blew across the holler. Within a couple of days the thick ice started to melt but refroze at night, making travel by horse or wagon impossible. Joseph repaired the broken window and then spent hours in the parlor playing checkers with Lark and Boots. Their infectious laughter floated through the house as Lyric baked and cooked, and she caught herself wishing the weather would worsen again. Joseph didn't appear to dread the approaching hanging; he kept his emotions on a tight leash. The more she was around the man, the harder it was to picture him being a hardened criminal. Losing one's memory surely didn't change an inherent mean streak, and Joseph didn't appear to have a cruel bone in his body.

She'd put a pork roast in the oven earlier and as the tempting scent filled the old house she mixed a batch of biscuits. When she stepped to the sink to wash her hands she caught sight of a lone figure struggling through the deep rutted path.

Katherine Jennings.

Thrilled for company, Lyric stepped to the back door and motioned her friend inside the warm kitchen. The young woman slipped and slid her way to the back door.

"Katherine! For heaven's sake, why are you out on a day like this?"

Breathless and red-cheeked, Katherine stepped inside and unwound her heavy scarf, moving closer to the fire. "I know — isn't this storm dreadful? But I had cabin fever so bad, I thought I'd risk the walk over."

Reaching for the coffeepot, Lyric poured a steaming cup and stepped to the service porch for cream. "How was the trip over?"

"Very slippery. I'm afraid this ice won't melt for another week or so, even if the sun stays out." Her gaze strayed to the sound of giggles coming from the library. "Is the stranger still here? I guess he couldn't travel in this weather."

"He's still here." Lyric pulled up a chair and sat down. "And no matter how happy I am to see you I hardly think you'd risk a broken bone for an afternoon chat."

Katherine cupped her hands around her cup and admitted. "The light came back again."

"Last night?"

She nodded. "We didn't go quite as crazy

149

as we did the first time, but it keeps us on edge."

"I know — it was here a couple of nights ago. Joseph shot out the upstairs bedroom window trying to run it off."

"Joseph?"

"I've given the stranger a name. He's lost his memory, you see." Clearing her throat, she busied her hands rearranging a spoon. "It seemed fitting."

If Katherine thought choosing a name for the man was a bit bizarre, she kept silent. She shook her head. "That doesn't work. Levi tried shooting it too."

Sobering, Lyric reached out to touch her hand. "What is it, Katherine? Does the light upset you that greatly?"

She nodded. "Ever so much. I've never encountered anything like it, and no matter how much I tell myself it won't hurt me I know it could."

"That's understandable; the unknown frightens most of us."

Leaning closer, Katherine whispered. "It's not the same between me and Levi anymore — we're always looking out the window or scouring the room with our eyes to see if it's there, and we don't laugh or joke with each other nearly as much as we did before that awful thing came into our lives." Lifting her cup, Katherine sipped her drink. "I honestly don't know what to think about any of it. At times I wish we hadn't built out here . . ." She glanced up. "Except for you. I am so thankful to have found you."

"And I you." Lyric shook her head. "I'm sure there's a simple explanation for the unusual light, though I can't imagine what."

Five days after the storm the ice had partially melted on the hillside near the barn, but the roads remained treacherous. If Bolton Holler craved a good hanging, Mother Nature was making them wait a while longer. Joseph was either living right or mighty lucky, Lyric decided as she rolled over in bed and opened her eyes to the sound of a hammer striking wood. Squinting, she noted the ray of thin light barely creeping through the room and wondered about the time.

Throwing back the blankets, she wiggled her toes into her heavy slippers and stood, stretching. The hammering came from a distance — in the direction of the barn. She stepped to the window and peered out at the slushy winter countryside. Who could be making such a racket at this hour?

Ten minutes later she let herself out the back door, shivering in the frosty morning air as she balanced two mugs of hot coffee. She had a hunch Joseph was the culprit; the man rose early and seemed restless now that he was starting to mend. The line still hung from the house to the barn but she couldn't use it with her hands full. Melted dark patches made travel easier, and if she felt herself falling she'd drop the cups and grab for support. Better to lose the coffee than break an arm.

Lord, we're barely into March. One more good snowstorm might do the soil good. Make the crops more fertile this year.

Making her way over the hill, she paused, her breath a white plume in the chilly air. By afternoon the temperatures would warm and make better headway melting the ice. Each new day brought Joseph's imminent demise closer, and the thought had now started to nag her, like a blister between her toes. Could she actually stand by and watch the sheriff hang this man?

Stepping into the barn she spotted the noise maker. Joseph had stripped the splintered door down to the frame and now planed the rough edges. "I thought it might be you," she teased. "Who else wakes with the birds?"

Without looking up, he smiled. "Did I disturb you?"

152

She walked over and set the coffee beside him. "No. I had to get up and look out the window to see who was making that racket."

Grinning, he reached for the cup. "Thanks. This should warm me up."

"It might be stone cold by now." She sat next to him, testing the brew. "Lukewarm."

"Better than nothing."

Her gaze rested on his work. "You're fixing the door." For one senseless improbable moment she wanted to throw her arms around his neck and hug him. If he were hanged, there would be plenty of funds for a new door but she knew in her heart she would never look at the barn entrance without seeing his face. Without wondering . . .

"It isn't too difficult. I looked around and asked that big hired hand with a gun you keep hidden down here, and together we found enough scrap wood to patch it. It won't be like new, but Rosie should stay warmer."

She blushed at the thought of the flimsy lie she'd given. Big, hard farmhand — not afraid to use a gun. He must think her very silly.

Her eyes moved to the horse. "What should we do about him?"

"Don't know. Do you need a horse?"

She shook her head. "I can barely feed Rosie. Truthfully, I've begun to wonder if he might be yours."

His gaze shifted back to the big stallion. "No. I wouldn't put up with a horse that cantankerous."

"Still, it makes sense. A saddled horse doesn't come from nowhere."

"He isn't my horse." His gaze skimmed the innocent-looking creature. "There could be all kinds of reasons he was saddled. Someone shot his owner. He threw his rider. His owner got occupied and the animal wandered off." He shook his head. "Do with him what you must; he's not mine."

"How can you be so certain?"

"I know, okay? A man would know his horse."

The animal shifted and stepped on Joseph's left foot and he smacked the stallion's rump. "Stay off my foot!"

"Now, now. Is it necessary to speak so harshly to him?" She had noticed that the two butted heads often.

"This animal doesn't like me."

"Now, honestly. Listen to yourself. Why would the horse have anything personal against you?"

"There are some animals that are cantankerous by nature, and this is one of them."

"Well, perhaps that's why his owner turned him away. But you would think he would have kept the saddle." She ran her hands over the rich leather and fine stitching and thought about the engraved initials toward the back that she'd noticed earlier. *J.J.* If it was his horse the initials were wrong. There should be a Y in place of the last J. He couldn't possibly be Jesse James. Jesse James had been shot and killed six years earlier.

"The owner probably couldn't get rid of him quick enough. If he were mine, I'd have sold him the day I bought him."

"Oh." She patted the horse's mane lovingly. "Don't listen to him. I'll bet you're a wonderful animal."

"I wouldn't bet anything more than a hickory nut."

"You surely aren't from these parts; we call them hicker nuts," she bantered.

"Then I must not be from around here."

The horse turned and nipped his hip and Joseph's face flushed scarlet. If she hadn't been standing there she could tell the animal would have gotten a blistering earful.

"So." She crossed her arms behind her back and circled the door frame. "You really think you can fix this?"

"I'm going to try." He paused, eyes focused on his work. "I like the feel of lumber, the smooth wood, the sweet scent of fresh shavings."

"Mmm. Perhaps in your former life you were a carpenter."

"Yeah." He chuckled. "I built furniture when I wasn't robbing, looting, or killing."

She sobered. "We don't know that you're an outlaw." It was the first time she'd let the notion slip out, and she hoped he wouldn't take advantage of her flagging suspicion. At this point she didn't know anything for certain other than the ice was melting faster than she'd like.

"You're right." He ran the plane over the weathered board. "We don't."

"Is anything coming back to you? Anything at all?" The blow to his head would knock anyone senseless, but Lark mentioned she'd read books about people who'd lost their memories and after a short while they had returned.

Other times they never regained their past.

God, perhaps that would be for the best. This man doesn't appear to be violent, and if he is hanged he will never recall his vile acts. On his behalf, I plead for mercy for his sins.

"Nothing."

His flat tone told her he was weary of the subject. She took another direction. "Did you see Katherine yesterday?"

"I saw her walking toward home. Why was she out in such weather?"

"She's lonely — and frightened. Seems the light paid them a visit too. Katherine's nerves were jangled and she was tied all in knots."

He paused and looked up at her. "Does the light bother you?"

"No. I've been around too long."

He nodded slowly, then cleared his throat. "Your mother. Is she . . . I mean . . . I wasn't expecting to bump into her."

"That she came to investigate the gunshot in itself was remarkable. She hasn't moved around for a while. You must have really startled her. I'm sorry if she frightened you. She has strange ways, and people mostly avoid us because of it."

"And that makes you a lonely woman," he said.

His keen perception surprised her. She tried to hide her longing to belong somewhere. Or to someone. Deep down she wanted to be loved and go to sleep every night knowing that in addition to God's love there was another person on earth to whom she mattered.

"Nothing wrong with being lonely," he said softly. "Just doesn't seem right that a girl like you should be cooped up here all alone."

She mustered a smile. "When Mother passes, Lark and I are leaving here — going as far as we can go. Maybe even to California."

"To start a new life?"

She nodded. "Of course Lark's at the age where she doesn't want to leave. She and Boots are close as bread and butter, but there comes a time when everyone has to leave someone they love. She'll make new friends."

"New friends." He shook his head. "Something inside of me says friendships are hard to come by — good friendships, that is. But I could be wrong. My thinking is muddled."

Smiling, she ran her hand over the front of her coat and eyed the door frame. Nothing on this earth could stop her from leaving once she was free to go. "Do you plan to work on this all day?"

"Do you have a better suggestion?"

"I thought maybe we could take a walk. It's going to be a lovely day, and maybe we can find some dandelion greens poking their heads through the melting ice. Lark and Boots found a sizable mess shortly before the storm."

"Thanks, but I'll work here for a while and then go back to the house."

"Are you sure?" She knew his argument — he needed to keep up his strength. How much strength would he need to attend his hanging? Yet he clearly wanted privacy.

"I'll see you for dinner?"

Nodding, he continued his work.

8

"Lyric's not going to be happy about this."
Boots trudged behind Lark, her scuffed red
boots leaving tracks in the melting slush.

"My sister won't know a thing about this
if you don't blab." Lark paused to catch her
breath. If her map served her right, the
Youngers all lived out this way. They were a
hardy bunch to be sure. If she and Boots
could get close enough to recognize features
she figured she could pretty well tell if Joseph was one of them. There would be
similarities — bold noses, hair color and
growth patterns, ruddy complexions, the set
of a jaw or a wide mouth and big teeth or a
small mouth and no teeth. The wounded
stranger was downright fine-looking, clean,
and had a good strong set of even white
teeth.

Lark considered herself to be above average in knowledge; she'd read her fair share
of mysteries, and she could spot a crook in

a crowd. There would be plenty today, and if those Youngers stepped a foot out of their houses she figured she could pretty well tell if Joseph was one of them. She shook the given name aside. Lyric had no call to give him a name; he had one. Her mission was to find it.

There was no use letting a good man hang for crimes he hadn't committed, and the more she was around Joseph the more convinced she was he wasn't evil. Pure instinct told her as much. And if he wasn't in a gang then Lyric could marry the fellow and they could stay here in Bolton Holler. A person would have to be in a walking coma to not recognize that Lyric had eyes for the stranger, and her sister was pretty enough, and thoughtful, and everything a man could want. They would be happy together and then Lyric would stop threatening to leave the holler. Always talking about leaving — it left her weary.

"You are as slow as molasses in spring," Lark called back to Boots. "Hurry up. It's going to be dark by the time we get there and walk back. And we have to go by Murphy's house on the way."

"Oh, good grief! You know you get on that boy's nerves."

"I don't *know* that. I keep him company."

161

"You keep him on the run," Boots accused. "He thinks you're a silly little girl."

"Maybe *now* he thinks it, but he won't someday. Someday I'm going to marry that man and he's going to wonder what hit him. I'll be seventeen in three years, after all."

"Oh, posh."

Murphy's place came into view. The unsuspecting farmer bent working on a plow. When Lark yelled, waving her hand in the air, he glanced up, dropped the rigging, and quickly strode toward the barn.

"Shoot. He didn't see me."

"He saw you."

"Did not."

Boots trailed behind, whining. "The sun might be out but it's still cold. My feet are blocks of ice."

"You need new soles on your boots."

"Grandpa doesn't have the money for new soles."

"Then wear thicker socks."

Something in the thicket caught Lark's eye. At first she thought it might be a piece of melting slush, but she detected a hint of color. Stepping off the road, she waded through the briars, her feet slipping on tricky ground. When she fell the second time her hand grasped the object and she pulled it up close. Why, it was a man's wallet!

"What are you doing off the road?" Boots called. "If you expect me to follow you through that brush you've got another think coming."

"I saw something in the weeds. Look." She held the item aloft.

Boots veered closer to the edge of the road. "Does it have any money in it?"

"I don't know." Lark pulled herself to her feet and waded back to the road. Unfolding the leather binding, she focused on the various pieces displayed. Mostly slips of papers with names written on them. Towns. Dates. A badge of some sort. She peered closer. A U.S. marshal badge. Her gaze scanned names but nothing registered.

One slip read *Ian Cawley* and had a Kansas address.

"Probably one of those Youngers stole it off a U.S. marshal and then shot him, took the money, and threw the wallet in the bushes," Lark mused.

"The lowdown no-goods," Boots concurred. "Shame. We could have used a few hundred dollars." She giggled.

"Yes, you'd buy new soles."

"Soles my foot; I'd get new boots. I'd have Earl order the best he could find."

163

"I found the wallet. Why should you get any money if there were any?"

"I came along with you. That should make the find half and half."

Lark stuck the wallet in her coat pocket and the girls moved on down the road, squabbling.

"What are you going to do with the wallet?" Boots finally asked.

"I don't know. Keep it, I guess. Maybe I'll write a letter to one of those names written on paper and see if they know an Ian Cawley and if they do I'll return it if he sends the funds to do so."

"Sounds sensible."

"Have I ever said or done anything dumb?"

"Too many to pinpoint."

"I'm hungry."

"Me too." Lark drew an apple out of her pocket. "Want to share?"

"Okay, but I'm not eating near the core this time. I get the part closest to the peel."

"Fine." Lark bit into the apple and juice spurted. "I'll just get it started for us."

Joseph opened the back door and stepped onto the service porch. Shrugging out of his coat, he stepped into the kitchen and warmed his hands at the cookstove. He'd lost track of time. How long had he been here? Days, he thought, maybe as long as a week or more. The pain was gradually subsiding to the point where he could sleep. Last night he'd awakened only twice but easily drifted back off.

The house was unusually quiet. No sign of Lark, Boots, or Lyric. The women must be out looking for greens in the snow.

After he poured himself a hot cup of coffee, he carried it to the parlor and closed the door. A fire blazed on the stone hearth and lent the room a pleasant feel. He stared at the cup in his hand and then at the polished table sitting next to the sofa. The furnishings were old but in good taste; best not to set the cup on the bare wood. Moving to the massive bookshelf, he chose a title and backed up until he felt the seat. Setting the book on the table, he then set his cup on top of it.

Settling in a wingback chair, he momentarily closed his eyes and savored the warmth creeping through his bones. After a bit, he sat up and reached for his cup, his eyes widening when he noticed he had company. Edwina was sitting opposite him, staring.

How long had she been there?

The cup rattled when he carefully replaced

it in the saucer and slowly got to his feet. "Ma'am?"

"Remove that cup from my table."

"Yes ma'am." He snatched up the china, clutching it to his chest. "I put a book under it."

The woman stared. The moments stretched. Joseph shifted. After a long moment of silence, he asked. "Is there something you need? I think your daughters are out looking for greens in the snow."

"Read to me."

"Read . . . ?" He glanced at the bookshelves lined with heavy volumes.

"Read."

"Okay, what do you want me to read?"

She produced a worn, tattered Bible. "Isaiah 53."

"All right." He opened the book and began flipping through the pages, scanning the notations that had been made beside certain verses in a bold but feminine hand. Someone had spent a lot of time in this book.

He found the book of Isaiah and flipped to the fifty-third chapter. He cleared his throat and began to read. "Who hath believed our report? and to whom is the arm of the Lord revealed? For he shall grow up before him as a tender plant, and as a root out of a dry ground: he hath no form nor comeliness; and when we shall see him, there is no beauty that we should desire him. He is despised and rejected of men; a man of sorrows, and acquainted with grief: and we hid as it were our faces from him; he was despised, and we esteemed him not. Surely he hath borne our griefs, and carried our sorrows: yet we did esteem him stricken, smitten of God, and afflicted."

He continued reading until he'd finished the entire chapter. When he looked up, he realized that the sick woman's eyes had filled with tears as she gazed into the distance. She was quiet for a long moment, and finally she spoke.

"Never used to understand how folks put so much store in that nonsense. Then that preacher came around one time. Tried to save my soul, and I laughed in his face. But he left that Bible and Lyric read it. Read the whole thing. She always said she liked that part. I've read it over and over and I just can't puzzle it out." She fixed on him. "Like that last bit. In plain words, what does 'he bare the sin of many, and made intercession for the transgressors' mean? Nobody's ever borne anything for me. I wouldn't let them. I've always taken care of myself. Haven't once asked for help from anybody and never will."

"In plain words? To be honest, Mrs. Bolton, I don't reckon I'm too good with meanings at the moment. But I can say what I think God is telling folks in this verse. I think He is reminding us that Jesus Christ took it upon Himself to die for man's sins — every last black sheep, providing they're willing to accept His offering."

Edwina's upper lip curled. "Every last black sheep. Well, I suppose I fit that order."

"It's called grace, Mrs. Bolton." He didn't know where the word came from; it was just there. The word had simply jumped into his mind. Did the woman sense that her days were few? Perhaps for the first time in her life her mind was dwelling on where she would spend eternity. Hadn't he been experiencing the same uncertainties?

An image flashed through his mind. Brief, but poignant — an older man holding a youthful arm, sawing a board. The ragged edge bit into the fresh lumber, moving back and forth, the implement held steady by a beefy, wind-chapped hand. And the man was speaking. Telling him about grace.

"Grace is a gift, son. All you have to do is accept it."

Edwina Bolton rose slowly, holding to the arm of her chair. Her hair was a fright and her bones thin as reeds. Joseph felt certain that a wispy breeze would blow her off her feet. He stepped up to assist her but she motioned him aside.

"I'm tired. I'll go back to my room now." She fixed her gaze on him. "Thank you for reading, young man. I'll think about these words."

She left the parlor. Returning to his chair, Joseph picked up the cup of cold coffee and sipped, musing over what had just taken place. Edwina was a lost soul, and he prayed that words stronger, more capable than his would reach her before she passed.

"Closer."

"We *can't* get any closer or they'll see us!"

Lark peered over Boots's shoulder. The girls were hidden behind a fat cedar, watching the Younger house. Already the sun was slowly edging closer to the west and they would be walking home in the dark. They'd been waiting behind the tree for over an hour and not a single soul had come out of the place known to belong to the Youngers. Their now almost daily vigil had produced nothing. They were no nearer to knowing Joseph's identity than they'd been a week ago.

The front door opened and Boots drew in

a sharp breath as a man stepped onto the porch, rolling tobacco in a thin white piece of paper. He stood gazing up at the sky as he worked, and then brought the cylinder up to his mouth and sealed the smoke with a lick. A match flared.

"Can you tell who he is?" Boots whispered. The girls had done their homework. They'd studied the posters tacked to the jailor's wall until he'd run them off yesterday, but not before he'd asked about the wounded stranger.

"Is he still alive?"

"He's alive but real sick."

"You tell your sister that he's got a few more days and then I'll be coming for him."

Lark's watchful gaze had shifted to the posters once more. "Lyric doesn't want me around him," she'd said. "Besides, he could be gone by now, dead as a doornail. He looked mighty puny this morning. Who knows if he's still alive?"

Which wasn't a complete fib. He'd been smearing molasses on a biscuit when she left the house this morning, but who knew? He could have died of any number of horrible accidents since then.

The sheriff turned a skeptical eye on her. "You'd better not be lying to me, Lark Bolton. I'm planning to ride up that way when

170

the weather breaks, and you people had better not be harboring a Younger."

She fixed him with a pout. "Didn't your mother teach you about Jesus and how we're supposed to love one another?"

"This has nothing to do with Jesus, missy. And anyhow, the Good Book says 'an eye for an eye.' "

"Then take Joseph's eye."

The man squinted. "Who's Joseph?"

"That's our man's name."

"The man you got at your place?"

"Yes, sir."

"I thought you said he was a Younger."

"Don't know that for certain — that's for you to prove."

"You're not making a lick of sense. Now you and Boots get on out of here. I got work to do. My word stands. I'll be up to get the prisoner as soon as I get a spare moment."

Like he had *so* much to do. He was scared to confront Joseph. Lark stiffened her spine, turned, and slammed out.

Nobody could ever convince her that their man was an outlaw. Lyric didn't really believe it either. Lark could see it in her sister's troubled countenance.

She hadn't mentioned the sheriff's threat to Lyric because it would only heighten that uneasy look she'd had in her eyes lately.

171

How long could a body stand at the window and look out and then pace the floor?

Her mind returned to the man standing on the porch smoking. He stood over six feet, was well proportioned, and had a fancy red kerchief tied around his neck. Brawny arms, thick neck. His features were well defined. Well cut lips, expressive mouth, prominent, rounded chin, sandy mustache —

Boots elbowed her sharply.

"What?"

"Stop ogling."

"I'm not ogling; I'm being observant."

"Do you recognize him from one of the posters?"

"Umm . . . he could Bob Younger . . . or maybe his younger brother, James."

Boots shook her head. "Is it Bob or James?"

"It's hard to say. The poster images aren't that clear."

The cabin door opened again and a second man joined the first. Both Lark and Boots wrinkled their noses. He wasn't nearly as pleasant to behold. Deep set eyes, a long, wide jaw, and heavy eyebrows. His eyes had a big long wrinkle over them, and the deep scars on both sides of his mouth made him downright scary.

"Recognize him?" Boots prompted.

"No — the hair is about same shade as Joseph's — or close — no. Our stranger doesn't look a thing like this man."

Boots checked the sun's location. "Okay. We have time to wait a while longer."

Activity started to pick up as the supper hour approached. Riders rode in and dismounted. Lark studied their appearances. One was tall and slender with a light complexion, and when he laughed she noted he had a couple of front teeth missing. Another had average height, stooped shoulders, a light complexion, and a heavy build. It looked like the last thing he needed was another pan of cornbread.

The two girls shared dubious looks and shook their heads.

Hoofbeats approached. This rider looked to be short, with dark hair and heavy eyebrows. His thin upper lip showed the effort of a sprouting mustache but the hair was thin and sparse. His long fleshy nose didn't fit Joseph's shapely one.

Boots perked up when a couple of men rode up and dismounted. Her eyes fixed on the taller one. "What about this fella?"

Lark studied the specimen. He was nearly as handsome as Joseph. He stood well over six feet and had an oval elongated face, high cheekbones, arched brows, deep set eyes, and dark reddish hair inclined to curl at the neck. He removed his hat and her face fell when he called to a friend in a thick Irish brogue, "A good evenin' to you!"

Boots groused, "Bejiggers! I thought we were close." Her animated voice echoed throughout the holler.

Heads snapped up. Hands moved to guns strapped on hips.

Lark grabbed Boots's hand and hissed. "Run!"

Lyric turned, spoon in hand, as Lark tramped into the kitchen. "Where have you been? I was worried sick. It's well past dark."

"I know — I'm sorry. Time got away from us." She handed her sister a limp clump of weeds.

"What's this?"

Cringing, Lark smiled uncertainly. "Dandelion greens."

"This is nothing more than wild grass."

"Really?" Lark shook her head and continued through the kitchen. "Well, we were picking after dark."

When she entered her room she kicked off her wet shoes and moved to the dresser, where she carefully tucked the wallet she'd found earlier in the top drawer.

Somewhere a man must be wondering where he'd lost or misplaced it.

9

Joseph was high on the rooftop fixing a hole when the day of reckoning arrived. The melting snow had caused so many leaks that Lyric couldn't keep track of them. The old Bolton place needed a man around. The fence was down, and the house needed so many repairs she'd stop counting.

Stirring gravy, Lyric hummed, casting a brief glance out the kitchen window. The spoon froze in place and she closed her eyes in sick despair. Three riders were approaching.

Sliding the skillet to the back of the stove she stepped to the back door and yelled up. "Joseph!"

"Yo!"

"Three riders are coming up the hill."

The long silence that followed allowed time for her panic to mount. "Did you hear me?"

"Yes."

"Crouch behind the fireplace flue. Lie flat."

"You don't want me to come down?"

"No! Whatever you do, *don't* come down." The old roof was steeply pitched with alcoves and angles — if the shadow was right a man could hide in the depths without detection. She might live to regret her rash decision, but so be it. She was willing to take the chance. Bolton Holler would witness no hanging today.

Boots and Lark. Where were they? Gone — they'd left earlier to do something. Pester Murphy, probably.

Moving swiftly to the front door, she opened it and nodded a greeting as the riders approached. "Good morning, gentlemen."

"Ma'am." The riders touched their fingers to the brims of their hats.

"What can I do for you this fine morning?"

The sheriff spoke. "We come for the Younger."

She frowned. "The Younger?"

"The wounded man. He isn't dead, is he?" Was that a hopeful tone she detected?

She shook her head. "I haven't buried anyone that I recollect."

The knot in the acting sheriff's throat

177

worked. "Then hand him over."

"Why, surely, but he isn't in the house."

"Where is he?'

"Who?"

"The Younger."

Her hand came to her chest. "Do I have a Younger?"

"Ma'am. Cut the act. Now hand the man over and we'll be on our way."

"Well, sir, if you think I have a Younger in my house you're more than welcome to come inside and get him."

The men eyed one another. One shook his head, conveying a silent warning. *Ain't goin' in that place.*

"You just bring him out here," the sheriff said.

"Who?"

"The Younger."

"Do I have a Younger?"

Climbing off his horse, the sheriff approached her. "Step aside."

"Yes, sir." She obediently complied.

Trailing the sheriff through the house, she chatted. "That was some storm. One of the biggest I can remember."

"Yes, ma'am." He cautiously opened a closed door, peeked inside, and shut it. Moving from room to room, he checked cubbyholes and drawn curtains.

"You'd know if he'd died, wouldn't you?"

"I think I'd have noticed." When they reached her mother's room she quickly stepped in front of him. "My mother's in here. She's been feeling poorly, and I'd prefer that you didn't disturb her."

His face drained of color. He gulped and gave a short nod. "I'll . . . uh . . . I'll just check the other bedrooms."

"Go right ahead," said Lyric. Joseph's room was neat and there would be no evidence of his presence. She made certain of that every morning.

While he made a quick pilgrimage she drew the window curtain aside and noted the two other men had gotten off their horses and were walking around the property, scouring the few small outbuildings. She heard her heartbeat in her ear when she noted they had started to circle the house, peering up at the roof lines. If Joseph pressed flat enough he might be overlooked since skiffs of ice still clung to the shingles. But if a man looked close enough —

She heard a door close softly and the sounds of boots thumping down the stairway. "Was he up there?"

"For the life of me I can't figure out why you'd be hiding him, but I have a gut feeling that you are."

The sheriff stalked toward the front door and slammed it closed behind him.

Hurrying back to the window she watched the three men retrace their earlier steps, peeking in holes and culverts.

God, please, please don't let them find him. She wasn't convinced the Almighty would grant her selfish request, but it couldn't hurt to ask.

That evening Lyric set a plate of stew and cornbread in front of Joseph. They were alone for supper tonight; Lark and Boots were extremely busy these days and she'd been meaning to ask her sister what preoccupied their time. Lark hadn't read a whole book in at least a week. "Did they walk around your side of the roof?"

Joseph nodded and reached for the butter. "They didn't spot me." He paused and then with head bowed said softly. "I'm much obliged. I would be hanged in the morning if You hadn't intervened."

She sighed. "I can't say if I made the right or wrong decision."

"I was speaking to the Lord, but I'm grateful to you as well." He poured cream in his coffee. "They'll be back. Then what?"

"I'll have to study on it." She had no idea

where this would go or for how long. What was she to do with a man with no memory? Just pray that in time it would return and her instincts had been correct? If they were wrong then she hoped he would simply walk away and never be seen in these parts again. Yet that thought didn't set well with her either.

She dished up her plate and poured a glass of milk. He shook his head. "What you're doing is chancy. You have no idea who I am or what I'm capable of doing, and you have your mother and sister to think about."

"And yet if I was wrong about this — if I helped an innocent man to hang — I'd never forgive myself."

They ate in companionable silence. When he reached for a second helping she smiled. He was getting much better, his color greatly improved, his wounds healing nicely. His eyes met hers. "I've been meaning to mention that your mother paid me another visit."

Lyric almost dropped her fork. "When?"

"A few days ago. I was in the parlor and looked up and she was sitting across from me. She comes and goes like a mouse."

"Did she say anything?"

"She wanted me to read to her."

"Read to her? Read what?"

"The Bible. She asked that I read Isaiah 53. She said it was one of your favorite chapters."

"That's right. Isaiah is one of my favorite books in the Bible." They ate for a moment longer before Lyric spoke again. "That was very thoughtful of you. Reading, I mean. It's important for Mother to hear the Word before she passes."

"I didn't mind. In fact, I rather enjoyed it. I know I've read that passage before, but when I couldn't say."

"Perhaps your memory is returning?"

He shook his head. "No, but the words meant something to me."

"How could anyone read that Scripture and not reap meaning?"

He glanced up and smiled. Such a normal act, but the smile cut right through her heart. She fairly burst when she looked at him. Was he taken? Did a woman with his children wait for him, peering out the window, praying for his return? The thought was almost as troubling as wondering if he were a wanted outlaw. If he was a Younger and her instinct proved faulty, she had only briefly saved him from a premature death. Outlaws didn't live long around here. She picked up the butter dish. "More?"

"Sure." He cut another slab. "Have I

mentioned that you're a good cook?"

"I don't believe you have." A prickle started at the bottom of her stomach and worked its way up.

His crooked grin touched her heart even more. He looked like a small boy, a boy she wanted to hug.

"You know what I'm thinking?"

She knew what *she* was thinking, and she shouldn't. "No. What?"

"I'm thinking it's a perfect night for fishing. Creek's up a little from all the melted ice."

"Fishing?"

"Creek runs right beside the house. The other morning I took a walk downstream and there's a fairly decent catfish hole down there. Want to come with me?"

"You mean — now?" She had never been asked to accompany a man anywhere and she wasn't sure how to answer. Nothing prevented her from accepting.

"I'll help with the dishes and then we'll get started. You have fishing poles, don't you?"

"Yes."

"I can seine a few crawfish and we'll see if we can catch a mess of sun perch. I'll even fry them up for you tomorrow. You got plenty of cornmeal?"

She nodded. He *was* asking her to accompany him. Where didn't matter.

"Sure, I'd love to go fishing."

She couldn't get another morsel of food past her lips after the invitation. She sat, pretending to eat while he polished off another plate of stew. Lark came in and took her supper to her room with a book.

After a bit, Joseph pushed back from the table and Lyric quickly gathered plates and stacked them in the dishpan. "We can do these later," she said.

Right now, she was dying to go fishing.

Moonlight lit the path as the two made their way down the creek bank. The stream was heavy from melting snow and ice, but it hadn't yet breached its banks. Lyric carried a bucket to put the bait in.

She held the light when they stopped and Joseph unwound the heavy piece of netting. Flying bugs darted to the light as she bent and watched him cast out the net into a shallow pool. He glanced over his shoulder. "Ever seined for bait?"

She nodded. "Sometimes, but I use worms. Mother doesn't like fish so I don't fix it often."

He tugged, slowly drawing the net toward him.

"I'm reminded of the apostles when I see you do this. Most of them fished for a living."

"That a fact?"

She nodded. "Oh, look!" The net drew closer and she spotted a handful of crayfish in the mesh. "You have some!"

He drew the seine closer, removed the crawling pincers, and handed them to her. Squealing, she let go and the bait fell back into the water.

"What happened?"

"One pinched me!"

"Sissy."

"Well, *you* handle the next ones."

"Well, I *will.*" He flashed another winsome grin that rocked her stomach. "We'll be here all night if I haul them in and you release them."

The thought of spending long hours with him didn't worry her, but those slimy pinching creatures were another story.

The net sailed through the air and within a half an hour the bucket contained enough bait to last for a while.

Trailing further down the creek, he led her to a spot she'd visited often. Moonlight shimmered on the water and a soft breeze ruffled her hair. She visited here often when she had serious thinking to do.

185

"There are a couple of big rocks . . ."

"Over here," she finished, and laughed. "I come here all the time — it's one of my favorite places."

"It's real nice," he agreed. "I've spent a few hours here."

"Really? This is where you come when I can't find you?"

"Most of the time. Can't tell you all of my secrets."

"I didn't suspect you were fishing."

"I haven't fished. Just sat down here and thought."

He didn't need to say where his thoughts led. His mind had to be so confused.

She located her rock and staked a claim. Setting the lantern on the gravel, she went to work putting a new line on her pole. She hadn't fished in ages and the old tackle was worn.

"Looks like you're a born fisherwoman," he observed when he came to perch on the rock beside her.

"I used to fish a lot when I was young. Lark and I would come here and she'd read and I would catch sun perch. We had fun." She drew her line through the eyehooks.

He studied her as he bent over the bucket. Absently he peeled the shells off the crayfish and put the meat on his hook. "Did you have a good childhood?"

Laughing softly, she glanced over. "No."

He nodded. "Your mother."

"My mother." She stood throwing the line and the bobber into the water to test it. The tackle merrily danced on the still water and then steadied. She drew the line back in. "Would you peel one of those for me?"

"You're a fisherwoman and you can't bait your hook?"

"With a worm," she noted.

"You have no trouble threading a needle through a worm's belly but you're squeamish when a crawdad gives you a little love pinch."

"Love pinch?" Her brow lifted. "He nearly took the hide off."

Reaching for the bucket, he readied the bait. "Maybe he fell in love with you real quick and that's his way of showing it."

"If a person loves me I'd prefer a gentle squeeze."

"I'll have to remember that." He stood and baited her hook. "There. I get whatever you catch for the effort."

"You're welcome to it." She threw the line out and then walked back up to the rock and sat down. Seconds later the bobber went under.

"You got one! Jerk!"

She yanked and hauled back. A perch flew up, swung back, and slapped Joseph in the face.

He batted the catch free of his eyes. "You jerked too hard."

"You said *jerk.*"

"I stand corrected." He calmly removed the flopping fish from the hook. "Tug firmly."

"Men." She sighed and glanced at him through lowered lids, grinning. "Never satisfied." She threw out again.

Backing up to his rock, he said quietly, "You know a lot about men, do you?"

"Nothing. You're the first man I've ever been around."

"What about your father?"

She shook her head. "Don't know a thing about him. He was never around and I learned not to ask questions."

"You don't recall a man in your life?"

She slowly shook her head. "I don't recall much of my youth until I was around seven or eight years old. That's when Mother started taking ill and the household and raising of Lark fell to me."

"Can't imagine one so young with so much responsibility. Did you resent the intrusion in your life?"

"Truthfully . . ." She jerked and missed

the catch. Bringing in her line she checked for bait, and then threw out again. "I don't recall ever having a childhood. Often Lark feels like my child. And Mother too."

"You have no other relatives?"

"None that Mother's ever spoken about."

"Has she always been this secretive?"

"Always. She's a bitter woman, I know that, but I care for her, and I try my best to love her. Sometimes she makes it hard."

The sounds of nature filled the air. A bullfrog croaked to its mate. It was too early for lightning bugs but they'd be around by the end of May, flittering about, flashing their tails.

"What're you thinking about?"

Joseph's voice brought her back. "I was just thinking about what a lovely evening it is."

Catching back a laugh, he baited his hook. "I suppose it is." A piece of bait dropped and they simultaneously reached to get it. Heads bumped. Lyric met his eyes in the moonlight and her heart hammered so hard she thought her chest might explode.

He leaned in closer and she shut her eyes in anticipation. When his lips touched hers she heard a soft sigh and realized it came from her. Not a friendly peck, but a man's kiss. He tasted warm and faintly sweet.

189

Their lips fit together as though God had made the mold. No awkward fumbling, only sweet, simple togetherness.

He wasn't in any hurry to break the contact. She wanted the moment to last forever.

If what she was beginning to suspect was true — that Joseph wasn't a bad man after all — then she knew God didn't drop men like him in a woman's path, not in Bolton Holler and not to a Bolton directly. This past moment was a gift. God had undoubtedly made her and Joseph for a purpose, but in her heart she feared this man wasn't intended for her. She couldn't saddle him and his future with the daughter of a madwoman.

Wherever his past or future lay she wasn't a part of it, though at this moment, every fiber of her being wished it could be so.

Life at the Bolton house settled to a more normal pattern. Joseph's wounds continued to heal and for the following week the sheriff didn't test Lyric's sincerity. She knew his suspicions ran high; the injured stranger was still alive and improving every day, but the sheriff would have to find him before she'd willingly hand him over. She had no doubt that Joseph had been right when he said it was only a matter of time before the man and his posse would be back, but for now all she could do was take one day at a time.

Ice patches melted and tiny fragrant irises poked their way through the newly awakened land. Lyric picked a huge bouquet of wild violets on her way back from milking, breathing deeply of the blue, sweet, intoxicating scent. The sun shone and the earth was coming alive. Spring was her favorite time of the year.

When she topped the rise she spotted Katherine hurrying toward the house. Elated to see her friend, she quickened her steps, smiling. The two women hurried toward each other, Katherine swinging the familiar wicker basket. Lark hoped it contained something special from Katherine's new kitchen.

When they met up breathlessly they embraced. Only then did Lyric spot the tears rolling from the corner of Katherine's eyes. "My goodness — is something wrong?"

Mutely nodding, Katherine reached into her light jacket and took out a crisp handkerchief. Lyric took special note of the intricate hand-stitched embroidered hem, most likely a gift from a doting grandmother. The tears came more swiftly now and Lyric took her friend's hand as they walked to the back porch steps. When they were about to enter the house, Katherine drew back. "Do you mind if we sit here in the fresh air?"

"Not at all." Had the town gossip begun to concern the Jennings? Lyric's heart sank. Did Katherine now fear that her friend was someone less than . . . normal?

But her opening words allayed the troubling thought. "Oh, Lyric. I'm going to miss you so much!"

"Miss me?" She flashed a consoling smile. "I'm not going anywhere soon."

"Day before yesterday?"

"Yes?"

"The light — it came back." She took deep gulps of breath. "I — we can't take it anymore! The thing literally scares us speechless — even Levi, who isn't afraid of anything."

Lyric sat up straighter. "Did it — threaten you?"

"Threaten us? It didn't rush us but it — it tormented us, Lyric. Bouncing here and there and peering into the windows."

"I've told you before it's playful."

"It's torment!" Katherine wailed. "It didn't come in the room this time; it just sat on the windowsill and shimmered. Then it left. But it returned last night and I

192

couldn't take it anymore. I begged Levi to leave." She broke down in heaving sobs.

Slipping an arm around her friend's waist, Lyric let her cry it out. There wasn't much anyone could do if a body couldn't take any more. If only that maddening light would go away. Who knew where it came from or why? There had to be a logical explanation buried somewhere in these hollers. If it meant harm, it would have acted long ago. The fact was, some things in life simply could not be explained.

"Where will you go? You've just built your lovely home."

"Back to Joplin. We'll have to live with Levi's parents until we can rebuild."

The words speared Lyric's heart like an ice pick. Her one and only friend gone, and it was only a matter of time before Joseph left too. She blinked back hot tears.

"And you know what else?"

"What?"

Katherine wiped her eyes with the end of the hanky. "I think I'm going to have a baby."

"A baby!" Lyric exclaimed. The news made Katherine's leaving even more painful to accept. Lyric would never have babies, but if Katherine stayed she could have helped care for the infant — pretend the child was hers . . .

"Oh, Katherine, I'm so happy for you." She leaned over to her friend and gave her a brief hug. "I've never been to Joplin and I know it's a far distance — but perhaps once the baby comes Levi could bring you here — permit me to see it?"

Nodding through glistening tears, Katherine nodded. "Levi and I are thrilled about the baby. I'll make him promise to bring me here, Lyric. I don't want to leave, and yet I can't live under these conditions. The light doesn't hurt us, but it keeps my nerves frayed until I can't sleep at night for fear the light will intrude. And now I'm afraid it will upset me so much it will affect my child."

"I know." Lyric patted Katherine's arm. "I guess I accept and ignore it because I've lived with strange circumstances for so long the light is barely noticeable."

"You know what?"

"What?"

"If it's a girl, I'm going to name it after you. Lyric. It's a beautiful name and your friendship has meant so much to me for the brief time I've been here."

"Yours has been the bright spot in my life," Lyric confessed. The two leaned together and hugged tightly for a long time.

Before Katherine or Joseph had come into her life, Lyric had been content with her lot; now she wasn't sure the loneliness wouldn't eat her alive.

"I'll leave the address where we'll be staying. You'd be welcome any time."

Lyric smiled, knowing that if Katherine mentioned the supernatural gossip surrounding Lyric and Lark they would be anything but welcome in the elder Jennings' home.

"Katherine, I haven't mentioned this but I have something of a secret that I've been keeping from you. The wounded man I've been caring for is most likely an outlaw." Lyric briefly explained why a suspected criminal now regularly ate at her table. "If he doesn't regain his memory he is doomed to be hanged once the sheriff has the gumption to take him by force."

Katherine's eyes widened. "Oh . . . how dreadful! You know for certain that he's an outlaw?"

"I thought I did, but now I have my doubts. I can't make myself turn him over to the authorities until he knows who he is."

"But he may never tell you even if he does regain his memory. My father knew a man once who lost his memory and it never came back. Lucky for him he was married with four children. His wife said the accident allowed her to fall in love with him all over again."

"That is a lovely thought and I've considered the prospect, but I believe he will be honest with me." If he never regained his memory it would be fine with her. Then maybe, just maybe, they could seek a life together with no jaded pasts to consider. His earlier kiss led her to believe that he had growing feelings for her — she couldn't mistake the way he looked at her or allowed his hand to brush hers at the most unexpected moments.

No. She shouldn't think that way. It wasn't fair to Joseph — or to her.

"Lyric." Katherine rested her hand on Lyric's arm. "Be careful. You never know — this man might be dangerous once his memory returns."

"I know." She'd thought of little else since he burst into her life.

"Do you want Levi to take him to the authorities?"

"No!" She met Katherine's stunned gaze. "No. I don't want him moved anywhere. Yet. And you're not to mention a word of this to anyone — even Levi, if you can bear to keep my secret."

"Yet?"

Katherine heard correctly. The hour was fast approaching when she had to decide to follow the law or follow her heart, but that hour had not arrived. Not yet.

"Not yet," she repeated aloud. "I have to know who he is for certain before I turn him over to the sheriff."

"You're a romantic, aren't you?" Katherine turned to study her. "You've fallen in love with this man."

"Guilty," Lyric confessed, and then felt her features crack. "Oh, Katherine, why do women do such foolish things when it comes to men?"

10

Joseph jabbed a hoe into the soft earth and then dropped a potato seedling into the black fertile soil. He'd spotted the box of plants on the service porch and instinct told him the weather was warm enough to get the early crop into the ground. The garden spot sat half overturned, bearing silent witness to the recent upheaval in the Bolton household. He had a feeling that normally the soil would have been tilled by now. Grinning, he thought of the imaginary help she'd mentioned — "a big man with a gun who wasn't afraid to use it" — and decided that he had begun to fill the job.

Lyric sat on the back stoop visiting with the Jennings woman. The two seemed to have a warm friendship. He struck the ground and an image of a young boy planting seed potatoes, standing beside a woman wearing a blue and white bib apron, flashed through his mind. But the picture disappeared almost as quickly as it had materialized.

Shaking his head, he poked another hole in the ground and dropped another seedling in a row running north to south. Today the effort to bend was less awkward; each new sunrise brought with it a bit more strength. For the first time since he'd come here he was starting to think that he might live long enough to be hanged.

And for the first time rebellion burned like hot coals in his belly. *God, if I am the man I'm thought to be, why didn't You let me die? Hanging is fair punishment, but now I'm left to watch the look on Lyric's face when I climb that platform. She's an innocent bystander. Why involve her in this?*

And he knew she would be there. Wild horses wouldn't keep her away, but he didn't want her to witness the ugly sight. Maybe that was God's punishment — to make him witness his sins in the most anguished way, through a woman's eyes. A woman who appeared to put her trust in him.

God, how I pray her faith isn't in vain.

He slowly moved down the row, planting, praying. After a bit he noted Katherine embracing Lyric and the young neighbor striking off toward home. Lyric slowly walked down the hill. When she reached the garden, she smiled. "Planting potatoes, I see."

"Hope you don't mind. I needed something to fill the time."

"I don't mind — but how did you know it was time to plant potatoes?"

Pausing, he pulled the handkerchief knotted around his neck up and wiped away the perspiration from his forehead. "Couldn't say. Instinct, maybe?"

Nodding, she reached for a seedling and followed him down the row.

"Did you have a nice visit with your friend?"

"Not really. Katherine's moving."

"Moving?" He dug another hole. "I thought you said they'd just settled here."

"They have, but the light keeps tormenting them."

He covered the hole with dirt. "That light again."

"*The* light."

Straightening, he met her eyes. "They've seen it too?"

She nodded. "Everyone's seen it."

Blue, yellow, bouncing. The image ricocheted through his mind.

"I wondered if my mind was playing tricks. That thing leaves you with a heck of a question in your mind."

"Well, it bothers Levi and Katherine to the extent that they're moving back to Joplin to live with his folks." She sighed. "And she's just discovered that she's going to have a baby."

"That's too bad — not about the baby, but allowing something that silly to scare them away." He paused, leaning on the hoe. "You'll miss her."

She sighed. "Very much."

"You honestly don't fear the light?"

"Joseph, nothing much frightens me except willfully disobeying the Lord or losing Lark. I think if the light meant any harm it would have done something by now. We've seen it over and over and it's always been harmless."

"Still, a light bouncing around like that —"

"Is disturbing. I can't fault Katherine for wanting to leave. I want to leave, but not because —" She caught back her words.

"Not because of the light," he finished.

"Correct. You want to see where some of the stories about the light originated?"

"Are the places nearby?" He glanced at the long row. "There are still a lot of potatoes to plant."

"I'll help later. Come with me."

He set the hoe aside and followed her across the field, feeling the heaviness that had been his constant companion start to lift from his shoulders.

They walked in companionable silence for about twenty minutes. Finally she paused, pointing to the ruins of an old cabin where only the rock chimney remained standing. "This is the old miner's cabin. There are all sorts of stories about miners carrying their lanterns across fields and disappearing, or this one particular miner whose home was raided by Indians while he was at work one night. His children were kidnapped and he never saw them again. It's said that it's his light that's seen, searching for his babies."

"That wouldn't explain the crazy way it acts."

"Nothing explains the light. People only tell stories. Stories help them stop being afraid."

A while later they stood at the foot of a high bluff overlooking a river and a cooling breeze lifted his hair. He had to admit she was good company.

Staring out over the river, Lyric's expression grew thoughtful as she continued sharing stories of the region. "This particular place is where the lovely daughter of an Indian chief met her death, or so it is said.

It seems her father was a selfish man and asked an exorbitant price for his daughter's hand. When the young brave couldn't pay it, the couple ran away and jumped to their deaths — kind of like Romeo and Juliet. The light is the ghosts of the young couple searching for each other."

"No way to solve a dispute." He shook his head, studying the high bluff. "That drop must be two hundred feet."

"I've heard that love makes you do strange things sometimes." Reaching for his hand, she continued the exploration.

It wasn't long later that Joseph and Lyric stood in a glade in a thick carpet of moss. Towering sycamores stood sentinel over what he thought might look like a tiny piece of heaven. Hyacinths bloomed; birds chattered overhead. The setting had to be one of the most peaceful places he could recall. "What happened here?"

Smiling, she turned to face him. "This is the most special place of all."

"Yeah? Someone lop off their head when the light appeared?"

"No. This is where you kissed me a second time."

Shaking his head, he gave a crooked grin. There was no way a man could spend the afternoon in her company and hold on to common sense. "You're awful sure of your-self, lady."

"Not in the least, but there's no law against hoping." A playful light was in her eyes. She was as sweet smelling and pretty as any rose that grew wild in the heavy thicket.

Joseph put his hands on Lyric's waist and drew her to him. His hold tightened as he brought her closer, their lips inches apart. "Do I have your permission to kiss you?"

"You didn't ask before."

"I didn't need to — your eyes invited me to do what I wanted."

"Kiss me, please."

His mouth closed over hers, and for a long moment neither of them could say anything at all.

Late that afternoon, Lyric dropped the last potato seedling in the ground and dusted her hands off on her long apron. "I need to get back to the house. Mother might be awake by now."

"Sure. Thanks for the excursion — and the planting help."

He watched her walk back up the hill. Another day, another time, another life and he wouldn't hesitate to take that woman in his arms and kiss away the sadness he saw in her eyes. The kiss in the glade had been warning enough that he was starting to care about her far too much for both their good.

Still, he wouldn't regret kissing her. He couldn't.

Mist hung over the valleys when Joseph slipped out of the house the following morning. It wasn't yet sunrise and no one else in the house had stirred. But he had an errand. A mission. If he was to be hanged he was going to make sure they had the right man.

He'd waited until everyone was fast asleep the evening before he gathered the necessary items. Lyric's oversized sunbonnet, a pair of her mother's work shoes, white gloves, a woman's purse, rouge, kohl, a pair of specs he found in the parlor, a pillow, and a piece of hemp.

He'd thought long and hard about what he was about to do. He was running a risk. If caught, he'd bring down judgment day quicker than he'd like, but if he played it right he could get a look at the sheriff's wanted posters and be out of there before anyone was the wiser. If he was a wanted man there would be a poster with his image on it. A fellow couldn't go anywhere in Missouri without seeing posters tacked to trees and buildings. If his picture was there and there was a bounty on his head he wanted the money to go to Lyric. If she followed through on the "new life" she talked about she would need money and lots of it. And if she didn't start that new life, well, she still needed a new barn door. Grandpa and Grandma had always made do on next to nothing. It wouldn't be long before they claimed their eternal reward, and they wouldn't want for anything where they were headed.

He paused. Grandpa and Grandma. It was suddenly clear he had them — but the image faded as quickly as it had appeared. Odd.

He walked to the barn and saddled the horse, smacking the animal smartly on the rump when he sidestepped each time Joseph tried to buckle the strap. If he owned this ornery son-of-a-gun . . . He flat-handed him again when the horse shifted to solidly plant a hoof on his left boot.

Minutes later he rode out of the barn, following the well-worn trail he'd seen Katherine walking.

Now all he had to do was pull this off without getting shot between the eyes.

Edgar Snood crossed his legs. "Well, I say

we ride up there and get him. You know he's there and the Bolton girl is protecting him like she would a chickadee. Who knows what's going on at that house, with that crazy lady throwin' her fits."

The jailhouse door opened and a woman — a rather stout woman — stood there holding a purse, her smudged kohl eyeliner and rouge standing out like a hen wearing a diamond ring. "Yes, ma'am?" the sheriff asked.

"Hello there, sir." She slammed the door. "I hope I'm not bothering you all but I'm trying to track down my nephew — the no-good one? If you don't mind, I'd like to have a look-see at your poster board."

"No, ma'am, don't mind in the least. That thar board's been a real source of interest these days." He chuckled to his friends and winked.

The two male visitors who sat in the office grinned. Elliot said, "Seems everyone's looking to collect a reward these days."

"Oh, I wouldn't take money for my nephew's capture." The woman spoke in a high falsetto. "I plan to personally wring his neck."

Joseph stalked to the board, heavy boots scraping the floor. He noticed the men's eyes fixed on his feet. Edwina Bolton's shoes were a little roomy even for him.

Pausing in front of the board he scanned the row of pictures for an image of himself. So far the sheriff and others hadn't looked past his boots, so if he was a Younger he'd so far managed to successfully hide his identity. It must be all that rouge.

His gaze traveled over the row of wanted notices. These men looked like fifty miles of bad road, but he didn't see his image, no one even close. Bending closer, he recognized the name John Jarrette, a man he'd come across about a month ago near St. Joseph. Jarrette. Joseph grinned to himself as it became clearer. The man had been shot and was dying; he'd offered his saddle if he'd bury him. He'd complied. Jarrette had a pretty hefty bounty on his head. Twenty-five thousand dollars. Joseph gave a low whistle. He knew where Jarrette was buried. Only thing was, the poster said he was wanted *alive.* There went twenty-five thousand dollars. His gaze shifted to the next poster.

And there it was: Jim Robert Cummins. The name stood out like the second coming.

He bent closer. "James, son of Samuel and Eleanor Cummins, rode with Quantrill and Anderson. $5,000 reward for cattle theft and spittin' on a sheriff."

Five thousand? He'd understood Cummins had at least a seven thousand dollar reward on his head.

He paused. He remembered . . . The road scuffle. The chase.

Norman. That rotten horse.

The light.

Memories rushed back like waves into a flooded cave. He wasn't a Younger or any outlaw at all. He was Ian Cawley, grandson of Irish immigrant grandparents who had raised him when his parents died of disease. Grandpa was a carpenter, made the finest furniture in the city.

The men's voices buzzed in his ear. He felt hot, then ice cold. He was about to be *hanged* with folks thinking he was a mealy-mouthed penny-ante outlaw?

He wasn't about to go down like that.

Trying to regain his composure, he turned back to the posters. The faces all seemed to blur together. Rubbing his eyes, he focused on Jim Younger's likeness. James Younger — known as Jim. Thirty-five thousand rested on his head. Now there was a bounty. He and Jim had a long-running feud. Both declared they would attend the other's hanging. Since Jim was on the opposite side of the law, Ian figured he would easily win the bet. He'd arrested Jim some years back and he'd done time for a bank robbery, but was released three years ago. The outlaw was thought to be still in the company of his gang here in Missouri.

Thinking straighter now, Ian turned on his heel and stalked back to the front door, opened it, and slammed it on his way out. Papers fluttered on the sheriff's desk.

"Who was that?" the first man asked when the door banged shut.

"Don't rightly know — ain't seen her around before. Got real manish features — and did you get a gander at those feet? Looked to be bigger'n mine." The sheriff got up to straighten the windblown papers on his desk.

"Don't mean to be hateful, but that thar's about the homeliest female I ever laid eyes on," Edgar noted.

"She could have used a good shave," the other man noted. The men chuckled.

"Well, as I was sayin' this minister and billy goat walked into a saloon . . ."

11

When Ian rode up to the Bolton house, Lyric was sitting on the back steps cracking walnuts with a hammer. A couple of sizable sassafras roots lay beside the stairs. Dismounting, Ian dropped Norman's reins and let the horse graze. During the ride home, the whole of his prior life had fallen into place, and he'd had to shake his head at the irony.

A U.S. marshal. He was anything but an outlaw. No wonder the title had been fitting like a horse collar around his conscience.

He stepped up and sat down beside Lyric, removing his hat. "Looks like you've been busy."

"We didn't gather enough walnuts this fall. Lark has such a sweet tooth that I've used all my supplies making fudge, and I found another bucketful this morning while I was digging sassafras root." She glanced over and her jaw dropped. "Joseph, why are you wearing a dress?"

"Oh, the dress . . . I had business in town."

"Wearing Mother's dress?" Her gaze moved to his feet. "And Mother's boots?"

"I needed a disguise. I wanted to get a good look at the posters on the sheriff's wall."

"You're not there. I've already checked."

"No, I wasn't there."

"Why would you take such a risk? Did anyone recognize you?"

"No, the sheriff had two visitors. They were too busy telling jokes to notice me."

"I want you to promise me you won't take such risks in the future. And never wear rouge again."

He tweaked her nose. "I promise, Mother dearest. What were you saying about the walnuts?"

Her gaze returned to the chore. "The meat may be dry, but there could be some good ones left."

"You said you were making fudge." He eyed her. "What is fudge?"

"You haven't tried it? It's a delicious kind of chocolate — quite the sugary treat. I'm told you can add all sorts of flavors but Lark likes vanilla with black walnuts."

"So you're getting ready to make this fudge?"

"No, I think I'll bake a chocolate cake instead and perhaps add a few nuts to the frosting, but I am boiling sassafras roots later. Would you like a cup of coffee?"

"In a minute — and don't go to any trouble. I can fetch it myself." He leaned back, stretching. It felt good to know who he was. His immediate urge to tell her about his memory returning faded. He had some serious thinking to do before he involved her any further in the misunderstanding. She would need to know that he wasn't an outlaw, but he needed at least twenty-four hours to come up with a solid plan for catching Jim Younger and avoiding a hanging.

Ian should have let Cummins go — he wasn't worth the chase and certainly not what the outlaw had put him through the past few weeks, but the little weasel had become a source of pride with him.

Five thousand dollars.

He shook his head, grinning at the irony.

She glanced over. "Something amusing?"

"No, just thinking." He focused on the brilliant sky, unusually blue this morning. "What are you going to do with the bounty money?"

Lyric furrowed her brow. "I haven't let myself consider that overly much. You're not well enough to be . . . hanged."

"How healthy does a man need to be? I figure I must be getting pretty close." He flashed a sideways grin. "All that fine cooking you've been feeding me is fattening me up." He patted his flat stomach. "They're going to need a stronger rope."

She calmly picked a nut from the cracked shell. "I hardly think that hanging is an amusing thought."

"Not amusing, but interesting." He shifted. "What brought you to the conclusion that I was a Younger — or that I was an outlaw, period? I had no identification on me, no horse — did I smell like strong drink?"

"No. I found a bank bag in your saddle roll that contained some money and the day's receipts. I . . . well, I assumed that nobody but an outlaw would be carrying that . . . plus tear my barn door off without being highly intoxicated, and nobody around here drinks to excess other than the outlaws."

"Without a horse, how would I have torn your door down?"

"Well . . ." She tossed the shells aside. "I realize now that I assumed quite a lot that night. Perhaps not all of it was true."

He caught her eyes and held them. "That's

good to know."

"How do you explain the bank bag?"

He could easily now, yet he couldn't without telling her his memory was back. "I can't, but maybe the bank bag wasn't mine. Maybe someone dropped it by the wayside and I picked it up?"

"Technically I suppose anything is possible." The color in her cheeks heightened. "Whatever I assumed that night, I don't feel that way now. I cannot make myself believe that you are a criminal."

Their gazes held for a long moment, and he wanted to take her in his arms and tell her the truth, kiss her fears away . . . but he wanted to protect her more. If he involved the Boltons directly in his circumstances they would be in real harm's way. When he had a plausible escape plan — a plan that would bring James Younger to justice while saving his own neck from the hangman's noose — then and only then would he tell her. When he was free of this situation he would explain everything to Lyric, and she would understand. A woman like her didn't come along every day, and he didn't intend to lose her through a misunderstanding. He trusted her with his life, but at the moment he had to regain that life in order to offer it to her.

He shifted and returned to star-gazing. "What would you do with thirty-five thousand dollars?"

"It isn't certain that you have a bounty on your head," she reminded him. "And even if there is, it wouldn't be that high."

"But if I do, I'm going to assume that I'm the biggest, baddest outlaw in these parts. What will you do with the money?"

"If that were true, I would leave here the moment I collect it. I'd take Lark and we'd go as far away as possible. Maybe if the bounty was big enough we'd go to a fancy school where Lark could get a fine education."

"What about your mother?"

Her gaze fixed on the walnut. "She gets weaker every day. I don't think it will be much longer now."

"You won't leave her here alone."

"Of course not." She tossed a nut into the bowl. "If the Lord hasn't taken her yet, there's a reason she's still here with us."

"How long has she been like this?"

"This weak? Maybe six months."

"What does the doctor say about her condition?"

"He won't come and examine her. He sent word that if I brought her to his office he'd do what he could, but she refuses to leave the house and I would have to carry her to a buggy with her fighting and screaming all the way. I'm sure you've noticed her labored breathing and the way she rarely talks for lack of air."

"Actually, no. She speaks in short distinct sentences when she makes her unexpected visits."

"Well, now you know why." She dropped another nut in the pan. "She can't get enough air for carrying on long conversations." Lyric offered him one of the shelled walnuts. "What would *you* do with a sudden windfall of money?"

He glanced up when she pierced his thought pattern. "Me? I'd spend it."

"On what? Suppose we're talking about a good deal of cash. Suppose — just suppose — your bounty would be very profitable."

"If we're going to suppose let's make it worthwhile. Let's say I'm worth fifty thousand."

She paused, the pick in midair. "That would make you a very bad person."

"Extremely bad." Some folks would give a hand or foot for that kind of security.

"All right, you're worth fifty thousand dollars."

"Thanks."

"And you're an extremely bad man who

shoots innocent people. And I have you, or I think I have you. What would you do if you were me?"

"Turn my sorry hide over to the sheriff."

"Even though I'm not certain that you're wanted for anything? And I knew they intended to hang you? For all I know, you could be a salesman traveling the country-side peddling your wares."

"Where's my wagon?" His eyes strayed to Norman. The horse was pulling up tender green shoots. He caught back a laugh at the thought of the animal subserviently pulling a peddler's wagon. That horse didn't do anything that wasn't to his liking.

"Perhaps something happened — you took a fall or someone knocked you on the head and your riding through my barn door was purely accidental, and now you can't remember up from down. What if you're a decent man trying to make a living selling vanilla and smelling salts and I turn you over to the sheriff and they hang you?"

He shook his head. "That's a lot of sup-posing."

"And you have a wife — and four — maybe five children waiting for you to come home?"

"What if I'm a black-hearted outlaw who would just as soon shoot you as look you in the eye? What if I haven't lost my memory at all, but I'm just biding my time until I take all the booty I can find and ride off?"

Her brow furrowed. "I don't think you're that kind of man."

"You can't say for sure." He could easily tell her he wasn't, but still he held back. He'd grown pretty fond of her — fonder than he cared to admit. Not only was she a pretty little thing, but she was as helpless in this holler as Norman would be on a pair of ice skates.

A smile quirked the corners of her mouth. "I don't fear that at all, certainly not from a man wearing a woman's dress."

"Well, I much appreciate your trust," he mocked.

"You've earned it." She stuck a bit of nut in his mouth. "Now, tell me what you would do with the money if it was yours."

"Me?" He thoughtfully chewed. "I'd give it to my Grandpa and Grandma — or at least a good amount of it."

"Are they in need?"

"Grandpa is a carpenter by trade. He's getting older but he still manages to bring in a little income and Grandma has her egg money, but they need a lot of things. A good plow horse, a new roof, and the old hen-house needs a match thrown on it." He sat up straighter. "And I'd buy Grandma one of those new sewing machines, the fancy kind that does a lot of different stitches. She'd be so happy the neighbors would complain her singing was disturbing their afternoon naps."

"Ahh, that's so thoughtful of you." She glanced up, curiosity mirrored in her eyes. "Wait — wait! How do you know all that?"

"How?" He scratched his uneven beard, searching for a plausible excuse and mentally berating himself for the slip. "I . . . I guess my memory's trying to come back. I can see Grandpa and Grandma in my mind, but I don't know where they are."

Her face lit, and Ian felt his heartbeat quicken. She was so lovely. He'd never seen such a smile. "That's wonderful!" she cried. "Then you remember who you are?"

"Don't get excited. I recall Grandpa and Grandma. Maybe that's a good sign."

"It's a wonderful sign! It means your mind is starting to clear."

Reaching into her pan, he selected a nut and popped it in her mouth. She grinned, chewing.

"Good?"

She nodded. "I love walnuts," she managed to say around the mouthful.

He scooped a handful and put them in

her mouth and she broke out laughing, catching the specks of nuts spilling out.

"Taste good?" he teased.

Waving her hand wildly, she shook him away and tried to chew. He enjoyed her antics, grinning. "Want some fudge with those nuts?"

Holding her hand to her chest she managed to munch and swallow the mouthful, still giggling. The sound of her laughter had the effect of a soothing balm. When he looked away momentarily her hand darted to his mouth, and she shoved a handful of walnuts inside.

They broke into laughter and playfully scuffled, upsetting the pan of nuts. When they bent to try to clean up the mess, their eyes met and the laughter died. For a long moment they gazed deep into each other's eyes.

What did she see reflected there? A scruffy, good-for-nothing outlaw, or a solid man — one she longed to know better? He knew what he saw: a lovely young woman who would turn any man's head. Trim figure, tiny waist, wide, trusting eyes rich as brown sugar beneath a crown of honey-colored hair. A woman he could easily take home and proudly introduce to Grandpa and Grandma.

"You look real kissable," he admitted softly.

"Then why don't you kiss me?"

"Because I'm not going to kiss you dressed like this."

"What if I just close my eyes?"

He bent closer, whispering, their lips a breath apart. "When this is over," he said, "I plan to kiss you once in the morning" — he touched her lips — "twice at dinner time" — he kissed her again — "and three more times in the evening."

"I'm thinking I'd need a few of those kisses you're doling out during the day to tide me over till suppertime."

"Yes, ma'am. As many and as often as you need." Her fingers slipped up to lightly thread through his hair, a silent but unmistakable invitation to draw her into his arms and hold her, to bury his face in that mound of sweet smelling honey-colored hair. He closed his eyes, willing strength. This mess was so close to being settled, so very close, but it wasn't. Not yet. And until he was free to claim her, he needed to keep his mind on business.

"Joseph?"

"Yes?"

"Would you please go into the house and change your clothing? I feel really strange kissing you like this."

"Oh. Sure." He broke the gaze, tossed the handful of nuts in the pot, and stood to go inside. He didn't feel good about keeping her in the dark about his memory returning, but it wouldn't be for long and it was to her benefit.

He'd have to remind himself of that often in the coming days.

12

Late that afternoon, Ian followed Boots and Lark through the thick undergrowth, swiping brush away from his face. The girls had insisted that he come with them, though he knew the trip was pointless. He knew his identity but he sure wasn't going to tell them. Not until the time was right.

He trailed Boots, who shoved the undergrowth aside and then released bare branches that smacked him in the face. He ducked when she did it a third time.

"Hey. Try to remember I'm behind you."

"Oh." She glanced over her shoulder. "Sorry."

Thwack.

Shaking his head, he shoved the briar aside. Walking through the woods with these girls was about as discreet as a rhino stalking a squirrel. They could be heard for miles around.

"Keep it down a little," he said. "They

can hear us coming."

"Sorry."

Thwack.

He blinked, trying to work a piece of bark from his eye. "Are you sure the Youngers live out this way?"

"Positive," Lark whispered. "We've been here before."

"When?"

"Last week. We wanted to see if anyone looked like you."

"Young lady, do you know how dangerous it is for two young women to be messing around alone in these woods? Lyric would tan your hide if she knew."

"We were doing a good thing," Boots argued.

"A real good thing," Lark echoed. "If we don't investigate, how will we ever know who you are?"

His conscience nagged him. These good-hearted girls were trying their best to help him . . . and all the while he knew exactly who he was. He wasn't going to keep misleading them — not if it meant putting them in harm's way. He couldn't.

"It's not worth the time and effort. Let's turn back."

"No way! It's not much further," Boots argued.

He stepped over a fallen cedar branch. "We can get ourselves in big trouble if anyone spots us. I'm turning around."

"Look — we're here." The girls paused behind a tall cedar. Ian had no choice but to follow.

"Did you recognize anyone last time?"

"Several from the wanted posters in the sheriff's office, but none that have your features."

They wouldn't. "Okay, we've been here. Let's go back."

"Not yet. We just got here." Lark eased a branch aside and peered through the cedar.

He spotted a structure a hundred feet ahead sitting in a thick sycamore grove. "Is that where they hang out?"

"That's it," Lark verified. "Don't look like much is going on right now." She lifted her hand to shade her eyes as she looked up. "The outlaws should be ridin' in for supper any time now."

The words still hung in the air when two men sitting tall in the saddle approached. One was a Younger, but Ian didn't recognize the second man. The riders dismounted and tied their horses to the hitching rail.

"Cole Younger is the bald one with reddish whiskers," Lark whispered. "I've seen so many posters of these men I know them by name."

Boots wrinkled her nose. "He's fat."

"Boots," Lark cautioned. "That isn't nice. He's . . . stout."

She shrugged. "They all look old and fat to me."

"Most of these men have a short life span." Ian couldn't think of many that survived their chosen lifestyles. They either died in prison on met their Maker in a public gunfight.

The two men walked into the house as others rode in. Lark softly called a few by name: "George Shepperd, Charlie Fletcher — he's the one missing an arm — Dick Liddil, Allen Parmer."

Boots stepped closer to Ian. "Are they really bad men?"

"Really bad, sweetheart," he said. "You girls are to stay far away from men like these."

The outlaws filed in over the next half hour. Ian had given up hope of seeing the man he wanted, but then a lone rider appeared. Jim Younger rode up and dismounted. He would know those lizard-skin boots anywhere. Ian had lost count of how many times Cole Younger's baby brother had eluded the law.

"Who's this one?" Boots asked.

Lark studied the man and then said, "Jim Younger. Wanted for just about anything you can think up."

"He's a mean one."

Lark turned to stare at Ian. "Do you know this man?"

"I . . ." He caught the near slip and retracted. "The name faintly rings a bell. I think anyone in these parts must have heard of Jim."

Drawing a deep sigh, Boots said, "I don't know why outlaws are so dumb. Don't they know they'll eventually get caught and either spend the rest of their life in jail or be hanged?"

"Bad men aren't dumb; they're wicked."

"What's the difference?"

"Ten to thirty years, most times."

So Jim was here, and his for the taking. The outlaw was hard to keep track of these days. Now all Ian had to do was draw him carefully into his snare without involving the Boltons. If the plan failed, which it likely could, folks couldn't blame Lyric and Lark for the daring escapade, but if the ploy were to succeed it would mean he wouldn't hang and both he and the sisters would pocket some hefty monies.

All he had to do was successfully make the plan work.

Ian parted ways with the girls on the walk home. That left Lark and Boots to make the journey back. At least an hour of light remained and the thought set easy on Lark's mind. Lyric wouldn't be too upset if she came in before supper.

Ambling along, Boots broached the subject they spoke about in whispers. "Lark, if Joseph is hanged — and it sure looks for the world like he's gonna be — then what?"

"I suppose we'll have to accept it, though it'll sure hurt."

"I mean what about our plans?"

"To run away?"

Boots nodded. "I was thinking, Lyric's going to be upset when Joseph . . . is gone. If we left now, she could get all the upset of losing him and you over at the same time."

Lark thought about it. Seemed reasonable, but cold. "That would be like heaping double trouble on her."

"Well, trouble is never good but I'm thinking if she's going to hurt she might as well lump all her troubles into one big grieving episode." They walked down the road, occasionally stepping to the fence line to yank up a dandelion green.

"I can't do that to her." Lark carried the handful of weeds. "It's going to be hard enough when Joseph goes."

"You changed your mind about going?" Boots stopped in the middle of the road to stare at her. "But we've always said —"

"I haven't changed my mind. It just doesn't seem right to leave now. Seems to me Lyric's got enough trouble on her mind — and who would help take care of Mother?"

"She don't need a lot of tending — just food and bathing."

Lark shook her head. "It's not the proper time, Boots."

"Okay." The admission came out on the heels of defeat. The girls walked on.

"And what about your grandpa? He's going to be upset when you leave."

"I know, but he's independent as a skunk, Lark. Sometimes I think I step on his nerves. He likes his quiet. And besides, he'll still have Caroline."

"He loves you; he'd fret if you weren't around to keep him company. Caroline's always mooning after some boy. She's not good company at all."

"I suppose you're right, and I sure don't want to hurt him. Grandpa's been good to me."

"And if the worst happens and Lyric forces me to leave, to start a new life somewhere else, we'll see each other again. I'll be grown before long, and I'll come back here. Maybe in two years — even less."

"Lyric won't sell the Bolton place?"

"Who would buy it?"

Nodding, Boots agreed. "Yes, who in their right mind would buy it?"

They walked on in silence.

"If I'm forced to leave, you promise me you'll make friends with Ida Summers," Lark said.

"Who?"

"Ida Summers. I see her occasionally when it's my turn to go to town. She's always in the store with her mother; she's real pretty and always friendly. One day she and her mother bought stick candy, and Ida offered me a piece. Of course I didn't take it because I'm not sure Ida knows who I am, but at least she offered."

"That was generous of her."

"So you promise you'll seek out Ida, and you and she can be best friends."

"Okay."

Lark stopped in the middle of the road. "Okay?"

Boots frowned. "Okay . . . I'll find Ida."

"Our *friendship* means so little to you that

you would *seek out* another friend that quickly? Just like that? I'm replaced?"

"But you said —"

"I know what I said, but I expected you to protest — to at least try and reason with me."

"Then stay. I don't want you to go, not ever. It wouldn't be the same around here if you left. I love you, Lark. You're like my sister."

Lark turned and walked on. "Sorry. I have to think of blood kin first."

"So you're staying?"

"Do I have a choice? Lyric makes all the decisions around here and if she says we leave I have to go."

"All right."

Her steps halted. "All right?"

"All right. You have to go."

She faced her defiantly. "You're not going to argue with me?"

"What good would it do? You just said you had to go."

"I love you. That's why it hurts that you'd let me go so easily." She sniffed. "I guess maybe there'd be no real harm if we left and Lyric had to grieve for everyone at the same time," Lark admitted. "But it will be a good grief — not a sad grief like she'll feel for Joseph."

"Do you suppose she's fallen in love with him?" asked Boots.

Lark nodded gravely. "That's another reason she'll have to leave. If they don't hang him she can't have him."

"Why not?"

Lark gave her a pointed look. "Now, why do you think? Lyric worries that Mother's illness might be passed down in families. She thinks she might go — well, what if she goes crazy someday?"

"So she'll never marry?" asked Boots.

"She says she won't. I will, though. I know I'm not mad. Murphy will wait for me — and I will come back. When I do, I'll paint our old house, fix the shutters, open the windows and let in fresh air, and plant pretty flowers. Everyone will forget the stories about the crazy old woman who used to live there."

"Have you talked to Murphy about this?"

"Heavens, no. He runs the other direction when he sees me coming."

"Then how can you be so certain that you're going to marry him someday?" Boots asked, her hand planted firmly on her hip.

Lark shrugged. "He's playing hard to get. He knows I have some growing to do — he's a patient man."

Boots paused again. "Then we *are* going

to run away — make a new life free of the Holler?"

Lark nodded the affirmative. "And I think we should do it now — not wait until they take Joseph away. It will be too sad."

"Okay. When?"

"Tonight, shortly after dinner."

"That quick? Shouldn't we stay around until this thing with Joseph is settled?"

"I see no reason to put ourselves through the agony. We've done all we can to learn Joseph's true name and we've discovered squat. They're going to hang him, Boots, and we can't do a thing to stop it." Her jaw firmed. "We leave tonight — exactly two hours after supper."

"Okay," Boots agreed. "We'll go tonight."

13

Fresh spring air floated through the bedroom lace curtain. Shortly after supper Ian had dragged the washtub from the porch to the kitchen and warned the females to stay clear. He was taking a tub bath. Clean-shaven now, he realized he had been starting to smell like a billy goat.

The women disappeared, but he heard giggles long after he'd heated water and sunk into the hot tub.

Now he lay in his bed, rinsed clean, his mind going over the slow-forming plan. He was figuring how to pull it off in tiny segments. If one thing went wrong he was a goner; he could figure on that.

Some parts came harder than others. Jim Younger would be an easy snare if the outlaw knew that Ian Cawley was going to hang with the sheriff thinking Ian was a Younger. Jim would be sure to attend, flashing a smile seconds before the trapdoor fell out from Ian's feet, smug in the knowledge that the holler had just hung a marshal. The occasion would provide full closure on the tit-for-tat relationship the two men had — *enjoyed* wouldn't be the word. Endured. That was the proper wording.

Stomached.

Younger wouldn't shed any tears when that noose closed around Ian's neck, and the same went for him . . . but how to draw Jim to the hanging without Ian confessing his real name? That was the problem.

The outlaw wouldn't waste time on a hanging — wouldn't risk showing his face — unless the victim was family.

Pulling the blankets closer around him, Ian stared up at the peeling ceiling plaster. The room was chilly tonight. Still hadn't replaced that window. He'd be sure to take care of it first thing in the morning. He recalled the black walnuts Lyric had been working on this morning and wondered if she'd ever baked that cake. He hadn't made it back from the garden in time for supper, but she'd left a note on the counter saying that his meal was in the warming oven. He hadn't noticed a cake anywhere.

A glass of buttermilk and a piece of chocolate cake would make him sleep better.

He got up and pulled on his trousers. When he crept into the hallway he paused. Edwina's bedroom door was wide open.

Perhaps Lyric's mother was having trouble sleeping?

He should check on her. He only needed to poke his head in. Lyric wouldn't want her mother to be uncomfortable.

Stepping inside the room, he quietly moved across the floor to her bedside. The woman was sleeping fitfully, tossing her head back and forth. She moaned quietly in her sleep.

Ian reached out a cool hand to touch her forehead. It was warm and damp. Edwina opened her eyes at his touch.

"Who are you?"

He saw no reason to lie to her. Why perpetuate a falsehood? Why tell a deliberate untruth to a woman whose mind was already lost?

"Ian Cawley," he said. "I'm a U.S. marshal."

"Are you here to harm us, Mr. Cawley?"

"No, ma'am. I mean you no harm." Stepping back toward the hallway, he quietly closed the door and then returned to her bedside. Whispering now, he said, "Hear me out before you call for Lyric."

He proceeded to tell his story, starting

with the accident. When he finished, Edwina shook her head.

"So you're not an outlaw."

"No, ma'am, I'm not. As I said, I'm a U.S. marshal. I make my home in Kansas City."

She shifted, her breathing slow and laborious. "Why the secrecy?"

"You've heard what the authorities plan to do to me."

"I hear things. I'm mad, not deaf."

He straightened and glanced toward the closed door before he continued. "I'm working on a plan to avoid the noose and help all of us, but I can't let anyone know that I've regained my memory until it's time to put the plan into motion." His gaze returned to her. "Will you allow me a brief time before you tell Lyric?"

"Who said I would tell Lyric?"

"I assume that since she's your daughter and she's a lovely, trusting young woman you'll want to tell her."

The woman closed her eyes and struggled for breath. When the spell passed, she said, "I'll keep your secret."

He nodded.

"But only because Lyric has bigger things to worry about."

He stepped closer, barely able to hear her soft reply. "I beg your pardon?"

"Lark and Boots have run away. I heard them leave earlier."

"That's not possible. They were giggling in the front room not two hours ago. Where have they gone?"

"Away. Lark refuses to leave Boots and she knows Lyric has fancy dreams for once I'm gone. Dreams to leave this house I built for them."

Fancy dreams? A longing to be free of this woman's legacy didn't seem out of place.

Edwina looked up though faded, haunted eyes and gave a maniacal laugh. "Fools — they are fools." The mirth faded to a dry cackle when the cough overcame her. Managing to speak, she whispered, "Laudanum . . . I need my laudanum."

He focused on the small vial sitting on the table. Unscrewing the cap, he drew a small amount into the dropper and placed it under her tongue. He turned when he heard Lyric's voice in the hallway. "Mother? I'm coming."

Stepping away from the bed, he quickly moved to the door to meet Lyric.

Lyric paused in the doorway, wearing a puzzled expression. "I'm sorry — did Mother wake you? It's those dreams again. They make her restless."

He took her by the arm and led her back

into the hallway. "But Mother . . ." She glanced over her shoulder.

"She's fine. I gave her a dose of laudanum. She'll be asleep shortly."

"But I should check on her — perhaps some warm tea would help . . ."

Gently taking her by her shoulders, he asked, "Where is Lark?"

"Why . . . in bed, of course. I was reading and just about to go up and join her. Why do you ask?"

"I think we'd better check." Together they moved to the rear of the house and the small room Lark claimed. When they opened the door, Ian noted it was clean, everything in place but for evidence of a teenage girl's hurried escape. A drawer half open. Empty chiffonier.

Lyric held the light higher, her jaw agape. "Where is she?"

"I'm afraid she and Boots have decided to run away."

"Run away!"

"I'll fill you in on the details later. Right now, throw some clothing on and I'll saddle Norman. They can't have gotten too far."

14

Heavy wind and rain rocked Lark as she held the lantern higher, trying to shield the flickering flame. "Drat this rain!" The pillowcase containing her belongings dangled around her waist where she'd tied it earlier.

"I told you we should have waited." Boots's red cowboy boots sank deep into mud. The cold spring rain was soaking both the girls through. "We'll never make it to Hornet tonight."

"We have to get out of the weather!" Lark called. "We can't spend the night in this!"

"There's a cave up the road, remember? Ordsman's Cave?"

"Oh, I hate that place. It's so big and scary — and has all those bats."

"We don't have a choice." Hail began to pepper the girls as they walked. "We'll be beaten to death!"

"Okay, run!" The girls set off, dodging deep puddles and clutching their hoods over

241

their heads. Boots dropped her valise and ran back to pick it up. Mud dripped from the bottom. "Oh . . . this was my mother's."

"We can clean it later. Come on, these hailstones are getting bigger."

It took a while to maneuver the muddy road and climb through rushing gullies and thick blackberry briars. Holding tightly to each other's hands they forded a creek and climbed a jagged limestone bluff to the cave opening. Crawling inside the crude shelter, Lark fell on her back. She tried to catch her breath and saw Boots was gasping for air as well.

The thought Lark most dreaded surfaced, of hundreds — maybe thousands — of bats hanging upside down on the ceiling. If she closed her eyes she would hear the sound of fluttering wings. The lantern burned so low it barely gave off enough light to make out their immediate surroundings. As she watched, the light went out and the cave went pitch black.

"Oh, dear," Boots said.

"I hate caves."

"Maybe we should have waited until tomorrow morning to leave."

"Probably, but the weather was fine when we left. I thought we'd have plenty of time to make it to Hornet."

"Yeah," Boots sighed. "Me too."

Only the sound of their ragged breath met Lark's ears.

The hail passed and a gentle rain fell on the limestone bluffs. "Most likely we'll have to spend the night in here," Lark said. "Are you up to it?"

"I . . . well, sure. If you are."

"Oh, I am. Totally up to it."

"Then we stay here."

After a bit, Boots said, "Are you sure we're doing the right thing?"

"Now, why would you ask that? We've got a plan and we're sticking to it. We hide out for a while, and then when Lyric gives up and moves on without me, we'll be free to go back to the old house — leastways I will."

"I would stay with you, but Grandpa really needs me, Lark. Honest. Caroline can barely boil water and I've been thinking I'm a big help around the house."

Lark shifted and rolled to her side. "I understand. If I had a grandpa like yours I would never leave. I'd just marry and move my husband into the house."

"That's what I plan to do — when I marry. Maybe four or five years from now." Boots turned the opposite direction, lying back to back with Lark. The two fell silent, but after a moment Boots admitted,

"Grandpa and Caroline are really going to be worried about me. I left a note — but they'll worry anyway. Grandpa especially. He's like that."

"Lyric too — in fact, she'll get one of her headaches that won't go away for weeks. I hate to do this to her, but she'll make do without us, Boots."

"Yeah, I know. It can't be helped."

Lark raised her eyes at the sound of soft fluttering overhead.

Yawning, Boots said sleepily. "When we marry, we can do all sorts of things together with our husbands. Go on picnics, attend church on Sunday, do our shopping together."

"You'll probably marry before I do," Lark confessed. "Since you're a little older."

"Yes . . . you're right. Do you think there are any rich men in Hornet?"

"Does a man's financial state matter to you?"

"No, but I wouldn't want him to be dirt poor," said Boots.

"Why not?" asked Lark. "It's the heart that counts, and the fact that he would be a God-fearing man would make you wealthy beyond your wildest dreams." She sighed. "It's such a shame Lyric won't ever marry."

"Bet she does," said Boots. "I bet she'd

marry Joseph in a minute if he wasn't going to hang soon." Boots rolled to her back.

"Could be — can't say I haven't noticed the way those two eye each other, like one was pancakes and the other was warm maple syrup."

"I've noticed that too. Shame he has to die, even if he is an outlaw. Could be if he met the right woman he would settle down and give up his wayward life."

"Seems like he's got good sense," Lark agreed.

"And he's a fine-looking feller," Boots said.

"Really fine-looking. Wish he had several brothers."

"Maybe he does."

Boots rose on one arm. "Maybe, and if he was your brother-in-law and he had brothers, then you could introduce me and we could still have husbands about the same time — if the brothers were close to our age."

"That's a thought."

" 'Course, rumor has it the Youngers aren't real well suited for matrimony. I don't think any of them live long enough to really settle in."

"True, and I'd want a man who could buy me a new dress at least once a year."

"Once a year?" Boots said. "Well, that wouldn't be asking a whole lot."

"It would for a Bolton."

Rain pattered softly on the soaked ground. The fresh-scented air drifted through the cave. The rain appeared to have passed but Lark was just plain too weary to walk back home.

"Guess we might as well stay here to-night."

"And then what? Continue to Hornet in the morning?"

"Let's sleep on the thought." If making a new life was this complicated maybe they should wait until warmer weather. "Right now I'm too cold and wet to think about anything but a fire and a mug of Lyric's hot tea."

"Me too. Maybe we should just go back in the morning."

"Maybe."

"You're not worried about the bats?"

"If I can't see them they won't worry me."

Lark just hoped the good Lord made her sleep like a log.

15

Ian's fingertips dug into the wet limestone as he scaled the bluff behind Lyric. "Are you certain there's a cave up here?"

"Positive." Lyric grunted, pulling her body steadily up the incline. "We've played up here since we were kids. A couple of years ago Lark declared she'd never come here again because of the bats so we haven't visited in a while, but if that hail caught the girls they'd have no other choice. This would be the nearest shelter." The couple slowly ascended the bluff. Overhead a thin moon appeared.

"I can't imagine what's gotten into Lark. I know she doesn't want to leave the Holler but we won't, not for a while."

Ian took a firmer hitch and hoisted himself to a ledge. "She's at the age where she forms close relationships; she doesn't intend to leave Boots."

The cave opening came into sight and

Lyric paused to take a deep breath. "There it is."

Pulling himself up beside her, Ian studied the entrance. "It's dark as a coal hole in there. Wouldn't they have carried a light?"

"One would think."

"Then again, they might not be there."

"It's possible, but since Boots ate supper with us and I saw her and Lark on the porch later, I assume they haven't been gone long enough to walk much further. I'll take a look." She reached for the lantern tied around his waist and he stopped her. "I'll check. There could be a bear or a rattler in there."

She took a step back. "All right. I don't like dark places anyway," she confessed. "Especially caves."

"You stand right here — I'll have to take the light. Can you handle the darkness while I'm gone?"

"Of course." She glanced at the sky and the sliver of moon. Thick clouds still churned overhead but a watery slit of light occasionally appeared. They'd spent half the night looking through hills and hollers before Lyric remembered the cave.

"Be back shortly." Taking the lantern, he ducked and disappeared into the cavern.

Before she could catch her breath, he

248

returned. "They're in there."

"They are!" Lyric started for the opening but he pulled her back.

"They're okay — both sound asleep."

"We can't leave them there overnight."

He glanced up, noting the moon's position. "Dawn will be here in another few hours."

"But Mother's alone in the house."

"She asked for her medicine and I gave her a dose. She should sleep the night through." He led her a short distance away from the cave entrance.

"I can't walk away and leave those two girls here alone," she protested. "Why not wake them and take them home?"

"Because I want those bats hanging from the ceiling to be the first thing they see when they open their eyes. Maybe they won't be so quick to take off next time."

"I can't go home without them."

"Then we sleep here tonight."

"Here?" She looked pointedly at her feet sinking into the soaked ground.

"It's not going to be comfortable, but dawn isn't far off."

"I suppose you're right." She sighed, pulling her wrap tighter around herself. "The girls do need to realize how foolishly they've acted. Where could they have been going?"

"I'd say they planned to get to Hornet tonight. By morning I suspect they would have headed back."

".Why would Lark want to run away? We're all each other has."

"You know she doesn't want to leave Boots; those two are inseparable."

"But leaving is in the future. I couldn't leave now."

He shrugged. "Apparently she doesn't want to risk it." He sat down and patted the patch of rock beside him. "Your bed, milady."

Eyeing the limestone mattress, she cringed.

"It's going to be a long night," he said, chuckling. "Longest two or three hours of your life."

Stirring, Lark opened her eyes to meet Lyric's stern expression. Dawn lit the cave entrance. Bolting upright, she murmured. "Don't be mad at me. I can explain."

"You'd better have a *good* explanation, young lady." Lyric's hand moved to her stiff back. "Scaring me out of my wits."

Boots sat up, rubbing sleep from her eyes. "Don't be upset, Lyric. We were going to turn back and go home but we were too tired."

"You were going to let me pace the floor all night, worry myself to a frenzy?"

"If the rain hadn't come you would have never missed me until this morning."

"That's your explanation? It's the rain's fault?"

"Ladies, it's too early in the morning to argue. Let's get your things and get out of here." Ian reached for the stuffed pillowcases and Boots jammed her feet into her mud-caked boots. All avoided eye contact.

"Those bats bother you any?" he asked.

Lark kept her head low. "I . . . I didn't look at them."

"Better take a look, girls. You were mighty brave to sleep in here with all that company."

Lark shook her head. "I . . . don't want to look."

"Me either," Boots echoed.

"Suit yourself, but they make quite a sight." He leaned back and stared up at the ceiling. "How many would you say are up there, Lyric?"

Lyric shook her head. "I wouldn't . . . care to say."

"Hmm. Guess a body couldn't say with any certainty." He glanced at Lark. "You girls ready to go home?"

"Yes," they answered in unison. Both heads were down and intent.

"Then let's head out."

Once they cleared the cave's entrance Lyric dropped back to walk with Ian. With the bedraggled girls out of earshot she whispered, "There wasn't a single bat up there."

He turned to look at her. "Did I say there was?"

"You asked me how many I thought were up there."

"And you said you didn't care to say."

"There weren't *any* up there that I could see."

"Me either." He flashed a grin. "Isn't that odd? They must have been further back in the cave."

"That's mean," she said crossly. "Allowing Lark and Boots to think that . . ." She paused when the little ploy sank in. "You are a sly one."

"Think so?" He grinned. "I think it's unlikely they run away again." He grabbed her hand and brought it to his lips. Warmth spread through Lyric as he kissed it.

Ian kept a tight grip on Lyric's hand as they kept walking toward home. The warmth inside her didn't go away.

■ ■ ■

The aroma of strong coffee brewing filled the Bolton kitchen. Boots had gone home and everyone had changed into dry clothing. Lyric had checked on her mother and found her still in a laudanum-induced lethargy, so now she joined Ian in the kitchen for breakfast.

Pouring Joseph a steaming cup of coffee, she said, "Ham and eggs all right?"

"I could eat a whole hog," he said.

Lark came down to join them, her features drawn from the night's soggy adventure.

"Did Boots go home?" Lyric asked, laying thick slices of ham in the cold skillet.

"Yes. She knew her grandpa would be worried."

Lyric dropped the subject. There would be time enough for punishment; at least the girls were safe and had suffered no harm from their escapade. When the meal was ready, the three ate together at the table, conversing in friendly tones. Lyric wondered if married life would be like this, a man and woman sitting in a warm kitchen having breakfast . . .

Moving his plate aside, Ian leaned back in his chair. "Lark, if you feel restless and want to do something, I have a job for you and Boots."

The girl glanced up. "A job?"

"Yes, a job. Are you interested?"

Lark glanced at Lyric, who lifted her shoulders with curiosity.

"What would I have to do?"

"Rob a bank, shoot a couple of deputies, push a couple of old women around, and steal a few horses."

Lark's jaw dropped.

Grinning, Ian continued. "When the authorities come for me, all you need do is spread the word that a Younger is going to hang. Note the exact day and hour — that's important."

Lyric half-rose, censure in her eyes. "Joseph!"

"I'm serious, Lyric. When they come to get me I want Lark and Boots to tack up posters in town, making clear the time and place of the hanging. And they're going to have to work fast. I want every citizen in the area to know about the hanging."

"Joseph . . ." Lyric protested.

"We can do that," Lark said. "But I don't want to think about them hanging you. They can't."

"They can, honey, but we might be able

to avoid it if you'll do what I say and do it right."

"I will." She nodded gravely. "Boots and I will do everything exactly as you say."

"It's imperative that you do." He turned his gaze on Lyric. "Relax. I don't plan to swing by a noose unless there's no other choice."

Tears welled in Lyric's eyes and she quickly wiped them. His features softened. "I know this is hard on you. I'm sorry."

Shaking her head, she got up and began to clear the table.

Mid-morning found Lyric pinning the wash to the line. Sheets flapped in the rain-bathed breeze. Joseph's words to Lark still rang in her ear. "You'll have to do exactly what I say . . ."

He didn't include Lyric in his plan, whatever that might be, and the thought stung. If she knew him like she thought she did, he had a recourse he was considering. Why hadn't he trusted her enough to confide his strategy? She should know by now that he wasn't the sort of man to stand idly by and be hanged because he didn't know his name, but did he honestly think that she would just hand him over to the acting sheriff without a fight? Didn't he know by

255

now that she would protect him any way she could? Maybe love blinded her.

Her hands paused in midair. Love. Was that what she felt for this man with no identity? True, abiding love?

Shaking her head, she picked up a dress, shook out the wrinkles, and pinned the garment to the line. In the distance the faint sound of approaching riders came to her. She stepped around the heavy line and frowned when she saw four men approaching. Dropping a wet towel in the basket, she started running for the house. "Joseph!"

The riders drew closer and her screams grew more frantic. *"Joseph!"*

He stepped to the back porch and opened the screen. "Yo!"

"They're coming for you!"

Hide. She must hide him. But where?

Under Mother's bed. The authorities wouldn't disturb a dying woman, especially Edwina Bolton.

She reached the porch and shoved past him. "Come with me. I know just the place to hide you. They can search the house and I'll tell them that I don't know what happened to you, that you were here and you must have run off . . ."

His arm blocked her. "You're not going to lie for me. The time has come for us to get this over with, Lyric. Let the cards fall where they may."

"We need to pray," she said. " 'Where two or three are gathered together in my name, there am I in the midst of them.' "

"Lyric." He focused grave eyes on her. "I'm not going to live my life hiding from the authorities." Their gazes met and held, hers swimming with tears. "God is fully aware of what's happening. Let's allow Him to settle the matter."

"But they're going to *hang* you, Joseph. Don't you realize what that means? You're going to . . . to . . . oh, I can't bear it."

"You're not giving the Lord much credit."

"You know they will. They've been biding their time until the sheriff couldn't delay any longer without looking like a fool."

"Get Lark. Tell her and Boots to do what I said. Tack a poster to every tree, storefront, and post in Bolton Holler, announcing the hanging."

Nodding, Lyric wiped her eyes on her apron. She couldn't fall apart now — not now when he needed her most. "I intend to help."

Smiling, he drew her close and held her. "I knew I could count on you."

"Oh, Joseph. You can't hang . . ."

He gently placed his hand over her mouth.

"Trust me. I know you've never been given a reason to place your trust in anyone, but I'm asking for that faith right now. Just do as I say . . . and it won't hurt to throw a lot of extra prayer in with your work." Giving her a final squeeze, he released her. "Go do as I say, and be sure you get it done before morning."

The riders rode up and reined in. The sheriff lifted his rifle. "All right, Younger. You're coming with us."

Lifting both arms in the air, Ian complied. "Can I bring my horse?"

"No, sir, you can't bring your horse." The sheriff sniffed at the suggestion. "You're not going to need a horse where you're headed. You're hanging at dawn."

Lyric stepped in front to shield him. "You have no proof of his identity. You can't hang him."

"Ma'am." He shifted in the saddle. "I can and I will hang him at dawn tomorrow morning."

"What about proof?"

"What about it? He can't prove he isn't a Younger."

Ian gently eased Lyric aside. "Who do I ride with?"

A smaller man patted the empty saddle space behind. "Climb aboard."

"No!" Lyric protested, clinging to his arm.

He took her gently by the shoulders and kissed her softly. Lips met again with more intensity. Moments later, he whispered, "Do as I say."

Close to hysteria, she drew back, catching a sob. "Yes . . . yes. You can count on me."

He gave her a wink, and then walked to the waiting horse and climbed aboard.

"Gone? Joseph's gone?" Boots wrung her hands. "But he can't be gone — they can't hang him without solid proof that he's a criminal! He isn't bad. I just know that he isn't bad!"

"Hush," Lyric said, starting to gather pen and paper. "They can and they will. They're going to hang him. Law doesn't mean much in these parts. We have to make posters. Quickly. We must have them pinned up before dark."

Chairs scooted on wooden floors and the women started to work.

YOUNGER HANGING, Lark wrote. "What time will they hang him?"

"Dawn," she said. Hangings were always at dawn.

Lyric's heart ached as she worked. Her mind refused to function. They couldn't hang Joseph — if it cost her life she wouldn't allow it. They'd run off. She would break him out of jail and then they would ride away and find a new life. He couldn't be a criminal. It wasn't possible. There was too much gentleness in him, and she knew — she just *knew* — that he was a good man.

You only want *him to be a good man,* her common sense nagged. *What if he isn't? What if he's cruel and despicable and every bit the criminal you first took him to be?* If she ran away with this man, thwarted the authorities in their evil pursuit, she could be opening herself — and Lark — up to a life with a wicked, cruel, merciless man. And they could hang her too if she was caught trying to assist him. Look how easily he had fooled Lark and Boots about the bats. Could Joseph be trusted?

Uncertainty ricocheted through her mind. *Oh God, help me,* she prayed. *I'm reasoning with my heart and not using practical judgment.*

Yet she scribbled furiously, one poster after another, matching Lark's and Boots's frantic efforts. Within the hour they had written enough posters to saturate Bolton Holler with the grim news:

YOUNGER TO BE HANGED AT DAWN.

Lark saddled the horse and brought it to the house, where the three women worked to secure the loaded basket of posters to the saddle. There was still sufficient time to nail up the posters and then turn to the matter of breaking Joseph out of jail.

"We could take Mother's gun and shoot him out of jail," Lark suggested.

"Two women against the town?" Lyric asked.

"Three," Boots corrected. "I'm in on this."

"A gun would be useless against the sheriff and his men. We'd run out of bullets and they would overcome us." Lyric had enough sense to know it was going to take sheer trickery if they were going to accomplish their bold move. "We have to create a disturbance. Distract them."

"It would have to be a big interruption." Boots shook her head. "Maybe I could talk Grandpa into coming to town and distracting the sheriff while we slipped inside the jail and got Joseph."

"We're not going to involve your grandfather, Boots. What we're contemplating could cost our lives — or at least land us in prison. Your grandfather doesn't need to be mixed up in that. I will be the responsible one if we're caught. I want you girls to stay back when the event begins to unfold."

"What event?"

"That's what we have to decide." They led the horse down the road, falling silent. Finally Lyric said, "First we have to create a huge scene."

"We already know that," Lark reminded her.

"No, I mean a really big diversion."

"Dynamite?" Boots asked.

"Do you have dynamite?" Lark asked.

"What would I be doing with dynamite?"

"Maybe your grandfather?"

"Grandpa and dynamite?" Boots laughed. "Have you seen the way he walks lately? He couldn't run fast enough to get away if he lit a piece of dynamite. Besides, what would he need dynamite for on his farm?"

"Dynamite would be destructive," Lyric admonished the girls. "We might kill someone. Even Joseph."

"True. Or us," Lark noted.

"Or us," Lyric repeated. This ordeal was turning out to be a nightmare. But Joseph trusted her. She'd never experienced trust like that before — except from Lark. Mother didn't trust her; the fact was evident in her eyes, though Lyric had never done anything to deserve the loss of her confidence.

The thought that a man like Joseph valued and placed faith in her, Lyric Bolton, the unlovable and unvalued, spread a warm glow throughout her body.

Whatever it took, she would defend and shield him till her last breath.

Within the hour the three women paused on the hillside, eyes fixed on Bolton Holler. "Won't the folks think it strange that we're nailing up posters about the hanging?" Lark asked.

"Stranger than they already think we are?" Lyric focused on the people of the holler going about their afternoon activities. The minute the Boltons walked into town the shoppers would scatter like chaff in the wind. Her eyes were drawn to the small brick jail and the one window with heavy bars. For a long moment no one said anything. Then Lyric spoke. "I have it."

Boots turned to look at her. "Have what?"

"I have the distraction."

"What?" both girls asked.

"Let's get the posters up and then I'll fill you in on the plan. It means we'll have to work through the night."

"I don't care. I'm not tired." Lark brightened. "You seriously have an idea you think might work?"

"I think so." She reached for another poster, Joseph's orders ringing in her ears.

Get as many posters up as you can. "If it doesn't work, you'll need to add our names to these before morning," she said grimly.

16

Ian paced the tiny cell, occasionally glancing out the window. Already the town was abuzz with word of the imminent hanging. He had to hope and pray the news had spread as far as the Younger place. His plan had more holes than a rusty bucket, but desperate times called for desperate measures.

The acting sheriff got up from his desk and stretched. "It's gonna be suppertime in half an hour. What do you want for your last meal?"

"Fried chicken, potatoes and gravy, hominy, three rolls and butter, and plenty of coffee." Ian had no intention that this would be his last meal, but as long as he was cooped up in jail, why not dine in style?

"Any dessert?"

"Chocolate cake, if they have it. Otherwise, pie — any kind."

"Geraldine makes a right good lemon pie."

"Don't care for lemon. Chocolate cake or any other kind of pie."

"Suit yourself. You take cream in your coffee?"

"Black."

"Alrighty then. I'll be back d'reckly."

"Take your time," Ian said under his breath when the front door closed. He stepped back to the window and released a pent-up breath when he caught a glimpse of a pair of red cowboy boots in the distance. The figure was nailing something to a tree. "Atta girl," he whispered. "Get those posters circulating." His gaze shifted and he spotted Lyric busy at work across the street. No doubt Lark was covering the other half of town. Closing his eyes, he whispered, "God, I sure could use Your help right about now. If You'll make certain Jim Younger gets the news, I'd be much obliged."

Smile fading, he wished that Grandpa and Grandma knew about his predicament — not that he'd want to worry them, but somehow he felt that their prayers always carried a mite more weight than his.

Returning to his bunk, he sat down. Everything in town would be quiet shortly. The day's excitement would die down and folks would turn in early in anticipation of the dawn hanging. That was exactly what he

266

needed. Complete calm. Jim Younger wasn't going to show his face unless he made sure he wasn't noticed, but if the news reached him of a Younger hanging he'd show up to see if the sheriff had actually captured one of his kin. Jim would make an attempt to rescue the poor soul. He'd pull his long brimmed Stetson low and possibly dress like a city man, but Ian would recognize the quiet, well-mannered Jim Younger a mile away.

What Ian needed was pure and complete calm; nothing to disturb the hanging. If everything went as planned, all Ian had to do was walk to the gallows, explain that his memory was back, and have the sheriff wire the marshal's office in Kansas City to confirm his claim. He allowed they might hang him and ask questions later, but with enough witnesses that wouldn't be likely. It was a long shot, though — and it seemed to get longer each time he meticulously went over the plan in his mind.

The bounty on Jim Younger's head would be enough to set a man up for life, if he played it right. Plus, he'd win the wager.

If folks in this town weren't scared of their shadows they would collect on a few of those hefty bounties waiting just down the road. They were spooked by an unexplained light and perfectly content to allow outlaws to live practically in their backyard. Neighbors, almost. He shook his head.

No wonder Lyric wanted to leave this holler. And he wanted to be the one to take her away.

Hold on, sweetheart. We'll get through this and your life will be different.

He refused to consider the possibility that his plan might fail. His gaze scanned the empty cell. Swinging his legs to the mattress, he laid back to wait for his fried chicken and potatoes.

Maybe he should have ordered that lemon pie. Grandma's lemon pies were always lumpy and tart — maybe Geraldine's would be different.

If there was ever a night to take chances, this was it.

"Go on! Git!" The sheriff tried to deter Lyric from nailing the last poster to a tree near the jail, but she persisted. "You want to join your friend?" he asked when she kept nailing.

"I'm not hurting a thing." She hammered harder.

"Why are you wasting time nailing up posters? Everybody around knows a man's gonna swing come dawn."

"Well, we wouldn't want anyone to miss the fun, now, would we?" She picked up another poster and moved to the next tree. White papers fluttered from every storefront and hitching post in town. The saloon had enough information tacked to its swinging doors that even the severely inebriated couldn't fail to take note.

The sheriff crossed his arms. "Am I gonna have to physically remove you, young lady?"

She turned and fixed a cold stare on him. "Am I breaking any laws?" She didn't like to use the town's misbeliefs, but if ever she could benefit from people's fears of her mother's illness, now was the time.

Turning on his heel, the sheriff stalked off, occasionally glancing over his shoulder, muttering.

Picking up her stack of posters, Lyric moved on.

Darkness overtook the women as they began the return journey to the Bolton house. They had walked as fast as the fading light allowed. In her haste to hang the notices Lyric had forgotten to bring a light, and clouds obscured the rising moon. "Walk faster," Lyric said. "We still have the biggest part ahead of us."

"Well, what is it? You can surely share your

plan with us now." Lark picked up her pace.

"Boots, you know those guinea fowl your grandpa has?"

"Those squawkers?"

"They make lots of noise, don't they?"

"Deafening. Grandpa likes to eat the eggs, and he keeps them for watchdogs around the goats. They'll run off anything that comes around."

"Good. How many would you say he has?"

"I don't know — maybe a couple of dozen." She paused in the middle of the road. "Are you thinking of using those nuisances in your plan?"

Lyric nodded. "We are going to catch every last one of them, haul them into town, and turn them loose the moment they open the door to lead Joseph out of jail."

"You mean we're going to let those noisy things loose?" Lark asked.

"Right smack dab in the middle of town. They'll cause such a ruckus that folks will be chasing them down, trying to drive them away. That will give us just enough time to slip in the jail and free Joseph. If everything goes as planned we'll have him out and gone before they miss him."

"Where are we going to put that many fowl?"

"I've been thinking about that. We'll have

to put them in tow sacks."

"They'll suffocate."

"Not if we punch holes in the bags. We don't have any other way to transport them."

Boots frowned. "Do you have that many tow sacks?"

"Of course. I have dozens."

Shaking her head, Boots sighed. "Grandpa's not going to like this."

Lyric dove, capturing another guinea by the hind leg. "Got ya!" she cried. The squawking and high-pitched squeals coming from the barn's direction were loud enough to wake the dead.

Boots arrived holding an upside-down fowl in each hand. "How many does this make?"

"Twelve."

Gritting her teeth, Boots whooshed. "How many more do we need?"

"As many as we can catch. Looks to me like your grandpa has several dozen here."

Lark approached, muddy and disheveled. "I chased this one clear down to the creek." She spit a feather out of her mouth. "They don't like to be handled."

"You're doing a good job, girls. I'm proud of you."

Lark grunted. "Let's hope it will be enough to save Joseph."

"He could use your prayers."

"I've been praying."

"Me too. A whole lot. If only he had some identification on him — something to prove who he was. Why wouldn't a man carry a wallet or something for security purposes?"

"Maybe he didn't want folks to know who he was," Lark said. "Or maybe . . ." She paused as though a light had gone off in her head. "Maybe . . ."

Her tone made Lyric pause. "Yes. Most men carry wallets."

Lark glanced at Boots. Her friend's jaw dropped. "Wallet. Do you think . . . ?"

"That would be too coincidental, Boots. A man with no memory, missing wallet, we find a wallet . . ." She shook her head. "It can't be his."

Lyric dropped another bird into the sack. "What are you two babbling about?"

"We found a wallet one day when we were hunting greens. It didn't have anything in it, no money or anything, but it had a name on a piece of paper. It had a U.S. marshal badge — Joseph isn't a U.S. marshal."

"We don't know who Joseph is. He could be anyone, Lark! Why didn't you mention the wallet earlier?"

She lifted both shoulders. "I forgot about it. It's in my top drawer if you want to see it."

Lyric's heart raced. *Don't get too excited. It's a wallet with no identification. It could be any man's wallet, and it was far too coincidental to take seriously.* Joseph's identity had not been sitting in Lark's top drawer all this time. That was improbable.

"I'll take a look at it before we leave for town," she murmured, determined not to get her hopes up. Or to have her worst fears realized. What if he was a Younger? Would she still adore him? Be totally and hopelessly smitten by his smile and the way little crinkles formed around his eyes when he laughed? The answer came swiftly. She would, and that would leave her worse off than now. There was a chance in a million that the wallet belonged to him. "Right now we've got to catch every single one of these guinea hens."

"Every single one?" Lark moaned.

"Every last one." Her mouth firmed. Whoever that was sitting in that jail cell, she planned to fight for him with every last ounce of breath left in her.

The moon slanted, slipping lower in the sky. Tow sacks of screeching guineas littered the field. Holding her aching back, Lyric dropped the last bird into the bag and heaved a sigh. "This should be enough."

"There are still two down by the creek. Want me to go after them?" Boots tied a knot in one of the sacks.

"Go ahead. I'm going to check on Mother before I hitch up the horse and bring the wagon here."

The girls struck off toward the creek and Lyric walked the scant half mile back to the house. Funny the Spooklight hadn't been around lately — or she hadn't seen it. Where was it when it could do some good? A showing at the jail right about now wouldn't hurt. There were times when the peculiar phenomenon almost soothed her, made her feel like her life was normal.

She had a deep ache for Katherine and missed her friendly chats. When Lyric left Bolton Holler, she would stop off in Joplin and visit her new friend, maybe stay as long as a week catching up on news. They would have a good laugh — or cry — about what Lyric was about to do in her attempt to save Joseph. The mood would depend solely on tomorrow's outcome.

When she reached the lane to the Bolton farm, she turned, surprised to see her mother's bedroom light burning. Quickening her steps, she realized that she had been gone a long time. Who had lit the lamp? Mother seldom left the bed these days.

Bursting into the house, she hurried up the stairway. "Mother? Are you awake?"

Only silence met her ears.

When she entered the bedroom she saw the thin figure slumped beside the bed. Was she gone? Compassion swept her and she knelt to feel her mother's pulse.

A thready rhythm fluttered beneath her fingertip. She was alive.

"Oh, Mother." Guilt overcame her as she managed to gently lift the frail body and slip her back into the bed. How long had she been lying here? Minutes? Hours?

Edwina stirred, eyes fluttering open. "Where have you been? I called and called."

"I'm so sorry, Mother. I've been away from the house longer than intended."

"Where's your sister?"

"She's with me." Lyric tucked the blanket closer. "I'll warm some broth. And run to the spring and get some cold milk."

Edwina brushed the offer aside. "Go away. I just want to get warm and sleep."

"But you haven't eaten —"

"Go away," she snapped.

Straightening, Lyric drew a tolerant breath. "Do you need your medicine?"

"Yes. And don't wander off again, you hear?"

"I hear." She opened the vial, inserted the dispenser, and placed it in her mother's mouth.

"Ungrateful girls," Edwina muttered, smacking the last of the laudanum off her lips.

"I'm sorry. I should have been more thoughtful," Lyric admitted. Her mind had been entirely on Joseph and saving his life.

Picking up the light, she turned and walked quietly to the door, her head spinning. Should she choose duty or love? If she couldn't leave Mother then she couldn't save Joseph at dawn . . . and she had given her word that she wouldn't leave. Lark could stay here and Lyric and Boots could attempt to divert attention, but the plan demanded more than two people to be successfully completed.

Hot tears coursed down her cheeks as she carried the candle down the stairway.

She had roughly four hours to make the biggest decision of her life.

"Where have you been? We've been waiting and waiting for you." Lark faced Lyric, her young face flushed with exertion. "Those guineas are going to suffocate soon."

"I know, Lark." Lyric wanted to wring her hands and scream. For the past hour she'd paced the kitchen floor, torn by duty but overcome by love. She couldn't let Joseph hang while Edwina slept peacefully in her warm bed; something about the situation seemed perverse. Yet she couldn't abandon her mother and save a man she knew practically nothing about.

Her sister stepped to the water bucket. "Boots can't take care of all those hens by herself. We either have to let them loose or take them to town. You decide."

Lyric's mind refused to function. Her heart said go, but loyalty said stay. If only she knew Joseph's true identity . . . Her jaw dropped. Of course! Why hadn't she thought of the wallet earlier? The questionable evidence was a longshot, but the found item might help. "Lark. Go get that wallet."

When her sister paused to drink from the water dipper Lyric swatted her hand. "Now."

Lark muttered as she stalked through the kitchen and up the stairway. Lyric could hear her grumbling as she entered her bedroom. Momentarily she returned and handed the wallet over. "Now can I get a drink of water?"

"Help yourself." A current shot through

Lyric as she held the rich leather — as though she had brushed Joseph's hand. *Please, God, let this be the answer to my prayer.*

Unfolding the pigskin, she shuffled through the few papers, coming across the slip that read *Ian Cawley,* followed by an address in Kansas City, Missouri. A shiny tin U.S. marshal badge winked up at her.

Ian. She tested the name on her tongue. *Ian Cawley. Are you the man sitting in jail about to meet an unjust death? The man without whom I'll never be the same?*

Softly slapping the wallet against the palm of her hand, she said, "Lark, there's been a slight change of plans."

Lark gulped water, lifting her brows with anticipation.

"Boots and I are going to have to do this job alone."

Lark lowered the dipper. "Why?"

"Someone has to stay with Mother. It was careless of us to leave her unattended. I promised her she wouldn't be left on her own again."

"If *you* promised why do *I* have to stay?"

Turning to face her, Lyric said softly, "You know how much saving Joseph means to me."

Her sister's features softened. "Means to

278

both of us. You're in love with him, aren't you?"

Lyric nodded. "Nothing will ever come of it, but yes, I love him no matter who or what he is, and I want to try my best to save him from hanging. And then — who knows? — maybe we'll be able to leave Bolton Holler together."

"If you ever make me leave Boots, I'll be sad forever."

"We both love Boots, and we'll save that talk for another time. For now, Boots and I will have to get those hens to the jail by ourselves."

"Would you let me and Boots try one thing before we drag all those birds to the Holler?"

"We have so little time —"

"It won't take long to see if this works."

"What do you have in mind?"

"Boots and I will take the horse to the jail and spring Joseph. Then he can ride away and hide and they'll never find him."

"How do you propose to do it?"

"We'll tie a chain to the cell bars and have the horse rip them out."

"Oh, Lark. That won't work."

"It'll work. The hero in my ten-cent Western novel did the same thing. A horse is a mighty power."

"I don't know — wouldn't ripping steel off brick make a lot of noise?"

"Everybody's sleeping at this hour. The sheriff goes home at night and the jail window is in the back of the building. We can try it, and if it doesn't work we'll still have time to come back and use the guineas."

Lyric's head pounded. If Lark's crazy plan worked Joseph could be well gone by dawn. If the scheme backfired, the younger girls could run much faster than she could. "All right — but you have exactly an hour and a half to get it done. If you're discovered, you come back as quickly as possible."

"What about the hens?"

"You'll have to have Boots's help. Hitch the horse and bring the sacks back to the house with you. I'll water the birds and be sure they have enough air. Now go. There isn't a second to waste."

Lark shot out the door, slamming it behind her. When Lyric stepped to the window she saw her sister racing across the field to Boots's grandfather's home.

Dear God, if this works it would be tantamount to You parting the Red Sea all over again.

Impossible? Of course it was. But her Bible taught her that with God all things were possible.

Awakened from a fretful sleep, Ian stirred as something struck the cell bars. What he assumed would be the shortest night of his life had turned into the longest. His supper sat untouched on the cell floor, a thick slice of uneaten lemon pie mocking him.

Rolling to his side, he wadded the thin ticking beneath his head and tried to get comfortable. The pillow was little more than a cloth napkin.

A stone hit the bar. He half rose on his elbow, wondering if it was hailing. But no — pleasant night air filtered through the iron rods. Rolling off the cot, he stood, stretching his strained back muscles.

When a third noise came, he stepped to the window. Moonlight lit the landscape. Boots's radiant face suddenly popped up, and he stumbled backward, his heart thumping. "Boots!" he hissed. "What are you doing here?"

"We're breaking you out." She motioned with her eyes to Lark, who stood thirty feet away holding the horse's reins.

"Go home," he snapped. "Now — before someone sees you!" He glanced over his shoulder. If the girls woke the sheriff his whole plan would be jeopardized. This hanging had to go off without a hitch until he reached the gallows and spotted Younger.

"Stand back. We'll have you out of here in a second. We packed your saddlebags with enough water and food supplies to see you through a week."

Before he could protest, her head disappeared. Helplessly he watched her approach Lark. The two girls conversed in hushed tones. Norman wouldn't pull those bars off the building; that horse didn't do anything that wasn't his idea. And he'd yet to find much that did appeal to that contrary animal.

Gripping the bars, he whispered in a strained tone, "Go home!"

The girls silently worked, attaching what looked to be a heavy rope around the saddle horn. His gaze fixed on the breakout effort and blood surged to his face.

Leading the horse to the window, Lark called, "Help us tie the rope!"

"Go away, Lark! Go home. Someone is going to hear or see you."

"Don't worry. We're prepared to run. You'll have to tie the rope around the bars real tight. We don't have enough strength to make it hold."

Stepping away from the window, he sat down on the bunk. If he ignored them they would go away. *Lord, let it be before they wake the whole town.*

A rope appeared on the windowsill. The hemp lay there and then slowly slithered to the ground.

The second attempt failed as well.

Ian sat on the cot, his gut twisting into a tight knot.

The third throw landed a piece of the rope inside the bar. Ian reached and shoved it back to the ground.

Seconds later an angry Boots showed her face between the bars. "Pick up that rope and tie it!"

He shook his head. "Go home and don't make a scene."

"You're going to hang in less than three hours!"

"Go home, Boots. I'll take care of this."

A second later the rope landed on the windowsill.

He pushed it off.

After the next attempt, silence reigned. He bided his time until he dared to lift his gaze to the window. Lark peered in, both hands cupping her eyes. Easing back in the shadows, he remained quiet.

"I know you're in there," she said.

He cracked his first smile. The girl was tenacious, like her sister.

283

"Answer me, Ian."

"Go home, Lark. You're going to make the situation worse . . ." He paused. "What did you call me?"

"Ian."

He swallowed back a mental groan. How did *she* know his name? "Where did you come up with that name?"

"I found a wallet when Boots and I were gathering greens. It has the name Ian Cawley written in it and U.S. marshal —"

"How long have you had the wallet?" he growled.

She picked herself off the ground and dusted the seat of her britches. "A while — when I found it I didn't think much about it considering the outlaws in the community. I figured someone had robbed a U.S. marshal and probably shot him and disposed of his personal belongings."

Ian shook his head. "Does Lyric know?"

"She does now. I gave her the wallet earlier — honest, I'd forgotten all about." She leaned closer and whispered. "Are you really a U.S. marshal?"

His heart sank. Lyric knew his identity.

"Listen." He pressed closer to the bars. "You have to promise me you *will not* speak a word of this to Lyric. I'm serious, Lark. If you do — I'll — I'll find that young farmer you're so smitten with and introduce him to the prettiest young woman I can find." That was the direst threat he had in his arsenal.

"It's true?" She gasped. "You really *do* have your memory back?"

"It's hasn't been back long, and I've kept it quiet for a reason."

Her youthful and slightly dirty features sobered. "You can tell me — I won't tell anyone. I promise."

"I trust you, Lark, but this time you're going to have to trust me. I don't want anyone to know about my memory coming back — not even Lyric. I can prove my identity to the sheriff when the time is right."

"But why? Lyric's protected you. She's trying to help you and find a way to get you out of here. She's in love with you, Joseph . . . I mean Ian."

The words sliced through his heart like a knife through warm butter. Closing his eyes, he wrestled with his conscience. Lyric would be fit to be tied when she learned his memory was back and he hadn't told her, but she'd be here now if he had. Spoiling his plan. "Listen to me, Lark. I don't want you or Lyric involved. Now go home until I come for you."

Boots called from the shadows. "When I throw this rope up to the window you latch on to it. Hear?"

"This isn't going to work, Boots. You're going to foul up my plan."

"You don't have a plan. You're going to hang in less than — well, I don't know the exact time you have left, but it will be getting light soon."

"I want you two girls to go home and stay there until this is over."

She shook her head. "Lyric won't permit it; she won't let you hang. Now here's our plan. We're going to hitch the horse up to the cell bars and rip them clean out. Once that's done, you're to get on the horse and ride like the wind. Boots and I will run home and the sheriff will never know who tore up the jail."

"Oh, wonderful. I'm sure he won't have the faintest idea who might do something like that."

"Well — he'll have an idea but he won't be able to prove it."

Ian glanced toward the darkness. "You tell Lyric for me that I said she is to stay away from here until I come for her. I want you to go now and bring me my wallet. Quickly." Having his badge on hand would be one more reassurance when the time came to reveal his true identity.

Lark's head appeared. "How can you possibly come for her if you're dead?"

"I can assure you that I am going to do all within my power to make sure that day doesn't come for many, many more years."

Lark sighed. "You won't let us help you?"

He shook his head. "Not this time, honey. Go home, get the wallet, and bring it back here before dawn. And pray that my plan works."

"Can't you give me a hint of what you're going to do? What kind of strategy is going to save you from a hanging?"

"A risky one, but I'm willing to take it." For her — for Lyric.

"Well, it had better be good enough," she said.

"It will be."

She eased away from the window and within minutes a rope sailed through the bars with a thump. Pesky female!

He sat for a moment, considering the odds. They were long; Younger had to know that one of his kin was going to be hanged this morning for the plan to work.

The sheriff would have to ignore the bloodthirsty crowd and agree to check his identity with the U.S. marshal's office. That might be the greatest variable of all: The acting sheriff was young and had a strong need to prove his worth.

Latching hold of the rope, Ian's protests dissolved in his throat. He had no assurance that Younger had gotten word of the hanging; he could have ridden out of town an hour after Ian last spotted him. And as Lark had pointed out, dawn was creeping up.

Maybe it would be worth trying to break out.

Just in case.

He grasped the hemp and wound it tightly through the thick bars, testing its strength. The knot held.

"Ready?" a soft voice called.

Sweat now puddled on his forehead. If he was caught he'd be shot on sight. "Where's Norman?"

"Who?" The hushed voice sounded like Boots.

"My horse. Norman."

"That's his name?"

"Where is he?"

"Standing right here beside me."

"Listen — he's contrary. When you start to pull keep your hand on his bridle. Tight. Don't let it go slack, or he'll throw the bit."

"All right."

Perspiration dripped in his eyes, and he wiped it clear with his right shoulder. If they woke the sheriff he was a dead man. His life hung in the balance between two flighty girls and a stubborn, cantankerous horse.

When had his life come to this? He'd once been an upstanding U.S. marshal, feared by outlaws and revered by his government.

He rechecked the rope's tension, thinking about Norman's fondness for water. Ponds. Creek beds. Fear struck panic. *Lord, please don't let there be anything close by. If the horse took a notion, he'd lie down in the creek.*

"There isn't any water nearby, is there?"

"There's a creek that runs by our house, but it's not close to the jail."

"Good." He swiped at the beads of sweat rolling off his forehead. If he ever got out of this mess he would leave this holler and never come back.

"Are you ready?"

"Let's get it over with. Ready."

Boots's and Lark's urging voices filtered through the bars. "Come on, Norman. You can do it!"

The rope grew rigid. Ian focused on the link to freedom as the thick hemp bit into the bars. Brick dust rose into the air.

The rope went limp. Activity ceased. Then it snapped rigid again.

Ian mentally strained with the horse's effort. "Come on, boy."

The dust was flying now, iron bars straining. Ian stood back, focused on the sight and prepared to leap to freedom. If Norman pulled this off it would be a miracle. Those bars were set in solid brick. Lark's pleading voice came to him. "Come on, you can do it — pull harder!"

"Harder," Boots's voice encouraged. "Give it all you got, Norman! Norman!"

"Norman?"

Ian froze when the rope went slack.

Stepping to the window he peered out. Had they been detected? Dread lodged in his throat. There wasn't much he feared, but that noose dangling in the wind unnerved him. Until this moment he didn't realize how much he wanted to live, to experience life with a wife and children. To take Lyric in his arms and hold her for the rest of her life.

Silence dominated the darkness. No shouts, no running feet. *God, let that be a good sign.*

Pressing close to the bars, he strained to see out.

"Hey!"

Boots's smudged face appeared in the window. Staggering backward, his heart lodged in his throat.

"Boots! For crying out loud — what's going on out there?"

"It's Norman."

"What about him? He's got the strength to finish the job. That horse is strong as an ox."

"You know that pond next to the jail?"

"You said there wasn't any water around."

"I know, but I forgot the pond."

Mentally groaning, Ian knew the words that were about to come out of her mouth before she said them.

"Norman's lying in the pond and we can't get him up."

"Drat that horse! Did you try swatting his rump with a willow switch?"

"We've tried everything, honest. He won't get up; he likes it there."

Agitatedly running a hand through his hair, Ian gave up. "He'll be there until he's ready to get up, and who knows when that will be?"

"What should we do?"

"Go home." He slumped against the cell window. No real harm had been done; the bars were still intact and unless the sheriff looked close nobody would notice any damage.

"Yeah, guess we should. We still have one more thing we can try."

"Boots!" He sprang back to the window,

hissing. "Tell Lark to go get that wallet."

He'd gone along with this foolishness, risked his life even further than required, and now they had to stand back and give his plan a chance to succeed. Granted it would likely prove as faulty as their clumsy jailbreak, but it was the last chance he had. It either worked or he hanged. Now that dawn approached the strategy sounded flawed. Could he really collect the Younger bounty money and go free?

"Can't, it'll be light soon." Boots's voice faded as she headed off.

"Boots!" Ian challenged in a loud whisper, but the girl was gone, swallowed up by darkness — the one last thing that stood in the way of life or death. Gripping the bars he wanted to shout.

Then cry.

God, I don't want to die. Not yet. If You could work it where I could be around a while longer, I'd be much obliged.

He dropped his head against the cold window bars as the first hint of dawn, a nearly imperceptible lifting of a thin, colorless veil, appeared on the eastern horizon.

Grandma's voice came to him, peaceful and soothing. "Life's a short walk, Ian my boy. Shorter for some, longer for others. It is well to love the earth and the things our

Maker put here — He made them for our pleasure, but life is a fleeting passage to your eternal home. It is there that you'll lay down your sword. If God gives you ten years or ninety, be glad and with great joy anticipate the day when all things good and pure become everlasting."

"I'm trying, Grandma," he whispered, but his heart wasn't in the promise.

His attention focused on the soft, muted light getting ever stronger in the east.

Lyric paced the kitchen floor, whirling when Lark opened the back door and stepped inside. Precious little time remained before the hanging. "Is he free?"

"No. For a while he wouldn't take the rope and help but finally he did. But the horse lay down in the pond and that was that." She shed her jacket and stepped to the cold cookstove. "Any biscuits left?"

Lyric shook her head. "You're worried about your stomach?"

"I'm hungry — we didn't have supper." She fished around in the warming oven.

"There's nothing there. I haven't fixed anything yet. Tell me what happened."

"Well . . ." Her tone turned evasive. "He said to tell you — actually all of us — to stay away from the town until he comes for us."

"Comes for us?" Lyric frowned. "How will he come for us?"

Lifting a shoulder in a shrug, Lark repeated the message. "He said to stay away. That's all I know."

"He doesn't want us to witness his death."

"Probably not, and truth be told I don't want to see it. I've never seen anyone hanged, and I don't want to start with a friend." Tears welled in Lark's eyes.

"I know." Lyric reached to take her in her arms and hold her. Tears rolled from both sets of eyes now. "I wasn't going to permit you to view the atrocity."

"He loves you." Lark hiccupped.

"He does? How can you be so certain?"

"Well — he just looks like he does. He goes all soft and mushy when I mention your name."

Lyric breathed out slowly. She closed her eyes and shook her head gently. "None of that matters now. He's such a fine man. Kind. Hardworking. Honest and totally trustworthy." Lyric's voice broke with emotion when the back door opened and Boots came in.

"The birds are all loaded. Do you know how much noise seven sacks of live guineas make?"

Lyric shook her emotions aside. Drawing

a deep breath, she turned to Lark. "Bake some biscuits and fry a slice of ham. Mother will be awake soon and she hasn't eaten a bite since yesterday morning."

"But Joseph said we were to stay here, Lyric. And he meant it. He doesn't want us butting in on his business."

"I don't give a fig what he wants. I will not stand by and let those imbecilic morons hang him. They're only doing this out of spite for the Boltons. And his being here makes them even more upset and determined to do away with him."

"But he said —"

"Boots, grab an extra lantern." Lyric dismissed her sister with a sharp look. "*You* bake biscuits."

Lark reached for her arm. "He needs his wallet."

Nodding, Lyric wiped her eyes on the hem of her soiled apron. "I'll see that he gets the wallet." Her eyes met Lark's. "Doesn't mean that the wallet belongs to him, Lark."

"But it does!"

"You don't know that."

"I . . . I have to keep a promise, Lyric, but you have to take that wallet to him right now."

"All right. I'm going, but I don't see how it can possibly change what's about to happen." Lark's former statement sank in. "What promise? Do you know something that I don't?" She met her sister's eyes.

"Just *go!*"

The urgency in Lark's tone set her feet in action. Lark was right; they could discuss this later.

17

Streaks of blue, pink, and orange gradually spread across the sky. Ian alternately watched the fingers of light splay the horizon and the back road leading to the jail. What was keeping Lark? She should be here by now. Pacing, he rubbed the back of his neck. This crazy plan was his and he'd own the outcome . . . but right now the scheme seemed doomed to fail.

The sounds of a gathering crowd outside drifted through the cell window. The scent of blood invariably attracted predators.

Ian sat back down on the bunk to await the time when the door would open again and they would come for him. Doubts assailed him. If Boots's and Lark's breakout plan had been successful, he would be ten miles away by now. He shook his head. It was a nice idea but it wouldn't accomplish his ultimate purpose. He wanted Lyric set for life if this was the hour the good Lord wanted him to exit this world.

Had Jim Younger even gotten wind of the hanging? His strategy was flimsy at best, but if he was going down he was going down alone. The Boltons had enough trouble without him involving them. His gaze shifted back to the cell bars. What or who had detained Lark?

Aware of the time ticking away, he focused on his boots.

In less than an hour, another man could be wearing them.

"Oh, turtle feathers!" Boots wrung her hands when the second sack split apart and feathers flew. Guineas scattered, their shrieks echoing in the holler.

The sun's rays had started to spread; tearing sacks had delayed the women twice. Guineas dangled by bound feet from Norman's saddle horn and stirrups. The white-breasted fowl squawked every time they added another hen to his load. Boots struck off to gather the strewn birds, trapping them between her feet. Her red cowboy boots were covered in dirt.

"We have to work faster!" Lyric fumbled to find an empty spot to tie a hen, keeping an eye on the sunrise. "The sun will be full up before we make it to town."

"I'm working as fast as I can!" Lark snatched a hen and tucked it under her arm. "I don't know why that horse had to go lie down in that pond. Who ever heard of an animal liking water that much?"

It seemed the whole world, not just the horse, was working against Joseph now. Lyric tied another bird to the saddle and bolted off in search of more.

The front door of the jail opened and the sheriff walked in, the smell of bacon and eggs lingering on his vest. "Howdy."

Ian didn't bother with niceties. He reached for his hat but the sheriff stopped him. "No need to take that, and leave your boots in the cell." He eyed the fine leather. "That's some good-looking leather — what's the size?"

"You couldn't fill those boots."

The sheriff appeared to catch the putdown and a growing grin spread across his youthful features. "Well now, I shore am gonna try, Mister, 'cause you ain't gonna be needin' 'em."

Ian got slowly to his feet.

"Might as well sit a spell longer. The mayor's still finishin' up his breakfast and the crowd's still gatherin'."

"I prefer to stand."

"I suppose I could offer a cup of coffee while we wait . . ."

The man's hospitable efforts were not only in vain, they were hypocritical. "No thanks." He glanced toward the door. "Sounds like a good turnout."

"Oh, it's a fine gatherin'. Standin' room only." The sheriff tossed his hat on the desk and walked to the gun cabinet. "A hanging's always good for business. Gets the folks moving about, and while they're in town they do their shopping."

The social chitchat rubbed Ian's nerves raw. The door opened a couple of times with men coming to check in. He tried to catch a glimpse of the crowd — see if he could spot Jim Younger — but his efforts were in vain. Crowd noises and the sound of someone tuning up a tuba met his attempts. Was Jim Younger out there waiting? Or was he fifty miles away, unaware he was about to win a bet?

The circus-like atmosphere grew louder. He needed order, calm, not folks milling around like this. Younger wouldn't announce his presence even if the townsfolk would choose to look the other way. The outlaw would disguise himself as an innocent bystander, merely here for the show, but Ian would be able to pick out his tall frame in a crowd.

Relax. Once the ruse was over and he informed the sheriff his memory was back, the authorities would have no recourse but to turn him loose, and then he would grab Jim and make the arrest. The bounty money would set him, Lyric, and Grandpa and Grandma up for life — if Lyric would have him. There'd been no time for proper courting, but he sensed that she shared his feelings. He'd seen it in her eyes. Felt it in her touch. He would forever be in her debt for the way she had shielded, nursed, and protected him, but gratitude alone had nothing to do with his feelings. She was the woman he wanted to spend the rest of his life with.

He glanced up when the door opened a third time and the hangman stepped inside. The man's grave features left no guessing as to his intent.

The sheriff glanced up. "Time to go?"

The hangman nodded.

"Then let's get a move on." The sheriff reached for the cell keys hanging behind the desk and then stepped to the heavy bars.

Ian stood up and handed his hat to the sheriff. He'd save him the trouble of stealing from a dead man.

"Thanks." The jailer eyed the prize.

"That's one of them true Stetson's, ain't it?"

"Bought it in St. Joe when I was up there this winter."

The man admired the souvenir. "I'll wear this real proud like."

Ian stepped past him and walked into the room. The hangman left, leaving the door open behind him. Ian waited until the sheriff put on the Stetson and admired the fit in the wavy glass hanging to the side. "Perfect fit."

"What luck."

The jailer tilted the brim just so before he straightened. "Well, can't keep the folks waitin' any longer. Guess I should tie your hands."

"Don't bother. I'm not going anywhere."

"Well — you're going *somewhere.* Guess it'll be betwixt you and the good Lord where that'll be." He picked up a piece of rope and bound Ian's wrists tightly.

Bright sunlight met his eyes, and he flinched as they stepped out of the building. A large crowd had gathered, and now a hush fell over the onlookers as the two men appeared on the jail porch.

"Just walk slowly and take deep breaths," the sheriff said in a low tone. "And remember I can shoot you dead if you try anything funny."

"I'd sure hate to be shot on the way to my hanging."

The men stepped into the street.

"Keep your eyes off the noose — that'll make it easier."

Ian felt the barrel of the sheriff's shotgun in the small of his back.

His gaze focused on the crowd, searching the sea of sober faces. *Come on, Younger. Don't let me down now.* Skimming the crowd he searched the back row, but no one even remotely similar to Jim Younger appeared present.

Walking slowly toward the platform, Ian focused on the left side. A man standing three rows back was about the right height, but he was too stocky to be Younger. His gaze moved to the left side. Short, tall, lanky, heavyset, old, and young.

Younger wasn't there.

A vision of Lyric momentarily blinded him, and he breathed a silent prayer. *God, let this work.* He didn't want Lyric witnessing this, but if he could look into her eyes, feel her strength like he had so many times in the past . . . He whirled when he heard a racket.

Guineas — more than he could count

303

swarmed the street, waddling frantically through the crowd, bald heads bobbing. Folks parted, stepping aside as the hens waddled through town, setting up a deafening racket. Feathers flew as men waded in and tried to capture the fleeing hens. The noise level turned raucous.

Ian watched the frenzy until he realized that all he had to do was disappear into the crowd. The sheriff and hangman had waded knee-deep into the fray, joined by deputies. Focused on the unexpected eruption, his mind raced. Where was Younger?

A man bent to recover a hen and the wind caught the hem of his long leather duster. Ian felt a jolt, experiencing the miracle he'd been praying for when he caught sight of the custom-made lizard boots. Nobody but Jim Younger wore those boots . . .

"Ian?" A hand touched his arm.

Turning, he faced Lyric, her hair tousled, dark circles shadowing her eyes. Her dirty dress had mud on it and her face was smudged. Folks were so preoccupied they didn't seem to notice her.

She was responsible for this commotion. He should have known she wouldn't stand by and let him hang without giving it her all to stop it. His features softened. "What are you doing here? I told you to stay away."

"It's true?" Her brow furrowed. A guinea feather was lodged in her hair. "You are Ian Cawley?"

Sobering, he realized that Lark had told her his identity. And considering her grave expression, Lark also mentioned that his memory was back.

"Lyric — I told Lark not to tell you until this was over."

"My sister didn't tell me. You told me. Just now, when you turned and responded to your name."

"Lyric, honey . . ."

She lifted a hand of protest, as though the truth pierced her like a sword. Their gazes met and held. If he'd experienced a moment this bitter he couldn't recall.

"You didn't trust me enough to tell me," she whispered.

"Trust had nothing to do with it. I'd trust you with my life, Lyric. I *have* trusted you with my life. And you've saved me up until now."

"But you couldn't trust me to secrecy?"

"I didn't want to involve you or your sister in this whole game."

"How long? How long have you known?"

"Only a short time — I promise you."

"Did you know the times you kissed me?"

He shook his head. "No. I kissed you

because you're a lovely young woman and that's what happens between men and women."

Her eyes searched his, begging for a better answer.

"I'm in love with you, Lyric." If both his hands hadn't been bound he would have drawn her to him, erase the look of betrayal in her eyes. "I love everything about you. Your hair, your eyes, the way you smell — the way you protected me and baked my favorite pies. I didn't tell you about my memory because I was trying to shield you. If this plan backfires the town will hang us all, they'll swear that you and Lark were in cahoots with me."

Chaos surrounded them and he had to shout to make himself heard above the fray. "When this thing is settled I want us to get married, build a house close to my grandparents."

She coldly slapped the wallet in his hand and turned away.

"Lyric. Don't go — not like this. Let me settle this and we'll talk . . ."

She walked on, clearly turning a deaf ear to his pleas, her small frame visibly shaken from the brief conversation.

A guinea shot through his legs and a man lunged after it, knocking Ian off balance.

He struggled to regain his footing, his eyes searching for that long brown duster and lizard boots.

A gunshot cracked the air and the mad scramble ceased. The sheriff stood on the porch, wild-eyed. "Stop it! We got ourselves a hanging. Leave these birds be until we get the job done."

The crowd gradually peeled away, allowing room for the outlaw and sheriff to proceed to the platform. Guineas clucked and squawked, fluffing indignant feathers.

The look of disloyalty that had reflected like a clear pond in Lyric's eyes haunted Ian. He should have told her. He should have included her in the plan . . . but she would have tried to talk him out of it, tried to find another way — and there wasn't one.

The platform approached, the thick rope noose swaying lightly in the early morning breeze. Delicate white alyssum lightly scented the air; red and white and purple tulips bloomed near the general store's front porch. When he was free, he was going to get some of those tulips for Lyric. All purple because he liked the color, all pretty and sweet-smelling like her.

18

Lyric led the horse out of the holler, tears blinding her. Joseph didn't trust her. He confessed to being in love with her, but he didn't trust her.

Did he think if she'd known that he was a U.S. marshal she would track him down and pursue him once he left? Did he think she'd make demands on him, reminding him that if it weren't for her he would be dead now?

Well, if he thought she would come after him, he couldn't be further from the truth. She wouldn't follow him. She'd never subject him to life with a Bolton — even though a Bolton had saved his skin.

Little did he know that she would have done the same for anyone — she did it for him, a complete stranger. She helped save his life. The good Lord did the healing. All she'd done was clean him up and force a few herbs and tea down his throat, but her efforts counted.

Tears blinded her and she reached up to brush them away. The horse plodded along beside her.

"He really doesn't like you any more than he likes me," she reminded the animal.

The horse shook his mane.

"No, it's the truth. I don't mean to hurt your feelings, but he doesn't care for you at all. Not one little bit." She paused to blow her nose.

What was she thinking? Taking her hurt and rejection out on a poor animal. Sighing, she wadded the handkerchief in her hand. "I'm sorry. I shouldn't take my resentment out on you." She tuned an ear toward the holler. How long did it take to hang a man? Silence met her efforts, so the deed wasn't over yet. There would be cheering and whooping when it happened.

What joy they'd take when the Bolton girls' outlaw had been hanged after all their efforts.

But Ian had the wallet and his identification. Chances were no one in town had ever heard of the marshal but they'd have to give him the benefit of doubt until they verified his claim, wouldn't they?

But then again, the hollers were full of outlaws and society misfits, men with prices on their heads.

Still no sounds of cheering. Had Joseph shown authorities the wallet, attempted to prove his identity?

I love you, Lyric. I love everything about you. Your hair, your eyes, the way you smell, the way you protected me and baked my favorite pies. . . .

Had he really said that to her or had she only dreamed that he confessed his affection? Her confused state couldn't sort through the fast pace of events. She wanted to believe him, longed to place her trust in him, but common sense told her that no man would want her. Not a Bolton.

Unconsciously she turned the horse back toward the town. What if the crowd and sheriff had no choice but to believe him about being a U.S. marshal and was forced to set him free? He'd have no way out of town. He'd be obliged to walk through that staring crowd with no horse and nobody who cared for him.

The animal plodded beside her.

The closer they drew to the town, the more Lyric mentally braced for the shout that would surely go up at any minute.

Ian paused before the platform steps and calmly faced the sheriff. "I hope you haven't gotten real attached to my Stetson."

The sheriff grinned. "Why's that?"

Ian presented the wallet with his bound hands. "When you open it you'll find my name, Ian Cawley, United States Marshal. My badge is there and I'll give you information about where and whom to wire for further confirmation of my identity."

Frowning, the sheriff slowly opened the wallet and leafed through the contents.

Ian spotted Jim Younger easing back now, eyes skimming for escape. Snatching his hat off the sheriff's head, Ian lunged, parting the crowd. Leaping around the startled townsfolk, he chased the outlaw who was now hightailing it out of town on foot.

Younger drew and fired, the bullet shattering a water barrel. Water flew and the barrel started to drain. Ian paused long enough to settle his hat and shout to a startled bystander, "Cut these ropes off my wrist!"

The man fumbled in his pocket and took out a small knife. In seconds the binds were slit.

Running again, Ian raced behind the escaping outlaw. It had been a while since he'd run like this, and his lungs were starting to remind him. Younger lunged for his horse tied outside the general store and mounted up, kicking the stallion into a full gallop.

Reaching the edge of town, Ian broke into a wide grin when he spotted Lyric leading Norman. When he reached her, he grabbed her by the shoulders, gave her a thorough kiss, and swung aboard the waiting animal. "You," he said, pointing to her. "I want to talk to you when I get back."

Jaw agape, she nodded.

Kicking his heels against Norman's flanks, he set off in hot pursuit. Younger had a good half-mile lead now.

Ian hadn't realized how much he'd missed Norman's easy stride. The horse's ways were the source of an inner battle. The horse could be the most ornery, uncooperative animal in creation, but every now and then, when he most needed the horse's strength, Norman gave it. Sometimes, like now, the horse could be noble. Proud. Free. Long, sleek muscles, easy, powerful stride, coat glistening with sweat as black fetlocks ate up the ground. Men had offered Ian a fortune for this animal, but there wasn't enough money in the world to buy him. Together, horse and man became one when the marshal was aboard.

He continued to hold the animal back, allowing time before he gave him his head. If he wasn't mistaken, this was the same road he'd lost Cummins on. The narrow road and towering oaks gave little opportunity for capture. He wanted Younger in the clear before he took him. No trees, no way of escape. He sat back and made sure Norman was comfortable with the pace.

Wind whipped the riders' eyes as the horses stretched now, flying hooves throwing dirt clods. Younger's stallion was a good match for Norman. The horse was powerfully built, auburn coat slicked with sweat, ears pinned back. Leg muscles strained and grew taut. Ian wouldn't be surprised if Jim had raced this animal for profit.

Trees and fence posts flashed by. He was eating Younger's dust now. Victory was not yet complete but he allowed himself one brief hope that the scheme had worked before he refocused on the arrest. But the words, "Thank you, God!" rang out.

The distance between the two riders widened and Ian said softly, "Now, Norman."

Responding to the command, Norman stretched out his hooves and gave Ian the speed he needed. A blur of prairie grass whipped by; Ian could feel the animal's powerful sides heaving as dirt pounded beneath his hooves. The distance between him and Younger faded and Ian prepared for the jump from Norman to the stallion.

He was going to break another rib, but sometimes life called for a little pain. With a lurch, he flew off Norman and soared through the air.

Head bent, Lyric walked up the hill toward the Bolton house. Angry, disillusioned shouts followed her. The town had been deprived of a hanging and their restless calls polluted the air.

Joseph was Ian Cawley. United States Marshal Ian Cawley. Overwhelming relief swept her. If he were telling the truth, he wasn't an outlaw. He owed no debt to society.

He was chasing someone — who?

Apparently he was a free man now. Free to come and go as he pleased. The sheriff wasn't on his tail.

Her throat tightened and she suddenly found it hard to breathe. What if he didn't come back?

"You. I want to talk to you," he'd said after that abrupt kiss.

She hadn't imagined those words.

No, he hadn't trusted her enough to share the truth, but he didn't owe her anything but gratitude. Yes, she had saved his life and he was beholden to her, but she shouldn't expect any misplaced sense of loyalty on his part. The shared kisses, the hours of enjoyable company . . . all of it had been perfectly proper. He had made no promises, and she had no right to pin all her hopes and dreams on him.

Removing a handkerchief from her pocket, she wiped her streaming eyes. *Get your mind on your work, Lyric. There are more important issues to consider now.* Would the man Ian was chasing best the U.S. marshal? Ian's injuries were still tender and his strength couldn't be normal.

The thought ricocheted in her brain, and she blinked back blinding tears. The two were noticeably bent on violence — that hadn't been hard to detect. It was as though the men were out to settle a personal vendetta.

Wiping her nose, she tried to gather enough gumption to collect the hens and be through with the whole matter. If Ian wanted to fight it out with some man it was none of her business.

"Lyric!"

Turning, she spotted Lark and Boots headed in her direction, both girls lugging sacks of screeching fowl.

Sighing, she wiped her nose again, squared

her shoulders, and went to deal with the hens — the only thing she felt qualified to control.

The sun wasn't yet high in the sky when Ian rode into town leading Jim Younger's horse with a bound Jim draped over the saddle.

Pausing in front of the jail, he waited for the acting sheriff to appear. When he did he scowled. "Why have you got that Younger strapped to his saddle? Ain't you caused enough trouble for one day? If you knew who you were why did you put us through all this trouble?"

"Because," Ian threw a leg off his saddle, wincing, and stepped down. "You're going to arrest this man and I'm going to collect the bounty money."

The sheriff backed up. "Now hold on. We don't mess with them Youngers . . ."

"Now, now. That was in the past. You're going to grow a backbone. You're going to arrest *this* Younger." He gave the stunned man a gentle pat as he walked by. "Think of it like this: You're coming up in the world."

The acting sheriff made fretting noises as Ian untied Younger and helped him to his feet. He led the outlaw into the jail, removed the wristbands, closed the cell door, and locked it. Stepping to the poster board, he grasped Jim's image and handed it to the sheriff. "I believe I'm due some money."

"I'll get you for this, Cawley," Younger called from the bunk.

"You're a sore loser, Jim."

The outlaw's sneer was as ugly as his soul. "You best watch your back."

"The one thing I refuse to worry about is the future." Ian grinned. Right now his future looked fairly bright. He'd find Lyric, they'd talk this thing through, and he'd make her understand the reason for his silence. He turned to the sheriff. "You are to leave this man in jail until I send someone to pick him up. Am I clear? If you release him, you're the one who's going to be staring through those bars."

"I ain't gonna release him." He dropped into his chair, staring at the reward poster. "It'll take me a day or two to get your money. And the wire just came. You're cleared; free to go."

"I'll be around." Ian glanced at Jim. "Take good care of my friend."

Younger's bitter tone followed him to the door. "Think you're smart, don't you?"

"Actually, I think I'm mighty blessed. This whole thing could have backfired real easy on me." So easy he didn't want to think about the narrow escape from the noose.

"Hey!" the sheriff called. "Where do I get ahold of you when I have the bounty?"

"Don't worry. I'm not in any hurry to leave."

First thing he was going to do was look up the doc and have him wrap the second — possibly third — rib he'd just broken.

His body was in a world of hurt.

By nine o'clock the women had dumped the last of the hens back in their pen. Boots slumped against a tree and announced, "I could eat a horse."

Lyric's stomach growled. They had worked all last night with only an occasional sip of water. "Come to the house with us and I'll fix breakfast."

When they entered the Bolton kitchen Lyric immediately headed upstairs. Mother was half awake and in an ill temper, her tone unnecessarily sharp. "I told you not to leave me."

"You weren't alone. Lark was here." At least for the better part of the night. "Did you call out?"

"I wanted *you* here."

Straightening the rumpled sheets, Lyric said softly, "I'm here now." And here she would be for the remainder of her life, but she wouldn't be the same naive child; boasting that she could live very well without love. Ian's brief time with her had proven that she was capable of falling in love, capable of spending the rest of her life with him if he had asked.

Despair overcame her. Fatigue from worry and the night's work shook her to the core and she rested her head on the mattress. How she longed to throw herself in a mother's arms and cry out her anguish. She couldn't recall a single time when she'd ever done that. She'd always had to be the strong one, the one who took over when life was good or bad.

Resting her head on the soft quilt, she blinked back hot tears. She never cried, and now she'd cried twice in one day. What was there to weep about? Life was peachy-fine, wasn't it? Ian would be leaving and she would be left with only his memory, a made-up name, and empty dreams.

A more distressing thought surfaced. What if Ian did come back to say goodbye? What if he acknowledged that the attraction wasn't one-sided, that they shared a mutual, strong desire? Love, even? How would she ever have the strength to turn him away? For turn him away she must. If Mother's illness had been passed along, Ian would be tying himself to a life with a mad woman. It wouldn't be fair to him.

She lifted her face, snuffing back sobs. She could never marry anyone. If Ian did return to say goodbye, she must let him go. A man like him deserved more than her.

She sat up suddenly. What if the Younger he'd been chasing had shot him and left him by the roadside to die? Both men had ridden out of town like their tails were ablaze. She hadn't thought to check the roads — she needed to check —

Stepping to the pane, Lyric tugged the lever and opened the window wide. Fresh air ruffled the curtain.

If only she had someone to ask for advice, a confidante. But Katherine was in Joplin and Lark certainly wasn't old enough to make mature decisions. If by some miracle Ian returned, should she confess her love? Tell him the truth in spite of the insanity that ran through the family?

She couldn't.

Absently patting her mother's pillow, she murmured, "Lark will bring your breakfast shortly."

"Make sure my toast is soft this morning."

"I will. You get some rest."

Her mind churned as she returned to the

kitchen. She had to get away from this house or she would burst. Lark turned from the stove. "Is Mother okay?"

"She's fine. Make certain her toast is soft this morning, and add a little jam. She loves that."

Lyric continued to the door, absently checking her appearance. Guinea feathers stuck to her skirt and her hair hung in her eyes, but her mind was intent on two things: getting somewhere outside to be alone with her thoughts, and checking the main road to see if there were any bodies lying around.

Three doors down from the jail, Ian stepped out of the general store. In under an hour the doc had wrapped his ribs and he'd made a purchase. He paused to check his vest pocket for the wedding ring. Paid a whopping price, but he could afford it now and Earl didn't balk when he asked for credit. The store owner had witnessed the whole scene this morning and knew about the coming bounty.

Ian walked to the hitching rail and offered Norman a handful of oats. He'd earned the reward. "Have I mentioned that you're occasionally one fine animal?"

The animal lifted his head, showed his teeth, and gave a loud whinny.

"Don't get too sure of yourself. Most of the time you're a walking glue factory. Bear that in mind the next time you lie down in the middle of a creek with me on your back."

Stepping off the boardwalk, he grabbed Norman's reins and mounted up, trying to muffle his groan of pain. He really was getting too old for this line of work. A bystander stopped him before he reined away from the post. "Mister!"

Turning, Ian searched for the source of the voice.

A man inclined his head. "That animal for sale?"

"Norman?" Ian's gaze dropped to the thick mane. There were times he would give him away. "No sir, he isn't."

The stranger approached, his eyes centered on the sleek stallion. "Mighty fine piece of horseflesh." He ran his hands over the front quarter and fetlocks. "Hear he runs like the wind."

"He can run," Ian allowed. "But he isn't for sale."

"I'll give you top dollar."

The man's features finally registered. Frank James. Known to be one of the finest horse purveyors around. And wanted for questioning in a case of suspicious trading.

As a U.S. marshal Ian should seize the moment, but he and the holler had had enough excitement for one day. Let James remain free for another young and industrious bounty hunter to capture. Ian had unfinished business with a lady. He clucked his tongue and turned Norman toward home.

"Sorry. The animal isn't for sale at any price."

19

The Bolton place looked eerily deserted when Ian tied Norman's reins to a low-hanging branch. If allowed to roam, the horse would eat his fill of the tender new shoots sprouting from the ground.

Stepping onto the service porch, he tapped lightly. Before, he would have walked in without announcement, but today was different. Today he knew his place. It seemed only fitting to knock.

His eyes took in the empty kitchen and cold stove, and a grin appeared.

He could have wrung Lyric's neck when she'd waltzed into town and set that mess of guineas loose in the streets.

And then he could have kissed her until she begged him to stop. Without the commotion, he doubted he would have spotted Younger lurking in the shadows. The uproar had routed the outlaw from the alley and into the fray — straight into Ian's plan.

Ian called out, "Lyric? Lark? Anyone home?"

Quiet met his efforts.

The girls must still be in town. Or else they were busy hauling all those hens back to wherever they'd gotten them.

He might check on Edwina. The past two days' excitement must have affected her.

He caught sight of Norman untying the knot in his reins with his teeth, and he stepped to the back door and called, "Norman!"

The horse dropped his head docilely.

Going down the steps, he crossed the yard to retie the animal. The ring sat in his pocket like a piece of hot lead. Would Lyric accept a worn-out battered man who wanted nothing more than to go back to Kansas City and build a little place next to his grandparents and care for them until they passed? She wanted a new life; would his suit her? He had a hunch it would. They'd take Lark with them, and life would be good.

Whistling, he retied the reins in a triple knot. Let Norman work on that for a while. "You are a real burr under my saddle, but you'll notice that I didn't sell you."

Norman whuffed.

"I could have, and for a right nice price.

Fool with me much more and you're gone. Understand? History. I'll buy a donkey if I have to."

Norman shook his head and whinnied. Ian ruffled his mane and went back into the house. He climbed the stairs up to Edwina's room and knocked on her door. "Mrs. Bolton? I just wanted to check in on you . . ."

His voice faded as his eyes fell on Edwina. Her eyes were closed, but not in sleep.

Half an hour had passed and there was still no sign of Lyric. Ian sat on the back stoop holding the letter he'd found at Edwina's side. He'd taken the letter and then respectfully covered Lyric's mother with the blankets.

He dropped his face in his hands, wondering how the girls would take the shock. *Thank you, God, that I got here first.*

The white slip of paper rested in his hands and he stared at the note. It had Lyric's name written on it, but maybe he should read it first, to spare her more heartache. Whatever it said could cause Lyric more pain or false guilt.

Then again, Edwina would have written his name if she'd meant the note for him.

Softly tapping the paper against his thigh,

he considered what he was about to do. If the message was kind — the sort of message a loving mother ought to leave to her daughter — he'd give it to Lyric. If it held angry, cruel sentiments, he'd throw it in the fire. It would be a simple matter to spare the woman he loved from this last bitter memory.

He unfolded the note. It contained three sentences in an almost indistinguishable scrawl:

I am not your mother. A woman from town left you and Lark with me one day and promised to return. She didn't.

Lyric raced over the new grass and along the path, finally flinging herself down on the ground when she reached the creek where she and Joseph — no, *Ian* — had once fished. She sobbed with great, messy gulps until her tears were all spent.

"Father," she prayed, "I think — no, I *am* — in love with Joseph. I think he may love me too, odd as that sounds, but I'm not certain. Keep him alive, Father. Keep him alive and safe." She wiped away the tears that had fallen on her cheeks. "And Father God . . . if he's alive, and if he doesn't return to say goodbye, would I be an utter fool to go after him?"

She looked out over the creek expectantly, as though waiting for an answer.

None came.

And then it came. Not a sound, not a voice, just a sweet certainty: *Go home.*

20

"What are you reading?"

Ian glanced up, startled by Lyric's voice. She stood before him, weary and dirty as a street urchin. Getting to his feet, he cleared his throat. "A note."

"A note?"

"Where have you been? I've been waiting for you." It was nigh on to noon now.

"I've been . . . out."

His gaze scanned her untidy appearance. "Looking like that?"

She focused on the paper in his hand. "What's that?"

How did he tell her? Did he hand her the paper and let her read the grim message for herself? Or should he blurt out the news and tell her what had happened? Neither way seemed less hurtful. "I'm sorry, Lyric. Your . . . Edwina has passed."

He put the note in her hand and watched as she read the three sentences. Jaw-dropping disbelief, and then puzzlement, clouded her eyes when she lifted her face. "I don't understand."

"I found her a little while ago, sweetheart." He reached to take her into his arms. "She must have known her time was near, and she used her last few moments to write that note. She wanted you to know the truth." Allowing time for the news to penetrate, he held her, brushing her damp hair free from her eyes. Seconds passed and she gave a tremulous sigh. Her shoulders heaved with silent sobs.

"Cry it out. I'm here for you," he whispered.

"Why would she wait so long? Why not tell me years ago?"

"You know Edwina. She liked things her way." He drew her closer to him. If she was going to fall apart he wanted her to do it now, when he could hold her. "Do you understand what this means? The woman you thought was your mother is no relation to you."

She shook her head. "Edwina never spoke of any of this."

"Maybe that's good." He tucked a strand of hair behind her ear and rubbed a hand across her back, their bodies swaying with the gentle breeze as Lyric clung tightly to his neck. He liked the feel of her dependence, welcomed it. If God allowed him, from now on he'd protect her, and never allow her to spend another day like the ones she'd spent in Bolton Holler.

"Lark will be along any minute." Lyric pulled away from his arms, wiping her nose on the handkerchief he'd put in her hand. "I'll need to tell her."

"I'll help you break the news."

Her eyes filled with gratitude. "I'm free now," she said.

Smiling, he drank in her spirit. "You're free." The way she said the word had such a soulful sound, and his heart sank within him. She'd spent her whole life here, catering to Edwina. Was it fair to tie her down to a husband and family now that she was finally free?

"Where is Edwina?"

"She's still in her room."

"We'll need to bury her." She paused, taking another absent swipe at her nose. "I've never buried anyone."

"I'll do that for you."

"There needs to be a wake."

A wake. He hated those things. "Lyric, do you really think that's necessary? The woman didn't have a friend on earth."

Shaking her head, Lyric said, "I'm going

to do this properly, Ian. There will be a wake. Tonight."

Later, Lyric set a damp cloth aside and studied the woman she'd called *Mother* all these years. Lark worked silently beside her. The girls had washed Edwina's hair and brushed the gray locks until they shone. Adding a touch of color to the woman's cheeks, she stood back and admired her efforts. "You are quite the deceiver," she said. Never once had Edwina let her deception slip — not even during the worst of her mad spells. What a sly fox she'd proven to be.

Resentment bubbled up in her throat but she swallowed it back. What was done was done. But why had Edwina hidden the truth all these years? Out of fear? Did she think the girls would desert her if they knew she wasn't their blood kin? Or was her motive one of pure self-interest? She had two girls who cared for her day and night, saw to her every whim. Cooked her meals and cleaned her house. Was that her reason for keeping the girls in the dark? Or had there been some part of Edwina that loved the girls?

Lark shuddered. "I don't know how you can talk about her so nicely. What's she's done to us is unforgivable and you know what? I'm *glad* she isn't our mother."

"It's not for us to judge," she reminded her sister. "Edwina was a very sick woman."

"A mad woman."

"Be that as it may, she will stand before the Lord and account for her life. We've only to answer for our own wrongdoings." Lyric set a small vase of wildflowers beside the crude coffin Ian had earlier built. "Is Boots attending the wake?"

"She said she'd come."

"Good. That will be four in attendance."

"Four friends she didn't have. I can run to town and spread the word. I guess someone might take a notion to be kind and come. It's kind of embarrassing to have someone die and nobody come to pay their respects. And I wouldn't mind having one of those chocolate cakes I hear Mrs. Grannier takes to folks when one of their kin dies."

"Lark, Mrs. Grannier is not going to send a cake. You should know that by now. You can go to town if you'd like, but don't expect cakes or mourners. There won't be any."

Lark set the brush aside. "You're free now. Are you going to leave with Ian and make me come with you?"

"Ian hasn't asked me to go anywhere with him."

"If he did, you'd go."

"Maybe."

Her lack of denial gave Lyric pause. What *did* she want — really want? Now that she was actually free of Bolton Holler, would she forfeit her plans for a new life with Lark to blindly follow a man she still knew so little about?

Love said she would, but love was fickle. For years she had loved Edwina in a strange, dedicated way, and now she discovered that her loyalty was misplaced. If she went away with Ian, would she come to feel the same about him, that she'd given her love and loyalty to a man she barely knew?

Boots arrived close to seven. Ian sat in the parlor, hat on his knee. Drapes and shutters were drawn. Heavy black crepe was tied to the front door as though there would be a flurry of grievers to weep through the night.

Mirrors and picture frames were covered with the same material. All clocks in the house had been stopped; ticking clocks would bring bad luck. The kitchen counter sat empty of casseroles, cakes, pies, or neighborly expressions of sympathy. Lark had made a trip to the holler to announce Edwina's passing, but as Lyric predicted the effort was in vain. Her sister returned in tears. "All Mrs. Grannier said was, "Good, the madwoman is dead.""

Boots scuffed into the parlor and took a seat in front of the casket, crossing her arms. Lyric and Lark sat down beside her. "Cross your legs," Lyric whispered.

Grunting, Lark complied.

After a bit Lark leaned over and whispered, "How long do we have to sit like this?"

"All night."

"All night!"

A moment later. "Is the coffin screwed down tightly?"

"Tight as a tick."

The moon rose higher. Lyric heard Ian occasionally shift in his chair. The old house creaked and groaned with the wind.

Around what she deemed to be midnight, Lyric served coffee and cold ham and biscuits. The mourners ate quietly and returned to the wake.

Lark dozed on Lyric's shoulder by early morning. Boots had slowly slid off her chair and now lay curled at the foot of her seat, snoozing. It would have been nice if one person from the town had come, if one pie or casserole had sat on the counter. After all, the town had been named after Edwina's great-grandfather who had supposedly been an upstanding citizen in the holler. He'd built the big house on the hill. He and his wife had formed the community. She turned her head slightly to see Ian and he smiled, encouraging her with his eyes.

Returning his grin, she softened her features.

He winked, flirting with her.

Turning back to the casket, she prayed for time to fly. Slowly, the minutes turned into hours. Lyric's back ached from sitting upright. There was no rule that one couldn't speak during a wake, but everything that could be said about Edwina had been voiced earlier and in a matter of minutes.

Lyric's head bobbed when she threatened to drift off. Jerking upright, she froze when she saw a prominent member of Bolton Holler had shown up. A gray — then green — light sat atop Edwina's casket, dimly blinking. The light — that silly, irrepressible light — had come to pay its respect to the Holler's most feared resident.

Lyric glanced around the room to see if others had spotted the nuisance. Ian's head lolled back and a half-snore escaped.

Boots buried her head in a blanket on the floor.

Lyric jabbed her sister. Lark stirred,

336

murmuring something, and drifted off again.

The light moved slowly, creeping along. Glowing brighter, it skipped to the top of the casket and appeared to sniff the fresh violets, then inched along the top of the roughly hewn box — momentarily disappearing inside. Eyes focused on the spectacle, Lyric watched in spellbound fascination.

When the brilliance emerged seconds later, it bounced up and down, up and down — higher and higher with each joyful bounce.

Then slowly it shifted in her direction. Pressing back in her seat, Lyric tried to avoid the encroaching radiance, for the first time in her life frightened by the object.

The dazzling ray adjusted speed and moved her way. In seconds she realized it was perched on her head. Not daring to move, she sat transfixed as it bounced, very softly, as though patting her head, offering tender sympathy.

This was *completely* insane. A light did not offer sympathy.

The light was some crazy phenomenon that had grown to inhuman proportion in people's minds. Yet she couldn't deny that a vivid object now lit the room, as though restoring happiness and life in this old house.

Then it was off, disappearing like a vapor behind a black-draped window.

Dry mouthed, Lyric tuned to see if Ian had witnessed the spectacle. His resonant snores filled the hushed room.

The light could be an angel. After all, God sometimes used strange means to send comfort to His children. Like the ravens who brought food to Elijah or the shining light at the Mount of Transfiguration. Lyric sat back and smiled.

21

Daylight spilled through the clouds and rays of warmth covered the earth. Lyric, Ian, Lark, and Boots carried the wooden casket to the waiting travois and then followed as Ian led Norman down past the barn a couple of hundred feet to a freshly dug grave.

As sunlight spread over the fresh green earth, Edwina Bolton's remains were lowered into the ground. Lyric had picked a few early blooming flowers on the way to the gravesite and now tossed them lightly into the yawning hole.

"You girls go back to the house while I cover the grave." Ian straightened, meeting Lyric's gaze.

"You need help."

"I've done this many a time. Go back to the house, Lyric."

Nodding, she turned hesitantly.

"It will take a while to complete the job," he said.

She left, realizing that she was dry-eyed and had remained so during the whole tragic ordeal.

That simple fact didn't seem respectful.

"Shouldn't we say one final word?"

Ramming a shovel in the mound of fresh dirt, Ian paused for a while and then recited the words he had once spoken to Edwina. "Surely he hath borne our griefs, and carried our sorrows: yet we did esteem him stricken, smitten of God, and afflicted. But he was wounded for our transgressions, he was bruised for our iniquities: the chastisement of our peace was upon him; and with his stripes we are healed."

They were both quiet for a long moment. Then Lyric nodded slowly. "Thank you, Ian. That's just right."

Joy bubbled in Lyric's throat and for the first time she felt almost hopeful as she removed the heavy drapes from the windows and black crepe from the front door. The clocks were set into motion, mirrors and picture frames uncovered.

It was finally over. Edwina was gone. And Lyric was free to pursue love, true abiding love.

Lark came into the room and started folding the mourning items. "We're free to go now, aren't we?"

Lyric nodded, almost bursting with happiness. "We're finally free to leave."

Lark's gaze roamed the cracked ceilings and warped walls. "We're going to just close the house and never come back?"

They could *leave.* The heady feeling swallowed her — and yet she couldn't leave without Ian.

Lark ripped a piece of crepe and flung it to the floor. "I don't *want* to leave."

Lyric paused, turning to face her sister. "Lark, please. Don't spoil this joyful occasion. We're free — after years and years of misery — to leave this holler. I know that you love Boots like a sister, but you can write, and one day when you're old enough I'll let you come back for a long visit."

"I don't want to leave, Lyric." The young girl's eyes filled with raw emotion. "Don't you understand that I love it here? This is my home. I know you don't feel that way, but is it fair to make me live the life you want?"

"Don't be silly — are you suggesting that you stay here, alone? You can't do that."

"I could stay with Boots and her grandpa."

Lyric shook her head. "Unthinkable. I couldn't do without you."

"But you could. You'll have Ian."

"I don't know that for certain." She wished it with all of her heart, but Ian hadn't spoken a single word on the matter since she'd returned to find Edwina dead.

"You do know it. You know he's in love with you and he won't leave unless you go with him."

Stepping off a stool, Lyric paused. "Lark . . ."

"Please." Lark crossed the room. "Please. Boots has already asked her grandpa and he said I'd be welcome to stay with them as long as I like. Just let me stay until you and Ian settle somewhere."

"I don't know that Ian —"

"He loves you, Lyric, and you two deserve time alone. I would only be underfoot and nagging you to move back here. You don't want that. I can't leave Boots and I can't leave Murphy. If you make me go I'll only run away and come back here."

For a long moment Lyric studied her. Her little sister was so much like her — determined, headstrong, and independent as an old billy goat. "I love you, Lark and I want the best for you, but I don't know what I'd do without you."

"You won't be without me that long. I think someday you'll come back to Bolton Holler."

"Never."

"You can't ever say never. And in the meantime, I'll live with Boots and help her take care of her grandpa."

"And annoy Murphy until he puts a warrant out for your arrest."

"I'll keep my distance."

"Lark — this is insane. For years we've planned this day —"

"*You've* planned it. I haven't."

Lyric shook her head, her argument fading. Lark spoke the truth. Lyric looked forward to her new life, but she really had no cause to plan her sister's. In another three years Lark would have the right to do what she wanted regardless.

"If Ian asks me to go with him I'll be both happy and sad. I don't want to leave you behind."

"I'll write every day, I promise." Lark stepped to take Lyric into her arms. "And three years is nothing. Time will fly past like — *whiff.*"

"Lark, I won't come back. I want to close the house and never think about it again. Nobody in their right mind would buy it, not with its legacy and the condition it's in."

"When I marry Murphy we'll live here together." She turned to fling open her arms to the bare walls and patched ceilings. "Some sweet day this old house will be filled with love and laughter and babies — lots and lots of babies."

"Oh, sweet Lark. You are such a dreamer."

Whirling, Lark grinned. "I can stay?"

Nodding, Lyric forced the dreaded words out. "You may stay — but you have to write often and —"

Squealing with joy, Lark flung her arms around Lyric's neck. "Thank you! I love you, I love you, I *adore* you!"

"Let's hope you can claim the same thing in three years."

And God have mercy on Murphy.

"I'll write twice a day!" She whirled and raced toward the door. "Wait until I tell Boots. She is gonna have a *calf*!"

Leaving the house, Lyric set off in a hurried run toward the gravesite, feeling as though everything had fallen into place. Now an invisible thread drew her to the man she loved. Over two hours had passed; the grave would be properly covered by now.

When she arrived at the fresh mound of dirt, Ian was nowhere to be found. The shovel lay at the foot of the grave. Her heart tripped. Had he ridden off? No, he wouldn't. She had seen the look in his eyes, experienced the way he'd comforted and held her earlier.

He was in love with her as madly as she was in love with him. Somewhere he waited for her to come to him. She considered the places they'd spent their best hours. And then, as though a voice beckoned her, she knew. Knew exactly where he waited for her.

She veered to a road that was overgrown, rocky, and hard to maneuver. At the end of her climb he would be waiting for her.

He'd want to pick a place free from reminders of tragedy in which to declare his love. Life offered more than misery and hurt. Their newfound relationship — if there was one — would be built on trust and faith in the future. She doubted that the marshal wanted any part of Bolton Holler and she didn't blame him. Wherever Ian wanted to go she would follow. If only he would ask.

He will, her heart sang. For the first time in her life she was willing to take a risk and find love. For too long she had steered clear of giving her heart to anyone, steeling her emotions to taunts and ridicule, but when this man forcefully rode into her life he had conquered her unwilling heart without lifting a hand.

The Spooklight had driven folks from

their homes, and hardworking families like the Jennings abandoned their homesteads in terror of the mysterious ball of light that bounced over hills and fields, but in a strange way the light had brought them together. Had it not tormented him the night he'd ridden through the barn door, she would have never met him, never found love.

She was almost there. She picked up her skirts and raced to the glade, the beautiful glade they'd visited one day where they'd dreamed of a brighter tomorrow.

When she burst into the clearing she saw Norman munching on a patch of grass, reins dangling. The shady clearing beckoned invitingly. Her gaze searched the lush hills and she spotted him kneeling by the shallow stream.

As she approached he said softly without turning, "What took you so long?"

"I wasn't sure where to find you."

"But you knew I would be waiting for you."

Her breath caught. "Yes, I knew." She had awaited him forever.

Lowering herself to the ground beside him she reached over and traced the firm line of his jaw. She bent and they shared a long, unhurried kiss filled with hope and promise.

"I've been looking everywhere for you," she whispered against his lips when the embrace ended. "What if I hadn't remembered the glade?"

"Then I would have come for you." He grinned, pulling her down beside him and tucking her in his arms. The fit was perfect. Lying back, they studied the sky — a tiny piece of vivid blue showing through the canopy of oaks and towering walnut trees. Squirrels chattered. Thrushes darted in and out of branches dressed in their spring finery.

"There are a few things we need to clarify," she said.

"I can answer any question you ask me. What's bothering you?"

"Your saddle, for one. It has the initials JJ engraved on the leather. Your initials are IC."

"John Jarrette. Met the outlaw on the road here a while back, drawing his last breaths. He'd been shot trying to rob a feed store. He said if I'd bury him I could have the saddle for payment. I didn't need compensation, but it didn't make sense to leave a good saddle by the roadside. Norman seemed to like the fit so I kept it."

"That sounds reasonable. Next, why would you lie to Lark and Boots about those bats? Even I believed you, and it's raised doubts in my mind if you might do the same to me. Try to mislead me about something."

"I don't think I said bats were there, did I?"

"Maybe not, but you led those young girls to believe they were."

"The mind can play strange tricks on a person. I'd rather your sister and Boots fear a cave full of bats than the imminent dangers they would have faced if their plan had succeeded."

He made perfect sense, and she'd told her fair share of half-truths during this whole escapade.

"Any more questions?"

"No, but I might think of others later." She snuggled closer. "I imagine you caught your man?" In all the commotion they hadn't spoken about the Younger capture. "That was really quite a plan on your part."

"The Lord looked after me that morning. The idea didn't backfire on me — but I was awfully grateful for your help, and for all those guinea fowl." He rolled slightly to gaze into her eyes. "Speaking of men, I heard you'd caught yours."

"Well, not yet, but I'm awfully close."

"What would it take to close the deal?" Tracing a finger along the ridge of her nose he said, "I'll pay any price you ask."

"Norman. I want Norman."

"Anything but my horse."

Grinning, she teased. "If I recall correctly, you don't like the animal."

"Who said I don't like Norman? I love that stubborn, ornery, oat-sucking fleabag."

Eventually, she sobered. "You know who you're getting?"

His eyes fixed on her. "A woman so beautiful, so good-hearted it takes my breath away. Someone I want to spend the rest of my life with."

"The daughter of nobody from nowhere. A woman who didn't want me or Lark."

"Your real mother is beside the point, Lyric. She gave up her daughters, but what about you? You want your freedom. Are you willing to give up your dreams for a broken-down old marshal who wants to go home and make furniture with his grandpa?"

Her hold on him tightened. "I can't think of a better new life than the one you just described."

"You don't fear being tied down with a family? Grandpa and Grandma are getting old, and there'll be some care involved."

"I would be honored to care for them, Ian. Your family *is* my new life." Her fingertips lightly threaded the thick mass of dark auburn hair. The depths of his love showed through the eyes that openly pledged his forever love. "I want to be all those things to you. I'll follow you to the ends of the earth."

"That would be Kansas City, to my grandparents' place. They've got a small spread outside of town. Grandpa is a fine woodsmith; I'd like to learn the craft. It's a good place, Lyric. A fine place to raise children, to make a home."

"I will love it — and your grandparents."

"And they'll love you. What about Lark? I know she doesn't want to leave the holler."

She shook her head. "She won't be coming with us. She asked permission to stay with Boots and her grandfather . . . and I said yes." Her gaze lovingly traced his features. "It's only a matter of time before she's old enough to make her decisions, and Boots's grandpa will provide a good home for her. The two girls — well, they're closer than sisters."

Smiling, he gently kissed the tip of her nose. "You're a wise woman and it won't be long before you'll be taking care of our babies. And the house?"

"For now I'll close it. Perhaps in time Lark will marry and reopen it, but I want to be free of all memories of the holler."

"She fully believes Murphy is her man, doesn't she?"

"I'm going to pray night and day that soon she'll outgrow her childish reasoning and come join us."

"Grandpa and Grandma would welcome her with open arms. They love kids."

She gently kissed him. "I want a new life — with you, Ian. If we stayed in the holler you would be subject to the same prejudices and superstitions that make my life so miserable."

"This part of your life is over; we'll be in Kansas City and you know Lark's going to hang around here and drive that young man out of his mind no matter what you say."

"I figure that's Murphy's problem."

"I'd say he's got a big headache."

"By the time Lark's old enough to marry that poor boy will have long ago found a mate." She paused. "Ian, can we stop in Joplin on the way to Kansas City and see Katherine?"

"If that's what you want."

"It's such a shame that Katherine allowed the light to run them off their land. They built such a lovely home."

They lay there for a moment, staring up at the faultless sky. A light breeze ruffled Lyric's hair and the scent of hay tickled her nose. Her life had experienced little serenity or such perfect peace, and she never wanted the moment to end. This would surely be the closest thing to heaven until she reached there.

"Honey?"

"Yes?"

"What do you really think that light is?"

"Well — I can't say what it is, but a very long time ago I decided there are just some things in life that aren't explainable. That doesn't make them bad or necessarily threatening — merely unaccountable. And look how God used that light to bring us together. What if you had ridden past here that night — never found me?"

He hugged her tightly to him. "Suppose God knows His business?"

"I believe He does. Better than we do, and maybe folks aren't supposed to have an explanation for everything God put on this earth. Maybe that's what He meant when He said that He works in mysterious ways."

Shielding his broken rib, Ian slowly eased to his elbow and fumbled in his pocket. She frowned. "Have you hurt yourself again?"

"Yeah, the sooner I give up this job the better. I'm running out of things to break. It's a good thing I've got a healer in my life." He fished out the ring and then turned to her. "Miss Bolton" — his gaze softened to earnest trust — "will you do the honor of spending the rest of your life with me?"

Hot tears rushed to her eyes. "I will, Mr. Cawley."

His mouth took hers and he deepened his hold possessively.

In the silence of the glade he whispered for her ears only, "You can call me Joseph."

■ ■ ■ ■

READER'S GUIDE

■ ■ ■ ■

1. Lyric and Lark suffer from the town's misperceptions of Edwina's mental illness. Have you ever made harsh or incorrect judgments about people?

2. When Lyric first finds Ian, she believes him to be an outlaw. What events or circumstances help her change her mind about him?

3. God uses unusual and unexpected circumstances to bring Lyric and Ian together. What were some of these circumstances?

4. Describe a time in your life when you saw God move in "mysterious ways."

5. The townspeople fear all the Bol-

tons because of Edwina's illness. Is it fair to lump family members together this way? Do you feel that you are defined by your family?

6. Before Ian regains his memory, he is willing to meet the hangman's noose because of sins he may have committed in the past. What does this say about Ian?

7. At the end of the story, Lyric chooses to leave Bolton Holler and all the painful memories behind. Lark decides to stay and try to make a new life for herself. In the circumstances, which life would you have chosen? Why?

ABOUT THE AUTHOR

Lori Copeland is the author of more than 90 titles, both historical and contemporary fiction. With more than 3 million copies of her books in print, she has developed a loyal following among her rapidly growing fans in the inspirational market. She has been honored with the Romantic Times Reviewer's Choice Award, The Holt Medallion, and Walden Books' Best Seller award. In 2000, Lori was inducted into the Missouri Writers Hall of Fame. She lives in the beautiful Ozarks with her husband, Lance, and their three children and seven grandchildren.

The employees of Thorndike Press hope you have enjoyed this Large Print book. All our Thorndike, Wheeler, and Kennebec Large Print titles are designed for easy reading, and all our books are made to last. Other Thorndike Press Large Print books are available at your library, through selected bookstores, or directly from us.

For information about titles, please call:
(800) 223-1244

or visit our Web site at:
http://gale.cengage.com/thorndike

To share your comments, please write:
Publisher
Thorndike Press
10 Water St., Suite 310
Waterville, ME 04901